THE CHOCOHOLIC MYSTERIES

The Chocolate Clown Corpse

"Well written and entertaining. . . . The story line is fun and the characters are well written. A truly enjoyable cozy."
—Open Book Society

"Carl has skillfully combined murder and humor with twists and turns to create a read that's hard to put down [and] the quirky characters are likable and realistic. The twists will keep you guessing until the end. You don't have to be a chocoholic to enjoy this tantalizing cozy murder mystery, just a fan of intrigue and mystery." —Thoughts in Progress

The Chocolate Book Bandit

"A nicely written cozy mystery with an interesting set of characters. . . . [It] will keep you entertained on a vacation or just sitting at home with a nice cup of coffee or hot chocolate!"
—Once Upon a Romance

"Carl's sense of humor shines through. . . . [She] writes sweet, tasty mysteries that include fun characters."
—Escape with Dollycas into a Good Book

"Carl knows how to construct a clever mystery that flows seamlessly with just the right amount of detail . . . [a] well-plotted cozy." —RT Book Reviews

The Chocolate Moose Motive

"In Carl's satisfying twelfth cozy featuring Lee McKinney Woodyard, the chocolate shop proprietor stirs up bad blood. . . . A recipe for Gran's Fudge rounds out the volume."
—Publishers Weekly

continued . . .

The Chocolate Castle Clue

"This book is a real winner. . . . [Carl] is a truly gifted mystery writer. One warning though: If you like chocolate at all, have a stash ready for when you read this book! Otherwise, you'll have to put this page-turner down long enough to run to the store when the chocolate cravings hit!"   —MyShelf.com

"An entertaining whodunit."   —The Mystery Gazette

"It has everything a cozy should: cute mysteries, fun themes, likable characters, and an interesting setting. If you are a chocoholic or fan of cozies, then you might want to try *The Chocolate Castle Clue*. It's a fun way to spend a few hours!"
                                                        —Booking Mama

The Chocolate Pirate Plot

"Cozy as cozy gets. . . . The perfect book to snuggle with to forget about any unpleasant winter weather while getting to know some of your favorite characters a bit better. Fireplace and hot chocolate are optional, but recommended."
                                                        —Fresh Fiction

The Chocolate Cupid Killings

"A chocolate-drenched page-turner! JoAnna Carl satisfies your sweet tooth along with your craving for a tasty whodunit."
                    —Cleo Coyle, *New York Times* bestselling author
                                of the Coffeehouse mysteries

"A deft mix of truffles and trouble. Chocoholics—this book is for you!"
                    —Laura Childs, *New York Times* bestselling author
                                of the Tea Shop mysteries

"Deliciously cozy. *The Chocolate Cupid Killings* is richly entertaining and has no calories."
                    —Elaine Viets, author of the Dead-End Job mysteries

The Chocolate Snowman Murders

"Dollops of chocolate lore add to the cozy fun."
                                                        —*Publishers Weekly*

The Chocolate Jewel Case

"[A] fun, very readable book, with likable characters that are knowable whether you've read all seven novels in the series or whether this is your first."   —Suite 101

The Chocolate Bridal Bash

"Entertaining and stylish. . . . Reading this on an empty stomach is hazardous to the waistline because the chocolate descriptions are . . . sensuously enticing. Lee is very likable without being too sweet."   —*Midwest Book Review*

The Chocolate Mouse Trap

"I've been a huge fan of the Chocoholic Mystery series from the start. I adore the mix of romance, mystery, and trivia . . . satisfying."   —Roundtable Reviews

The Chocolate Puppy Puzzle

"The pacing is perfect for the small-town setting, and the various secondary characters add variety and interest. Readers may find themselves craving chocolate, yearning to make their own. . . . An interesting mystery, fun characters, and, of course, chocolate make this a fun read for fans of mysteries and chocolates alike."   —The Romance Readers Connection

The Chocolate Frog Frame-Up

"A fast-paced, light read, full of chocolate facts and delectable treats. Lee is an endearing heroine. . . . Readers will enjoy the time they spend with Lee and Joe in Warner Pier and will look forward to returning for more murder dipped in chocolate."   —The Mystery Reader

The Chocolate Bear Burglary

"Descriptions of exotic chocolate will have you running out to buy gourmet sweets . . . a delectable treat."
                    —The Best Reviews

The Chocolate Cat Caper

"A mouthwatering debut and a delicious new series! Feisty young heroine Lee McKinney is a delight in this chocolate treat. A real page-turner, and I got chocolate on every one! I can't wait for the next."
—Tamar Myers, award-winning author of *The Death of Pie*

Also by JoAnna Carl

The
Chocolate
Clown Corpse

A Chocoholic Mystery

JoAnna Carl

AN OBSIDIAN MYSTERY

OBSIDIAN
Published by New American Library,
an imprint of Penguin Random House LLC
375 Hudson Street, New York, New York 10014

This book is a publication of New American Library. Previously published in
an Obsidian hardcover edition.

First Obsidian Mass Market Printing, November 2015

For more information about Penguin Random House, visit penguinrandom-
house.com.

ISBN 978-0-451-46618-1

Printed in the United States of America
10 9 8 7 6 5 4 3 2 1

PUBLISHER'S NOTE
This is a work of fiction. Names, characters, places, and incidents either are the
product of the author's imagination or are used fictitiously, and any resem-
blance to actual persons, living or dead, business establishments, events, or
locales is entirely coincidental.

*To the Mystery Book Discussion Group
of the Herrick Library, Holland, Michigan,
mystery lovers who know how to have fun*

Acknowledgments

The unnamed hospital used as a fictional setting in this book has no relationship to the real-life, much-respected Holland Community Hospital. No such shenanigans as the ones in this book could ever occur in that outstanding institution.

I owe thanks to Susanna Fennema, who tips me off to suitable Lore items; to my real-estate adviser, John Naberhaus; and to Dr. Rosemary Bellino and nurses Vanessa Lipe and Dianna Smales, who plot efficient kidnappings but whom I still trust with my health. Michigan friends were a big help, as usual, particularly Tim and Laura Raubinger, Rob and Loren McCaleb, Robin Williams-Voight, Susan McDermott, and Tracy Paquin. Also assisting were Dave and Rosalie Bentzin, who live where winter sports are popular; my daughter, Betsy Peters, who knows a lot more than I do about chocolate; and chocolatier Elizabeth Garber, who allows me to copy the product line of her company, the Best Chocolate in Town, which is based in Indianapolis.

I would also like to thank Ruth Dishman, who made a generous contribution to the Lawton, Oklahoma, Arts for All campaign in honor of her grandchildren, Kyle and Paige Walters, whose names appear in this story.

Chapter 1

I don't usually answer the telephone at the Warner Pier police station.

Warner Pier is a small town, true, and my aunt is married to the police chief, true, and somehow I wind up at the station now and then. But the PD has staff—the chief, four patrolmen, and a clerical assistant. The 9-1-1 calls go to a county system twenty-four hours a day, and after the office closes at five o'clock, ordinary business calls are caught by an answering machine after two rings.

They don't need a volunteer to answer the phone in Warner Pier, Lake Michigan's most picturesque resort.

But that day I was sitting around the station at five fifteen, the only person there, waiting for my aunt and uncle and my husband so we could all go out to dinner. I had plopped into a chair next to the empty desk usually occupied by the secretary. When the phone rang my mind was in three other places, and after just one ring I automatically picked it up.

"TenHuis Chocolade," I said.

I'd not only answered a phone I shouldn't have, I'd answered it the way I do for my job.

The caller, a woman, gasped. "Oh! I was calling the Warner Pier Police Department."

"And you reached it. I'm not the regular person who answers the phone, so I said the wrong thing. But I'll try to help you."

"Oh. Well . . ." The caller had an odd, whispery voice. "I wanted to ask about a crime that happened about a month ago."

"I can refer your question to the right person."

"It was a violent death."

Hmmm. Warner Pier doesn't have all that many killings. Or did she mean an accident? "Yes?"

"The murder of Morris Davidson. The clown. A month ago. Do you remember it?"

"Oh yes. It caused quite a stir around town." I looked at the caller ID on the secretary's phone. The little screen held a number with an area code I didn't recognize. "Where are you calling from? I'm surprised the Davidson killing got any attention outside of Warner County, since it was not too unusual."

She didn't answer my question. "Not unusual? Why do you say that?"

"It was the proverbial break-in with the burglar reacting violently when surprised by the homeowner."

The caller gasped. "Is that what people think happened?"

"After the confession, there wasn't much else to think."

"Confession? Confession! You mean someone confessed to the murder?"

"Yes. He's now in jail."

"Oh." I could barely hear her. The woman's voice was more than surprised. It was amazed. Maybe beyond amazed.

"Who is this?" I asked.

She spoke but again didn't answer my question. "In jail! But that's awful!"

"It's pretty standard procedure," I said. "If you confess to killing someone, you are sent to jail. Can you give me your name?"

The only answer was a click as the woman hung up.

I stared at the silent receiver. "Weird," I said.

There was a knock at the door, and I looked up to see my husband, Joe, through its window. I let him in and immediately told him about the phone call.

"Isn't that strange?" I asked.

Joe shrugged. "You say there was no name on the caller ID?"

"Right. There was a number, but no name. Is that suspicious?"

"Not necessarily." Joe is a lawyer who has some experience as a defense attorney. Plus, he served as city attorney of our little town for a couple of years, and his office was in the same building with the police station. So he's drunk a lot of coffee with cops.

"The call was probably made from a pay phone," he said. "There are still a few around."

"But the woman sounded so amazed to learn a burglar had confessed to killing Moe Davidson."

"We were all astonished, as I recall."

"I admit I was."

Joe grinned. "Lee, when the guy everybody loves to hate is murdered, every single person in town is a suspect. So finding out that Moe was taken out by someone who didn't even know him—well, Agatha Christie wouldn't have approved." He sat down in one of the visitors' chairs and picked up a magazine. "So I tend to agree with your caller."

"What do you mean?"

"Just that the whole situation was astonishing. Not satisfying." Joe looked into space for a moment before he spoke again. "Frankly, I don't think the guy—Hollis? Is that his name? I don't think he has good representation. If I were his attorney, that confession would never have been made, much less accepted as true."

He gave a short laugh. "Although he'd probably still be right where he is now. In jail. And he may yet be sent for a decent mental examination."

My uncle and aunt, Hogan and Nettie Jones, arrived then, and the four of us went out to dinner. I told Hogan about the odd phone call, but he simply shrugged.

"Some curious person. But Davidson's death was surprising all around. His whole life was surprising."

"Surprising how?"

"First off, how could such an annoying guy be so funny?"

When the caller had called Moe Davidson a clown, she hadn't been slamming his intelligence or personality. Moe had literally been a clown. He'd dressed up in a comic hobo outfit and marched in parades under the name Hobo Moe. He had done pantomime jokes. He'd pulled quarters out of kids' ears. He'd walked an invisible dog. He'd bragged that his makeup—including the row of painted teardrops near his left eye—was registered with a national listing of clowns and could not legally be copied by any other clown.

Moe had even run a clown business, Clowning Around, which happened to be located in the shop next door to TenHuis Chocolade, where I'm business manager.

Moe's store offered clown paraphernalia and collectibles—dolls, games, costumes, DVDs, figurines, notepaper, and a million other items. He provided a clown act for parties. Anything to do with clowns was available at his store.

But Moe was equally well-known in Warner Pier for his nonclown activities. When he wasn't being funny, Moe was one of the most annoying cranks in town. At one time or another—when he wasn't wearing his clown outfit—all of us could cheerfully have killed him, or at least yelled at him.

As far as I know, Moe Davidson never hit, stabbed, shot, drowned, or otherwise physically attacked anyone. But, by golly, he hurt a lot of people.

Moe's weapon was his tongue. He could figure out where anyone's sensitive spot was, and he knew just what to say to make that sensitive spot hurt. He whacked my ego with a verbal crowbar every time he walked into TenHuis Chocolade, and he seemed to walk in there a lot more than I wanted him to.

I have this problem talking. I mix up my words. The highfalutin name for it is "malapropism," named after a Mrs. Malaprop in an eighteenth-century play by Sheridan. She made *Bartlett's Familiar Quotations* for describing a fellow character as "headstrong as an allegory on the banks of the Nile."

I once remarked that an unusually kind person had "lots of apathy." Personally, I don't find Mrs. Malaprop very funny. To me the condition is embarrassing, not humorous.

I control this most of the time; it comes out mainly when I'm nervous. And I never once spoke to Moe Davidson without feeling nervous. He laughed whenever he saw me. That made me nervous, and I misspoke.

Once he came into TenHuis Chocolade for a pound

of truffles, and I recommended the "Asexual Spice—I mean, *Asian* Spice!" Another time, he approached me with a formal document he wanted to present to the Warner Pier City Council, and I said, "Oh, I'm sorry. I make it a rule not to sign petit fours—I mean, petitions!"

Moe would laugh at me and tell everybody in town what I'd said. He became the only person in Warner Pier I actively tried to avoid. And I couldn't avoid him, since he worked next door. When he wasn't too busy with civic affairs to open the store.

When Joe was serving as city attorney, he couldn't avoid him either. Moe Davidson was that annoying citizen who got up at every civic meeting and opposed something. He also frequently telephoned Joe to gripe, and he wrote letters to the local newspaper. He even gave money to the causes he supported.

At a public meeting, the most maddening thing about Moe was that he always started out by saying, "My family has been in business in Warner Pier since my great-great-grandfather came here in 1845."

Joe said he always had an awful time not breaking in to comment, "So has my family, Moe, and none of us was ever very successful either."

Because despite the Davidson family's long history in southwest Michigan, no one in the clan ever became very prominent. They were farmers who didn't own much land, operators of barbershops and dry cleaning establishments, managers and clerks for small retail businesses. None of them was in "the professions"—law, medicine, theology, engineering, and such. Joe could never understand why Moe thought an ordinary middle- and working-class background—even one covering one hundred seventy-five years—qualified him as an authority on civic affairs. A civics class would have been more impressive, and Moe didn't even have that in his background.

Both Joe and I also found Moe lacking in common sense. His positions on the city's doings seemed to come out of left field, or sometimes right field. One time he'd be strongly pro-environment. When the next issue came up, he'd take the position that government was putting environmental issues in front of individual rights. No one could ever predict if he was going to be pro or con on any particular issue until they saw his name on the list of donors.

But despite his fanatic and sometimes fantastic views on how to run the city, Moe never ran for office; he lived outside the city limits. He remained simply an interested local businessman and public-spirited citizen who always got up and spoke his piece. By doing this, he managed to infuriate everybody at one time or another.

Moe might have been run out of town if it weren't for his clown act. At every community parade, carnival, or celebration, he painted on a smile and a row of tears, put on his Hobo Moe costume, and made all the children—and most of the adults—laugh. As long as he kept his mouth shut he was hilarious.

Moe Davidson was a strange combination of qualities, so maybe it was poetic justice that he died strangely and that his death led to a strange phone call.

I probably would have forgotten the whole thing— call, killing, and clown—if three things hadn't happened.

First, Aunt Nettie and Hogan took their dream trip to the South Sea Islands.

Second, a For Sale sign went up next door.

Third, Joe was dragged into the case.

Or maybe he jumped in willingly.

Chapter 2

In midwinter in Michigan, we all dream of the South Seas.

Snow usually starts here in November. In December it's fun—skiing, snowmobiling, skating, and Christmas. January . . . Well, by then the winter routine has set in, and we can live with it. February is a good time to catch up with your reading and to watch a bunch of DVDs; plus, I'm usually busy then because Warner Pier holds its annual winter tourism promotion that month, and I serve on the tourism committee. But when March starts, and the snow and cold seem to have no end, that's when most of us are ready for the funny farm—as long as that farm is located someplace warm.

Joe and I usually take a vacation in December or January. I need to check in with my parents in Texas, and from there we go on down to the Gulf of Mexico or over to Phoenix or someplace else that is warm and sunny for a couple of weeks. Then we can face February or March, when Aunt Nettie and Hogan try to get away. It's best for TenHuis Chocolade if Aunt Nettie and I don't leave town at the same time.

This winter Aunt Nettie and Hogan had decided to splurge on Samoa and Tahiti—and they were going in late February. They were even booked for a week on a sailing ship, completely out of touch with civilization. No phones. Limited e-mail. Hogan found a retired sheriff's deputy to stand in as police chief, and they began to pack lightweight clothes in flowery patterns.

As usual, TenHuis Chocolade and I were both up to our ears in the annual winter promotion of the Chamber of Commerce tourism committee. This year the theme was Clown Week, so our shop was full of foil-wrapped molded clowns and molded clown hats in one-inch, two-inch, and four-inch sizes.

Not only was I heavily involved, but my best friend Lindy and her whole family had also been sucked in. Lindy and I have been friends for half our lives, and we're an example of how small-town lives can become entangled.

Lindy and I worked together at TenHuis Chocolade when we were both sixteen. At eighteen she married Tony Herrera, who just happened to have a close friend named Joe Woodyard. Twelve years later I married Joe Woodyard. (It gets even more complicated.)

Lindy and Tony have three kids. Tony's dad, Mike Herrera, is a successful restaurant owner, and Lindy is catering manager for her father-in-law. Mike was elected mayor of Warner Pier, and in the middle of his third term he married my mother-in-law, Mercy Woodyard.

Anybody who can understand all this without drawing a diagram is a genius. And it largely came about because Joe and Tony both went out for high school wrestling.

So I wondered what was going to happen when

Lindy told me her son, Tony Junior, now in ninth grade, had signed up for the wrestling team at Warner Pier High School.

"I'm almost surprised," I said. "His dad will be a hard act to follow, after competing on the team that won State . . ."

"Oh sure. Haven't you and I heard about that glorious event a million times?"

"At least half a million, anyway." I laughed. "Is Tony Senior excited about Tony Junior—"

"Puh-leeze! There is no more 'Tony Junior.'"

"What's happened to him?"

"Now that he's a high school athlete, he's known as T.J."

"Hmmm. It's a good enough nickname, but how is Tony Senior taking it?"

"About like you'd expect. He doesn't say much, but he doesn't know whether he should be angry or hurt. Anyway, he accidentally pushed Ton—I mean T.J.—toward wrestling because they're having a long-term hassle."

"What about?"

"Wrestling! Professional wrestling."

"I'm under the impression that all amateur wrestlers hate the pros."

"You're pretty close to right. Tony—Tony Senior— froths at the mouth when he catches T.J. watching those shows. Uses words like 'stupid' and 'phony.' It's caused some homemade matches I haven't enjoyed. The kind that include yelling and pouting."

"Doesn't Tony see that if he'd drop it, T.J. would probably lose interest?"

"Heavens! I wish one of them would lose interest. They're driving me nuts. That's why I talked both of them into working on Clown Week. But not together."

"What are they going to do?"

"Tony has agreed to supervise the skating rink."

"Oh good! Joe says he was always the best skater in their gang, growing up. And he's big enough to keep any rambunctious skaters in line."

Lindy nodded. "And T.J. is going to work on the sledding hill."

"Learning to handle the public, huh? His grandfather will have him working as a waiter PDQ."

"Oh, Marcia's already going to work at the Sidewalk Café during Clown Week."

Marcia was Lindy's older daughter, now sixteen.

I laughed. "Send her around if she wants some hints on how to get good tips. Waiting tables saved my bacon several times before I landed in the chocolate business."

Between Clown Week and Aunt Nettie and Hogan's trip, I nearly forgot that odd phone call to the police station. A few days after it came, Joe and I drove Hogan and Aunt Nettie to the Grand Rapids airport and enviously waved as they lugged their carry-ons down to the departure gate. When they reached Sydney they e-mailed to let us know they arrived safely and were about to set sail.

Their first day at sea was the day Moe Davidson's store went on the market.

As business manager of TenHuis Chocolade, I had long lusted after the building next door.

Moe Davidson had owned that building, but I didn't know who inherited it. He was survived by a wife, Emma, and he had two grown children from a previous marriage. The Warner Pier gossip mill reported that Moe and the kids had hardly spoken for years. Both son and daughter were in their early thirties. I hadn't ever seen Moe's daughter, but I had heard that her name was Lorraine. I had met the son, Chuck, briefly, when he visited the shop.

Emma and Moe had been married about two years, and she had occasionally worked in the Clowning Around shop, but nobody in Warner Pier knew her well. The Davidsons hadn't spent the past two winters in Warner Pier; lots of tourist-oriented businesses close up in the off-season. Emma and Moe had gone to her home in Indiana. In addition, Emma hadn't taken much part in local affairs when she was there. I'd never met her, and I'd heard she didn't have much to say for herself.

In September Moe had closed the store for the winter, though he had originally planned to reopen for Clown Week. None of us knew if that would work out now. The apartment over the store, a common facility in downtown Warner Pier, had been vacant for a couple of years.

Even though I didn't know just who now owned the building next door, I knew I wanted to buy it from them. So the new For Sale sign got my attention fast.

Nearly forty years earlier Aunt Nettie and her first husband, Phil TenHuis—my mother's brother—had spent a year in the Netherlands learning to make luxury, European-style chocolates. They then rented a shop in their hometown and opened a business catering to the tourists who visited one of Lake Michigan's prime resorts, Warner Pier.

Due to Aunt Nettie's and Uncle Phil's hard work and expertise, plus the good business climate of Warner Pier, TenHuis Chocolade had prospered. As time went by they had bought the original building, the shop had expanded to fill its whole downstairs, and they had remodeled several times.

Five years earlier Uncle Phil had been killed in a traffic accident. By then I was a five-foot-eleven blond divorcee with an accounting degree, so I moved up from Texas and joined TenHuis as business manager. I met Joe, got married, and settled into the community. I was proud of being part of TenHuis Chocolade and proud because we had tripled the mail-order side of the business. Today the business depends on mail order as much as on tourism. This keeps us busy year-round, unlike the Warner Pier merchants who depend solely on summer visitors.

I thought TenHuis had lots of potential for even more expansion, and to expand we needed more space. I needed a larger office staff, but we had no place to put desks or people. We needed at least one sales rep out there calling on corporations and convention planners. We needed a larger shipping department. We needed a catalog and direct-mail department, a catering specialist, a larger workroom for producing truffles and bonbons, and a dozen other things that we couldn't have because we had no place to house them.

So I'd had my eye on the store next door as an investment for TenHuis Chocolade ever since I came to work for Aunt Nettie. It would double our available space while keeping TenHuis in its prime location, in the heart of Warner Pier's picturesque business district. We could expand without the inconvenience of changing our address.

However, I had always thought of the building as a purchase for TenHuis as a company. But the company couldn't buy a pricy piece of property—and I'm happy to say that downtown Warner Pier property is expensive—without Aunt Nettie's approval. She is president of the company.

But if the building went on sale while Aunt Nettie was out of the country, and I had to move quickly to get it—well, I might have to buy it on my own.

The thought was terrifying. I'd have to talk to Joe, of course, since he'd be linked to me as a purchaser. I'd also have to consult my banker. But a sale was probably doable. I fought down a panic attack, took two deep breaths, and called the Realtor.

That the sign even went up showed how out of touch Moe Davidson's kids—or wife, or whoever was handling his estate—were. Warner Pier is small enough to rely on word of mouth. If a piece of property in the business district goes on the market, the rest of the business community gets advance warning in the post office line or the drugstore or the coffee shop. Rarely do we find out something's for sale by seeing a sign.

At least the name of the real estate firm was familiar. I'd served on a Chamber of Commerce committee with the local agent, Tilda VanAust.

I saw the sign at ten thirty and was on the phone with Tilda by ten thirty-five.

"How did the Davidsons get the store on the market so fast?" I asked.

"Actually," Tilda said, "Moe had signed the property over to Emma for tax reasons, so it didn't have to go through probate. Emma's signing it back to Chuck and Lorraine. She's here to help them close the building out, but she won't share in the proceeds."

"Interesting. How much are they asking?"

I held my breath. The asking price she mentioned was, of course, way too high, but I told her I'd definitely like to view the property.

I tried to sound cool. "Of course, Tilda, you know that business was not so hot this year in Warner Pier. But my aunt and I would like to consider expansion at some future date. So we might look at it as an investment."

"Lee, you know that this property is in a prime location. There's been a lot of interest in it already. I'm expecting an offer this week."

Sure. As if I believed that, since nobody had known it was going on the market. But now that it was officially for sale, I expected Tilda would be getting some calls. I definitely wanted to be first in line, but I didn't want to act so eager that Tilda saw me as a sucker.

Tilda said she had some time that very day, so we agreed to tour the building at three o'clock.

As soon as I hung up I tried to figure out what time it was for Aunt Nettie and Hogan. Actually, I decided, it didn't matter. The best way to reach them was by e-mail. Hogan had said he'd check that whenever he had access to it. I fired off an electronic message.

Then I sat back and faced facts. I was on my own. It was unlikely that I'd be able to reach Aunt Nettie to get her approval in the next few days.

If I wanted advice, I had a perfectly good husband who had a law degree and also knew a lot about construction. Joe would be glad to advise me. Besides, if I had to act on my own, any buying I did would involve him legally, so he'd have to go along with it anyway.

Joe works three days a week for an agency similar to the Legal Aid Society. It's located in Holland, thirty miles away, and specializes in poverty law. I picked up the phone and called his office.

"Sorry, Lee," the administrative assistant said. "He had to go see a judge down in Warner County."

"In our county? But nearly all his cases are in Holland."

"I know. He was surprised by the call. But he went. You could call his cell."

"I don't want to do that. Either he'd have it turned off or I'd interrupt something he doesn't want interrupted. I'll send him a text. But if you hear from him, ask him to call me."

I hung up and began to chew my nails and consider the possibilities.

I might not be able to talk the Davidson family down to a figure I thought was fair, and I'd have to give the whole project up. But even if we did reach an agreement, Aunt Nettie might not think it was a good idea.

Or if I couldn't reach Aunt Nettie, I could decide to buy it on my own, only to find that Aunt Nettie didn't want it.

Joe and I would wind up owning a downtown building we didn't really want. Then we could either resell it or rent it out. It might be a good financial investment.

Or we could fail to find a buyer or a leaser and lose a lot of money we couldn't afford to lose.

Looking at the purchase from several angles, it could be either a real winner or a serious loser. I bit another nail.

When the time came to meet Tilda, I asked one of the ladies who make the chocolate to watch the counter. I also told her where I'd be and asked her to pass that news on to Joe if he showed up. Then I took a deep breath, put on my jacket, and headed next door.

The entrance to Clowning Around was ajar, so I walked right in, then came to a complete stop.

All I could see were clowns. Clown dolls, clown masks, clown puppets, clown pictures, clown books. They hung from the ceiling and were stacked in shelves along both side walls. They were piled on tables in the middle of the room. There were white-faced clowns, hobo clowns, even a mannequin of a dog wearing a clown costume. There were girl clowns and boy clowns. Harlequins and Pierrots. And the centerpiece was a large portrait of Moe himself, wearing his Hobo Moe outfit.

Crazy colors and wild shapes were everywhere. The bizarre decor of the shop made the first sound I heard fit right in. It was a loud, piercing whine. The noise sounded like a siren, but I quickly realized it was a human voice of the high-pitched and annoying sort.

"Honestly! The mess! This place is nowhere near ready to show to potential buyers. That agent must be crazy."

A deep and melodious male voice replied, "Cleaning is our responsibility, Lorraine. It's not up to the Realtor. And I'm not getting rid of anything until we get through this Clown Week promotion and see if we can't sell most of the stock."

"Nobody would buy those idiotic clowns! God! I've gotten to the point where I hate these things. They're just reminders of what a jerk we had for a dad. And nobody will be interested in the building in the shape it's in. It needs to be staged."

"Staged?" The deep voice chuckled. "You've been watching too much HGTV."

"You haven't been watching enough, Chuck. Things have to look attractive if they're going to sell."

I'd apparently interrupted a family quarrel. I quickly slammed the door behind me, just to make a noise, then called out, "Hello! Anybody here?"

I heard a gasp from the back room, and the face of a blond woman appeared between two clown masks. The light was so lousy I couldn't see her clearly, but when she spoke the voice was the one I'd heard earlier.

"Hi, there! Are you Mrs. Woodyard?"

"Yes, I'm Lee Woodyard, your next-door neighbor. I was supposed to meet Tilda VanAust."

"She got held up, so she sent us to open up. I'm Lorraine Davidson."

The woman edged out of a curtained door that obviously led to the back room. She hit a switch and light flooded over her. The effect was that one of the clowns had come to life.

Lorraine was one of those women who apparently believe that if a little makeup enhances her appearance, then a lot will make her a raving beauty. She wore heavy blue eye shadow, and blush was slathered on in exactly the wrong part of her cheeks. Her eyebrows looked as if they'd been painted on with a Magic Marker. Her hair had been bleached until it would have tempted any healthy horse to have a bite, and she wore it in a fluffy, "big hair" style.

In other words, her appearance matched her voice. Loud, brassy, and unpleasant.

I blinked. Then I saw a man behind her and realized it must be the guy with the voice as melodious as Lorraine's was raucous.

"Hi," he said. "I'm Chuck Davidson."

Chuck matched his voice, too. He was tall, nice-looking, and neatly dressed, with dark hair and even features. He came forward and we shook hands. He had a pleasant smile.

"And this," Chuck said, "is our stepmother, Emma."

For a moment I couldn't figure out whom he was talking about. There was no other person present. Then there was movement among the clowns, and a small woman came from behind the counter.

Mrs. Davidson couldn't have offered a greater contrast to her stepdaughter. Lorraine was tall. Emma Davidson was short. Lorraine was thin, almost skinny. Mrs. Davidson was plump. Lorraine had long, bleached hair. Her stepmom's hair was a mousy brown and was short and straight.

Mrs. Davidson didn't speak, but simply nodded.

I hadn't come to talk to these people. I hope I greeted them pleasantly, but I was there to look around.

So we looked. I told the three of them that I wanted to get an idea of the building and to visualize the changes that would be required if we expanded into that space. I led the way, looking at the shelving, then going into the back to judge the amount of room. I had brought a flashlight, and I investigated the basement, making sure there were no damp spots and taking a look at the furnace. Chuck accompanied me. I addressed questions to him, but he was vague about details such as utility bills and taxes. I'd have to get those figures from Tilda.

I wasn't paying him much mind, actually, until he caught my attention with a strange remark.

"Of course, I know that cost is no object to you, Lee."

I turned to look at him, and I'm sure my amazement showed. But I tried to turn my reply into a joke. "Chuck! I'm an accountant! I assure you that even if my last name were Rockefeller, cost would matter to me."

He smiled. "I know you and your husband are major benefactors of Warner Pier."

For a moment I felt more amazed than ever. Then I got it. "Oh. Someone has told you that Joe donated the Warner Point Conference Center to the city."

"It was a terrific gift."

"Joe inherited that property unexpectedly, and he didn't want to own it. In fact, because of the taxes and upkeep he couldn't afford to own it. He says he gained financially by giving it away. And he donated it with the understanding that his name would never appear publicly in connection with the center."

"I'm sorry! I didn't know the background."

"That's quite all right. There's no secret about any of this. But I assure you that Joe and I personally are like most people. We live paycheck to paycheck. As for the possible purchase of this building, that would be a business decision for TenHuis Chocolade. I certainly have no interest in becoming a downtown landowner myself."

I had to admire Chuck. Although I had tried to speak pleasantly, I had definitely told him where to get off. A lot of people would have been crushed by my little speech. Chuck didn't turn a hair.

"I'm sorry I misunderstood the situation. I guess I'm used to my dad."

"Your dad?"

"Oh yes. I'm sure you know he was always giving money for community projects. But he would want full credit and a picture in the newspaper."

I'd observed that particular trait in Moe myself. But I decided I'd better not comment.

"I guess I'm ready to look around upstairs," I said. "Is the stairway near the rear entrance?"

Chuck followed me to the back. I had stopped for a look at the staff bathroom when I heard the front door open. Good, I thought, it's Tilda. Now we can get down to cases.

Instead, I heard Lorraine's raucous croak. "Of all the nerve!"

The voice that replied to her was deep and familiar. "I beg your pardon?"

"You've got gall, coming here to harass us!"

"I'm sorry—I was told I would find my wife here."

It was Joe, and for some reason Lorraine Davidson was angry with him. I headed for the front of the store.

Chuck called out. "Lorraine! Calm down."

But Lorraine seemed to be doing the opposite of what he suggested. She was working herself up. Her voice grew shriller, angrier, and ever more raucous, calling Joe every name in the book.

I burst into the front section of the store. "Joe! Ms. Davidson! What's going on?"

Joe shrugged. "Don't ask me. I just got here."

"You know why I'm angry!" Lorraine was nearly screaming. "You're the dirty dog who's trying to get our father's murderer off! You should be strung up! Just like that creepy homeless guy should be!"

Chapter 3

If Lorraine was going to keep yelling, there didn't seem to be much point in hanging around. I mouthed, "I'll talk to you later" to Chuck and followed Joe out the door.

On the sidewalk I paused, and an odd thing happened. I heard Chuck's voice. "That's enough, Lorraine!" Then complete silence fell behind us. Not a sound came from inside Clowning Around.

"Lorraine has stopped howling," I said quietly. "What was that all about anyway?"

"I don't have the slightest idea. Who are those people?"

"The younger ones are Chuck and Lorraine Davidson, Moe's son and daughter. The older woman is their stepmother, Emma Davidson."

"Older woman? I didn't even see an older woman." Joe shook his head. "I guess I can explain the hissy fit. Let's get off the street, and I'll tell you."

I led the way to TenHuis Chocolade, and neither of us spoke again until we were seated in my office, with our heads close enough to speak quietly. My office has glass walls that don't reach clear to the ceiling, and it's in a corner of our retail sales area. People who work in glass offices shouldn't speak loudly if they want privacy.

So I kept my voice quiet. "What caused all that, Joe?"

"Lee, I wouldn't have gone near Clowning Around if I'd known the Davidson family would be present. Why were you over there anyway?"

"They put the store up for sale today, and I was having a showing. You know I've always wanted to acquire that building for TenHuis expansion."

"I may have scotched that deal. Sorry."

"What kicked off Lorraine's tirade? You're normally pretty tactful. I can't believe you just walked in the door and said something she didn't like."

"I didn't say anything. But the three of them were in the courthouse when I went to talk to the judge. I saw them sitting there, and I guess they saw me walk by. They were strangers to me, but somebody must have told them who I was."

"Who *are* you? Why did the mere sight of you send Lorraine into a swivet?"

Joe answered, but his reply didn't make a lot of sense. "Royal Hollis' attorney has stepped down," he said.

"Royal Hollis?"

"The guy who confessed to killing Moe Davidson."

"Oh! That homeless guy?" Joe nodded, and I spoke again. "You said he deserved better representation. But what does that have to do with anything?"

"Doke Donovan is retiring."

"The lawyer?"

"Yeah. He was Hollis' attorney."

"Now I remember. Court-appointed. But what does that have to do with you?"

"I thought Doke was doing a halfhearted job for Hollis. Now Doke has health problems, and he's stepping down."

"Joe! Quit stalling! How do you fit in?"

"Apparently I'd talked to Doke about the case sometime—I don't even remember doing that."

Joe still wasn't giving me direct answers. I stayed quiet, trying to be patient.

Joe went on. "It was at the bar meeting, he says. Now Doke wants me to take over. The judge has okayed it, but I said I'd have to think about it."

"Oh." I began to see what was going on. Lorraine was obviously not happy about Hollis getting a new attorney, and Joe had been suggested for the job, and she didn't like that either. Her incoherent tirade had apparently been intended to tell Joe what she thought.

This was Joe's problem, not mine, but if Joe took Royal Hollis' case, the Davidsons might not want to deal with his wife. I could see my dream of owning the Clowning Around building collapsing.

Joe frowned. "Lee, if it's going to mess up this deal for the Davidson store—well, I know that's important to you. We can talk about it."

He looked serious. Maybe he looked miserable.

I thought about it. Hollis' new trial was right up Joe's alley. He would be representing a homeless man for a fee set by the judge. That might not sound like a very tempting case to the typical lawyer, but for Joe— well, he's always for the underdog. He doesn't see law as wills and deeds and property settlements. He sees it as the last protection of the little guy against the big one, of the helpless against the powerful.

Heck, Joe sees himself as a knight in shining armor, and the sword he wields is the law. He uses that sword to protect the helpless. Making sure that Royal Hollis got a fair trial would be better than a million dollars to Joe, even if Hollis still wound up in prison.

Was Joe offering to refuse the case just to please me?

I didn't know whether I should laugh or cry. All I knew was that one of the major reasons I loved Joe was that knight-errant complex of his. That and a great pair of shoulders. I was really lucky to have such a guy, and I knew it. He was a lot more important to me than any building could ever be.

I leaned over and kissed him. Smack on the mouth. Right in my glass-sided office, right in front of God and everybody, including all the ladies who make chocolates, and anybody passing outside on the street.

"Joe," I said, "you feel strongly about this case, and you need to take it."

He grinned broadly, and I knew I'd said the right thing. "I said we could talk about the case," he said. "I never said I wouldn't take it!"

I grinned back. "Nice to know that you haven't changed our whole relationship over this. Justice comes first! Will you have to drop your job at the agency for a no-pay?"

"Oh, I think I can keep my job at the agency. And I will get some kind of a fee. The State of Michigan doesn't demand charitable donations. I may have to cut back on my time at the boat shop."

"I hate for you to spend less time at the boat shop. You claim the boat shop keeps you sane. It would be a pity if you lost your mind over a court-appointed case."

"If I feel my sanity slipping away, I'll tell the judge that Royal Hollis needs a different attorney, one in his right mind." Joe sighed. "And now I guess I'd better go

back to Holland and tell the agency what's going on."
He kissed *me* that time, then headed for the door.

On the days Joe's not practicing poverty law, he runs
a boat shop, restoring antique wooden power boats.
Yes, it's an odd combination of careers, but Joe finds it
ideal. The days of working with his hands, he says,
give him time to assimilate the intellectual and emotional challenge of trying to help people whose lives
are often pretty messed up.

A typical client for his agency is a single mother trying to dig child support out of her ex-husband, or an
elderly woman who's trying to get her landlord to fix
the roof. The poverty law agency doesn't handle criminal work, so I knew Joe couldn't take Hollis' case as
part of his regular load there.

I seated myself in front of my computer and tried to
look like a business manager, even though my mind
was two other places: at Clowning Around and headed
for Holland with Joe. I gave a mental shrug and tried to
think philosophically about the building next door.

If the Davidsons wouldn't sell it to me because I was
married to Joe, well, the world wasn't going to come to
an end. It would be inconvenient, but life would go on.
My brain toyed with the idea that somebody I was
friends with—maybe somebody like Joe's stepfather,
Mike Herrera—would like to buy it. Then I could take
it off his hands at some future date, when Royal Hollis'
fate had been settled. Hmmm. I doubted the Davidsons
would fall for that; the personal connections of a town
like Warner Pier are too transparent. They'd see right
through my plot.

It finally occurred to me that I ought to tell Tilda
VanAust what had happened. If one of her clients was
nutso, she needed to know.

Tilda wasn't in her office, but the receptionist referred me to her cell phone. Tilda listened to my report on the showing at Clowning Around. My description of Lorraine's tirade was greeted with complete silence.

I began to fear that our connection had been broken. "Tilda?" I said. "Are you there?"

"Oh yes, I'm here. Your story left me speechless."

"I know Lorraine and Chuck are your clients." A Realtor has to protect her clients. I knew that.

"I'm sorry you and Joe had this experience."

"We'll live."

"I didn't want the Davidsons to show you around, but I was going to have to cancel, and Chuck insisted they could handle it."

"He tried to calm Lorraine down."

"She's the—well, the emotional one."

For "emotional," read "crazy." I didn't say that out loud.

"And Emma never says a word," Tilda said.

"I certainly didn't hear a word out of her."

"Chuck works as a salesman. He's been fairly polished the few times I've met him. But believe me, that's the last time the Davidsons will show that building themselves! Or their house."

"Oh, the house is for sale, too?"

"Right. They're clearing out of Warner Pier. But I'm surprised to hear about Lorraine's fit of temper this afternoon. Chuck came by a few minutes ago, and he didn't mention it. I was under the impression that things had gone pretty well."

"They did until Joe came in. Then Lorraine cut loose."

"Chuck seemed to think you were definitely interested in the building."

"At the right price I would be, Tilda. But I was left with the impression that, once they realized I was connected with Joe, they didn't want to deal with me."

"Personal feelings shouldn't interfere with business dealings. I'll talk to them."

I hung up knowing that at least Tilda wasn't against TenHuis Chocolade purchasing the Clowning Around building. Then I glanced at the clock and realized I needed to go to a meeting of the tourism committee. Back into the ski jacket and out the door.

I drove the few blocks to the Chamber of Commerce building. At least I didn't have to wear my clown outfit for this event.

Yes, for Clown Week all the members of the tourism committee were dressing up like clowns. And that was just the beginning of our activities.

Warner Pier's whole downtown—all twelve square blocks of it—was going to be turned into a winter funhouse. The four tennis courts in the park along the river had been flooded and were festooned with lights to become a skating rink. Three horse-drawn sleighs had been hired to roam around offering rides to visitors. At the high school, on a hill overlooking the downtown, the gym had become a snack bar and souvenir stand. Central heating was available there, so people could warm up after walking from shop to shop spending money.

But the star attraction was the sledding hill. Three blocks long, it ran from the high school down to a big open area next to the skating rink in the park. Giant inner tubes, plus sleds and snowboards, were provided. Teenagers such as Tony Junior—I mean T.J.— had been drafted to accompany young or inexperienced sledders. Helmets were provided. Even to a nonsledder like me, it looked like a lot of fun. Plus, our committee had rented a snowmaking machine to ensure plenty of snow.

I was a big supporter of the sledding hill, even though

the thing scared me to death. The first year I'd lived in
Warner Pier I went sledding with Lindy, Tony, and their
three kids. On my first try I flipped off my sled and was
buried in a snowbank. Tony and T.J. had to dig me out.
They thought it was hilarious, and I vowed never to
head down another slope without a snow ax to stop myself. So far I had kept my vow, despite a lot of teasing,
particularly from T.J.

Anyway, there was a lot going on with Clown Week.
That afternoon the tourism committee gathered officially to meet our professional clowns.

The theme of the annual midwinter promotion had
been set two years in advance, and we'd hired our out-
of-town talent the previous summer. We'd signed a con-
tract after seeing them in a video, and today we were to
get our first real-life look at Kyle and Paige Walters, a
brother-and-sister team of professional clowns. They
were to do eight performances during the next week,
providing informal floor shows in several different
restaurants.

On Friday, promotions committee folks were supposed to attend the opening event wearing clown costumes. Earlier in the week we were also to wear
costumes to visit the children at an area hospital for a
photo op. I had borrowed a costume for those events.

I had helped plan all this, and now I had to support it.

As I came in the front door of the chamber building,
I heard music. Someone was pounding the old piano in
the meeting room, and as I went into the session, singing began. It was the old standby "Make 'Em Laugh,"
the one Donald O'Connor sang in *Singin' in the Rain*. I
paused just inside the room to watch.

Well, the singer wasn't Donald O'Connor, but she
was pretty good. It was Paige, the sister, and she could
belt it out. Her costume was covered with big purple

polka dots, and she wore a little green hat with a white pompon on top. She had a cute face, and she hadn't covered it with grotesque makeup.

Her brother, Kyle, was playing the piano, and he joined in on the chorus. His costume had green polka dots and a purple hat. They were attractive, not the scary sort of clowns. Paige pranced and kicked joyously, and after the first verse she began to do clown tricks. She pantomimed carrying in a heavy bucket, convincing the audience it was actually full of water. When she finally threw it at the audience, everybody squealed and ducked as confetti flew at them. She shot a pistol, and a sign reading BANG! popped out. She did several other traditional tricks.

Then she and her brother exchanged places at the piano, and Kyle juggled Indian clubs and tennis balls, first separately, then together.

The act went on for just about ten minutes. After their applause, the two of them explained that they were just giving us a taste of their work, and that the acts they'd be doing for the formal presentations would be longer and different.

I felt a great sense of relief. They seemed to be just what we needed: family entertainment.

After the performance, we all turned to the coffeepot and a plate of cookies, plus a tray of chocolates I had contributed. At the refreshment table I found myself talking to Tony Herrera—Tony Senior.

Tony is a big guy, at least six foot three and even more muscular as a machinist than he had been as a high school wrestler. Even more agile, as well, I'd guess. At least he can still ice-skate like a demon.

He grinned at me, and I saw why Lindy fell for him when she was sixteen. He's a lot more rugged-looking than he used to be, but they seem to be just as crazy about each other as they were then.

"Hey, Tony, I saw you practicing at the skating rink yesterday," I said. "You still have it, guy! Did you ever play hockey? Speed skate?"

"Nah, in those days my dad hadn't given up on getting me into the restaurant business. He had me busing tables from the age of twelve. I only got to wrestle because the coach begged."

"Coach spotted you as a comer, huh?"

Tony laughed. "No, but I could always sit on the other wrestler. I was the biggest guy in the ninth grade."

"T.J. has really shot up this year."

"Yeah. He's gotten dumber, too."

"Aw, Tony! He's a good kid."

"He used to be. But now—whatever I say, it's wrong. And he's still watching that stupid wrestling."

"I think he just does that to get your goat."

"If he doesn't do a good job on the sleds, I'll get his."

Tony growled and moved toward the coffeepot. I turned and found myself face-to-face with Chuck Davidson.

He greeted me with an outstretched hand, so I shook it. "I'm so sorry about Lorraine losing her temper," he said.

"It wasn't your fault, Chuck. Of course, at the time I couldn't figure out what was going on. Since then Joe explained that he's been asked to represent Royal Hollis."

"Yes, he came through the office when we were over at the courthouse, and the prosecutor—he'd called us in to explain what happened—said he was to be the new defense attorney. He didn't mention his name, so we didn't know he had any connection with you. When your husband walked in over at the store, it caught us all by surprise."

"I can see that it would."

"It's all such a mess! I may be called to testify. And I'm sure your husband doesn't want to get involved either."

"He can refuse the case if he doesn't want to take it."

"Oh? Then he hasn't agreed to represent Hollis?"

"I don't know exactly how things stand, but I think he does plan to take the case."

"Why would any lawyer want to represent an obviously guilty person?"

"Joe has to speak for himself, but this is the United States, Chuck. Even the guilty are entitled to a defense. And that means some lawyer has to provide it."

It was time to change the subject. I turned to the refreshments table behind me. It included a tray filled with TenHuis bonbons and truffles. "I brought some chocolates. What would you like?"

I can always distract upset people with chocolate.

Chuck halfheartedly declined, but I talked him into an Amaretto truffle ("milk chocolate filling flavored with almond liqueur, in a milk chocolate shell, and embellished with chopped almonds"). He almost rolled his eyes in ecstasy as he bit into it.

As soon as he had his mouth full, I spoke. "My concern in all this is the Clowning Around building. Would you still consider TenHuis as a buyer?"

Chuck savored his truffle, then spoke. "I'd have to talk to Lorraine and to Emma. But I see no reason not to. I just wanted to apologize for the emotional scene, and I guess I ought to commiserate with your husband because he got stuck with a hopeless case."

I smiled. "Joe always wants to see justice done. He'll handle the situation."

I left then and drove back to the office. Because it was nearly quitting time, I parked on the street instead of in my reserved spot in the alley. As I walked toward the entrance of our shop, I saw something interesting.

Tilda VanAust was coming out of Clowning Around. And she wasn't alone. With her was a tall man. He wore a good-looking jacket and a fur hat and in general had a prosperous appearance. The two of them were pointing and gesturing, obviously talking about the Clowning Around building.

My competitive juices started to flow. If he was a potential buyer, I wanted to know.

Chocolate Chat

The early growers of cacao were, of course, those exotic Central American peoples. In fact, their names and cultures are so exotic that those among us who are not experts on history or anthropology find them quite confusing: Olmec, Maya, Aztec, Toltec.

Scientists claim to have at least partially analyzed the Olmec vocabulary, and they say it contains the first use of the word "cacao."

The Olmecs lived three thousand years ago. Their domain (south of today's Veracruz, Mexico) was ideal for wild cacao trees, providing lots of hot, humid, and shady places for them to grow. Since the Olmecs were an agricultural people, they may well have been capable of domesticating the plant, but some scientists believe the Aztecs achieved that feat.

Today the Olmecs are remembered mainly for creating gigantic, and beautiful, stone heads.

Chapter 4

It certainly looked as if Tilda was showing the building— "showing" in the real-estate sense.

Tilda had been "too busy" to show me the building. But she had found time to show it to some other person.

Fleetingly, my feelings were hurt. Then I decided to laugh it off. Just because Tilda had a conflict at three o'clock didn't mean she wouldn't be free at four. I was being silly. Besides, the man might not be thinking of buying the building. He could be bidding on repairs. Or inspecting the plumbing.

Or he could be an agent from Holland or Kalamazoo who was looking for a suitable building for a potential client. In fact, a white van with a magnetic sign on its side was parked at the curb. The sign read P.M. DEVELOPMENT.

Hmmm. Maybe Tilda hadn't been jazzing me when she said there was a lot of interest in the building.

Whatever was going on, I was going to play it cool. I walked by, giving Tilda a casual wave, and went into

TenHuis Chocolade. I hung up my coat and went directly into my office. If Tilda looked in my window, I wasn't going to give her the satisfaction of seeing that I was taking any interest in the man who had visited Clowning Around.

But as the man moved toward his van, I could hardly resist peeking at him. He had parked directly in front of our show window, and I could see him from my desk. Not that I could see much. I got a glimpse of bushy black eyebrows, but the hair around the edges of his brown fur hat seemed to be silver gray.

I ducked my head and concentrated on my computer. At least I could look as if I were working.

But I had barely booted up the computer when the front door opened, and a woman I had never seen before came in. I put on my greeting-a-customer face and moved to the retail counter.

The newcomer was a woman of forty or so. She was wearing a camelhair coat with a mink ascot—I'd call it a bib—tucked inside the neckline. Her hair and makeup were perfect. In fact, she looked almost too perfect. I wondered if she'd "had work done," as they say.

"May I help you?" I asked.

"I hope so. I was told that I might find a Joe Woodyard here."

"Joe is my husband, and he did drop by earlier. But he went on to his office."

"His office? And where is his office?"

"In Holland." I gave her the address.

She sighed. "Oh, I hoped I could find him before it got too late. I haven't checked in anywhere yet."

"I can try to call and tell him you want to see him. It takes about half an hour or forty-five minutes to get there. But if you are planning to stay in Warner Pier, Joe might meet you down here."

"I hate to trouble him."

"We live in Warner Pier, so he'll be coming home."

She sighed. "It's rude of me to expect him to meet me so I can fire him."

"Fire him?" I said the words out loud, then waved a hand dismissively. Lawyers' wives have to learn not to ask questions. "Sorry. It's none of my business."

"I'm sure he'll tell you about it. I'm Royal Hollis' daughter. I just found out that your husband has been appointed to defend him." She dropped her eyes. Evidently she was finding this conversation unpleasant. "Now that I've found out about my father's problems . . . Well, I can afford to hire a *real* attorney for him."

I resisted the temptation to snap at her, *Joe is a* real *attorney, witch!*

Maybe I wouldn't have used the word "witch." I might have used one that rhymes with it. Just who the heck did she think she was, anyway?

But instead of spouting off I remembered my business manners, smiled slightly, and spoke. "I'll try Joe's cell. Since Mr. Hollis' case won't be handled by the Holland agency Joe usually works for, he might prefer to meet with you down here in Warner Pier."

"What do you mean it won't be handled by the agency?"

"Joe works for an organization that offers legal services to low-income individuals and families. They don't do criminal cases."

She looked wary. "What kind of legal problems do poor people have?"

"The same kinds the rest of us do. Divorces, custody disputes, even wills and deeds. Please have a seat, and I'll try to reach Joe."

She sat in one of the two chairs we keep for customers, and I went into my office and called Joe. He said he was just about to leave his office.

"There's a new development with Royal Hollis," I said.

Joe listened while I described Hollis' daughter and reported what she had said.

Then he laughed, sort of. "Tell her I'll head right back and meet her about six o'clock. Find out where she'll be." Then he hung up.

I reported to Hollis' daughter.

"Where were you planning to stay?" I asked.

"I suppose there are hotels in this town."

"What!" I laughed, or pretended to. "Warner Pier is the tourism capital of Southwest Michigan! We have motels and B and Bs on every corner. And at least half of them are open at the moment for our annual winter promotion. Of course, you might find someplace less expensive if you went into Holland."

"I don't care about the cost. What's the most comfortable place?"

I suggested either the Inn on the Pier, a motel that's near the downtown, or the Peach Street Bed-and-Breakfast, run by Sarajane Harding, one of Aunt Nettie's best friends. I even found a map of Warner Pier to give her; what's the use of being on the Chamber of Commerce tourism committee if you don't have some materials to hand out?

She looked a bit worried. "I guess I can find the B and B," she said.

"Would you like me to call and make sure they have a vacancy?"

"Oh, would you?"

"Sure. What's your name?"

"Oh! I'm sorry. My name is Belle Montgomery."

I called Sarajane and learned that she had a room for

that night and the next three. For a price. But the price
didn't seem to bother Belle Montgomery. She waved it
away calmly. "Tell her I'll be there shortly." Then she
frowned at the map. "Which way do I turn when I
leave here?"

I guess that was the remark that made me offer to
show her the way. Or maybe it was my Texas upbring-
ing. We're taught to be kind and helpful—even to
someone who said she intended to fire my husband.
Besides, it was after five o'clock, and I was ready to
leave the office anyway.

Or maybe I was just being nosy. I'm afraid that's
been known to inspire my actions.

Anyway, I wound up leading the way to the Peach
Street Bed-and-Breakfast with Belle Montgomery driving behind me in a Cadillac sedan.

Mrs. Montgomery found the room she was offered
up to her standards, so I helped get her hand-sewn
leather luggage inside, then called Joe to tell him where
she was. As soon as she'd had time to freshen up I escorted her to a small study off the main parlor. Sarajane
had said she could use that to meet with Joe.

I was ready to leave, but Belle—by then we were on
a first-name basis—kept asking me questions about
Joe.

Where had he gone to law school? Answer: University of Michigan.

How long had he practiced criminal law? Answer:
Three years. That was before I knew him. But recently
he'd been at the poverty law agency.

Why did he change? Answer: Ask him yourself. The
real answer is that Joe was once married to a well-
known defense attorney. He didn't like the way she
operated professionally, and that was a factor in why
they split up. He was so disgusted he dropped out of

law completely for a while. Which introduces the boat shop. There's no secret about any of this, but Joe doesn't always want to explain it all.

As we talked, Belle's eyes got bigger and bigger and her hands shook. If Belle wasn't a woman who was upset and scared to death, she was doing a good imitation of one. Despite her obnoxiousness when we first met, I felt sorry for her.

When we heard Joe come into Sarajane's living room, Belle jumped to her feet. When he came into the study, she wrung her hands.

I was almost surprised to see Joe looking quite spiffy. He had apparently dropped by the house to change his shirt and tie, and had even picked up his dressy overcoat, a gorgeous garment his mother had given him for Christmas, saying, "Every lawyer should be prepared to face the Supreme Court." As far as I knew it was the first time Joe had ever worn it. A heavy ski jacket is usually more practical in our area. He wears any kind of an overcoat only if he's going to court; a poverty lawyer doesn't want to look too much wealthier than his clients.

I recognized the feeling that inspired the overcoat. Joe didn't want Belle Montgomery to think he was some hick backwoods lawyer. Joe can play games with the best of them.

So I hid a smile as I spoke. "I'll say good-bye."

"Oh no! Please stay." Belle was still sounding panicky.

"Joe may prefer to speak privately."

Joe took off the overcoat and tossed it casually over the back of a chair. "It doesn't matter. Mrs. Montgomery isn't a client."

"I'm not?" She looked surprised. "But I'm willing to finance my father's defense."

"That's nice, but if I represent your dad, I'll be working for him, not you. It doesn't matter who foots the bill."

"Oh."

"Plus, he has the final say on who his lawyer is."

"Oh?" It was more of a squeak than a word. I began to hope Joe wouldn't be too tough on Belle. Her eyes were the size of Frisbees.

She sounded plaintive when she spoke. "Do you think my dad has any case at all?"

"I haven't looked at the files yet. And if he wants a different lawyer, of course I won't bother."

"Oh."

"I plan to interview him in the next few days. You can go along, if you like."

"Oh!"

"If Mr. Hollis accepts your offer and wants a different lawyer, I could suggest some names. But in the meantime I would be happy to file a petition for his release on bail."

"Release!" I thought Belle was going to faint. "Release! You mean he might get out of jail?"

"Maybe. While he's awaiting trial."

"But he can't get out! He can't get out!" Belle burst into tears.

Joe's big-time lawyer act almost deserted him. He reacted like a typical man faced with a crying woman. A look of panic flashed across his face, and I got a pleading look from him. Then he gathered his wits and sat back in his chair, looking confident.

I moved to Belle's side and did all the dumb, ineffectual things we do when people are deeply upset. I patted her hand, found her a tissue, and said, "There, there." That's a fat lot of help. But Belle continued to cry, and I began to understand what was going on.

Belle didn't want her father to get out of jail. Belle thought he was guilty. She might even have been afraid of him. All this get-him-a-lawyer and spare-no-expense stuff was pure pretense.

Her whole point was to make herself look good while keeping her dad locked up. When she was told he might be released, she was sorry she had come, sorry she had offered to pay her dad's expenses.

It was at least three minutes before she spoke again. "I'm sorry," she said. "I shouldn't have lost control like that. I was just so surprised. But if he got out, where would he go?"

"We'd have to find a place for him," Joe said. "But that's not happening yet."

"What do you mean?"

"Frankly, it's extremely rare for a person accused of a crime this serious to be released while he's awaiting trial."

"Didn't he confess?"

"According to his earlier attorney, Doke Donovan, Mr. Hollis doesn't always think clearly. Doke believes that your dad said things the sheriff misinterpreted."

"But the jury would have to hear them."

"He needs to have a proper mental evaluation before he can go to trial."

Joe leaned forward and looked at Belle closely. "Mrs. Montgomery, have you visited your dad since he has been in jail?"

She shook her head.

"Was he around when you were growing up?"

She shook her head again.

"Have you seen him in recent years?"

Another headshake.

"Just how well do you know him?"

This time she ducked her head and looked at her hands, twisting them in her lap. She didn't shake her head, but it was a long moment before she spoke.

"I've never met him," she said. "I've never even seen him in my whole entire life."

Chapter 5

Neither Joe nor I said anything, but I guess we both looked amazed. I know I was surprised. Here Belle was offering to spend a lot of money to help out her dad, and she had never even met him?

As the silence grew, Belle stood. She held her head up high, and she spoke calmly. "I think I'd better go up now. I'll have to explain later."

And with great dignity she walked out of the room. Belle had time to reach the stairway before I again heard a noise that sounded like crying. I took a step, starting to follow, but Joe shook his head.

"I'll talk to her tomorrow," he said. "Let's go."

Joe followed me home, and after we pulled into the sandy lane that led to our semirural house, I saw his truck stop. I felt sure he was getting the mail, so I drove on.

We've set aside a parking area next to the house, creating four spots—two for us and two for visitors. When my headlights hit the area, I was surprised to see an SUV sitting in one of the extra spots. A Warner County logo was painted on its side, topped with large letters that read SHERIFF.

My heart sank. I was tired and hungry. I didn't want to have a session with Warner County's sheriff, Burt Ramsey. We'd had plenty of run-ins with him in the past.

My aunt's husband, Warner Pier's police chief, didn't have much use for Ramsey. His main problem, Hogan said, was that he was an elected official. Ramsey felt compelled to get along with the voters, and he seemed to think this meant groveling.

Hogan had spent his entire adult career in law enforcement. He had a bachelor's degree in criminal justice and a master's in public administration. He had worked a lot of years for a major police department. He got along with the public, but he relied on acting professional to do that. He never . . . well . . . sucked up to citizens. The only people he needed to suck up to were Warner Pier city council members and, frankly, Hogan had whipped them into line during his first year on the job.

Ramsey, on the other hand, had never worked in law enforcement before he was elected sheriff. He'd been a small businessman, running a convenience store and gas station. Ramsey had just enough training to gain law enforcement certification, but basically he was a politician.

Outwardly, Hogan and Ramsey were united in trying to serve the public. They were both pro–good guys and anti–bad guys. However, I believed that inside, Ramsey felt threatened by Hogan's very existence. And maybe Hogan felt a bit condescending toward the county officer. He was polite, but I always felt he had to keep reminding himself to act nice.

Because of these undercurrents, the connections Joe and I had with my uncle by marriage made us unpopular with the sheriff. He seemed to suspect us of plotting to undermine his authority and to make him look bad in front of the voters.

Maybe he was right. I thought Ramsey was a jerk, and if he made himself look bad, so be it. However, I tried not to do anything obviously mean to this poor excuse for a lawman. But he was always on the defensive around me or any other connection of Hogan's.

As I drove up, Ramsey got out of his SUV and stood waiting, hands on hips. He looked as if he were ready to make a quick draw. His stance was not welcoming, but I reminded myself that he was at my house, on my turf, and a man's home is still his castle. A woman's, too.

As I got out of the van, I saw that Ramsey wasn't alone. A second police car was parked on the other side of Ramsey's SUV, and a uniformed officer came around to stand beside him. After a second I recognized him as Clancy Pike.

Pike had been one of Ramsey's deputies—the best one, Hogan thought—until he recently retired. He had been the only trained investigator in the sheriff's department. He didn't have a lot of experience with administration, but Hogan had asked him to stand in as Warner Pier Police Chief while he and Aunt Nettie were gone.

I called out in what I tried to make a pleasant voice. "Hi, Sheriff Ramsey. Hello, Clancy. Sorry we weren't here to greet y'all."

Ramsey yelled his reply. "Where's that husband of yours?"

"He's right behind me. I think he stopped for the mail."

"I've got a few things to say to him."

"You're welcome to come on in the house and say them."

"Out here's better."

After that I couldn't think of anything else to talk about. Well, maybe the weather, but that didn't seem suitable. I did turn on the outdoor lights, which can be done with a remote control. That gave me a better look at the two lawmen.

Ramsey was a fair-skinned man with sandy hair, a couple of inches shorter than I am. Clancy, in contrast, was a hulk. Not a hunk. A hulk. He was at least six-four, with giant muscles and a completely bald head. And he was ugly, with a threatening look in his eye, though I'd never known him to be anything but polite. Chillingly polite.

Of course, I couldn't see either Ramsey's fair hair or Clancy's bald head at the moment. The temperature was in the low twenties, and both of them were wearing warm winter hats. Ramsey's was knitted, a sort of watch cap, and Clancy's uniform cap had furry ear-flaps that snapped on top. I was wearing a knitted hat, too, and a ski jacket.

The three of us stood beside our cars and waited until Joe pulled in and parked.

Joe got out of his truck wearing his lawyer face, the totally deadpan one. He nodded to Clancy and spoke to Ramsey. "Hi, Burt. What can I do for you?"

"You can tell me why the hell you've taken this case of a bum killing a prominent citizen!"

"Everybody seems to be mad about that today."

"What did you expect? Do you think the people of this county want to waste money on this crazy man who murdered an important businessman?"

"Well, Burt, if he is crazy—"

"He's crazy like a fox! You know what I'm saying! He's trying to get off on a technicality!"

"He's not getting off at all, Burt. Not so far. He just gets a new lawyer because his old one got sick."

"I've already had a dozen complaints about this!"

Joe gave a humorless chuckle. "People are funny about these things, aren't they? They're always yelling about constitutional rights, but when someone actually invokes them, they get all bent out of shape."

Ramsey looked as if Joe had slapped him. His head snapped back, and his eyes popped. "Constitutional! Constitutional! I'm talking about money out of the public pocket! Useless expense!"

Through all this yelling from Burt Ramsey, Joe had never raised his voice. He hadn't changed his deadpan expression. Now he spoke again, and once more his voice was very quiet.

"We need to follow the law, Burt."

"He'll be found guilty! He has no defense!"

"He has me, Burt. I'm his defense."

"The evidence is all against him!"

"I haven't had a chance to read the files yet."

Ramsey looked so frustrated I thought he was going to jump up and down. I was afraid he was going to punch Joe. I felt pretty sure Joe could protect himself if the sheriff punched him, but Ramsey had a gun and an unreliable temper.

He leaned over, putting his face close to Joe's, and for the first time he spoke quietly. "Me and my guys, Joe, we didn't do anything wrong. That confession was right according to Hoyle. Clancy here took it, and he doesn't cut corners. You're not going to be able to prove a thing."

"I'm sure Clancy did everything just right, Burt." Joe didn't mention Ramsey's doing everything right. He simply went on. "It's my job to make sure Hollis gets a fair shake."

Ramsey and Joe stared at each other for at least thirty seconds. Then the sheriff clenched his fists and shook them in the air. "I'll get you for this!" He yelled the words. "You're not going to get away with this!"

He swung around, climbed into his patrol car, and started the motor. The car shot backward, nearly hitting a tree on the other side of the drive. Then he took off, throwing sand and snow. Luckily, it didn't hit any of us.

Clancy hadn't said a word. He, Joe, and I watched Ramsey leave.

Joe turned to Clancy. "I hate quarreling with Ramsey," he said. "But I suppose he'd never believe that."

Clancy shook his head. "You can see why he's upset, Joe. He thought he had this case all set. He was already talking to the prosecutor about sending the guy up for life. Now you take over and make remarks about a completely new investigation."

"I have total confidence in whatever you did, Clancy. But I've been handed this job, and I can't do it right if I don't look the evidence over. And Hollis definitely needs a mental exam. Come on in the house. We'll have a beer."

Clancy shook his head. "I'd better go hold Burt's hand. He'll need it. And, Joe, I have to back him up on this, you know."

"Sure, Clancy. I understand that. It's what the citizens expect."

Clancy leaned toward Joe. "But I'll be glad to talk the investigation over with you. Any time."

"Thanks."

Clancy got in his car—actually it was Hogan's car—and drove away. At least he didn't throw sand at us.

"Clancy always scares me," I said.

"You're just intimidated because he's one of the few guys around who's taller than you are."

"You're taller than I am, and I'm not scared of you."

"Yeah, but Clancy's taller than I am." Joe laughed.

"Let's go on in the house. We may be in for a lot of hassles this evening."

"Hassles? What do you mean?"

"If Ramsey stirs people up, we may get some phone calls."

"Drat!"

"Do you want to go out for dinner?"

"No. It'll be worse if we're in a public place."

I could remember the days when Joe was city attorney. If he made some recommendation one faction or another didn't like, citizens didn't hesitate to collar him at a restaurant to tell him about it.

Sure enough, when we came through the kitchen door the phone was ringing. Joe answered, but the caller wasn't anyone we knew. After two more calls Joe pulled the plug. "They'll call back," he said. "But I don't have to listen to them tonight."

And true to his word, he didn't plug the phone back in until the next morning. Then it rang almost immediately, and the person on the other end of the line was his mother.

You can't hang up on your mother. Plus, Mercy Woodyard Herrera needed to know the whole story. People were probably asking her about the situation, so she'd better understand what was going on.

Joe explained, and I was standing close enough to hear her voice as she replied. It wasn't a happy voice. "Well, Joe, you have to follow your conscience."

"That's how you brought me up, Mom."

"Don't blame me for this!" Mercy laughed. "I don't know what help I could be, but if you need anything give me a ring."

Mercy owns Warner Pier's only insurance agency, and she makes a profit every year. She long ago gave up on her dream of Joe becoming a wealthy corporate attorney.

Joe put on his jacket, and he was reaching for the door handle, ready to leave for work, when the phone rang again. He gave a deep sigh and stared at the instrument. I could see him debating whether to answer it.

I reached around him and stretched out a hand toward the phone. "I'll tell them you're gone," I said. "Hello."

The caller gave a little cough, then spoke in a gruff voice. "Is Woodyard there?"

"This is Mrs. Woodyard."

"Your husband. Is he around?"

"He just went out the door. You'll have to call his office."

"Nah. Just give him a message." He coughed again.

"Certainly."

"I'm a friend of Royal Hollis."

"Yes?"

"If he really wants to help Royal, check out the wife."

"Who is this?"

"That don't matter."

The line went dead.

I repeated the conversation to Joe. He frowned.

"What did that mean?" I asked.

"Is there anything on caller ID?"

"Just a number."

Joe took the phone from me and punched the proper buttons to call the number back. The phone seemed to ring repeatedly. I moved my head close to Joe's, trying to hear who answered.

"Holland Help for All Shelter," a recorded voice said. "Our office isn't open now."

Chapter 6

Joe's reaction surprised me. He pulled off his necktie. Next he picked up the telephone and called his office. It wasn't open yet, of course, but he left a message saying he wouldn't be in that morning.

"Please ask Teresa to talk to Mrs. Bailey about her child support. Cancel anything else. I'll call in at noon." He hung up.

"What are you doing?" I asked.

"I'd better stay home this morning and read up on Royal Hollis. If everybody in the county wants to tell me all about this case, I guess I need to give it the once-over so I'll know what they're talking about."

He went to the dining table, which doubles as a workstation at our house, opened his briefcase, and took out a thick file.

Joe obviously didn't need me. "See you later," I said. "I'll come home for lunch."

When I came back at quarter after twelve, he was

still sitting at the table. It was now covered with papers, and Joe had added his laptop to the mix.

"I brought sandwiches," I said, "but I don't see anyplace to put them."

"Pour some Cokes and I'll clear a spot."

"I can see you've been busy."

"I may need to bounce some ideas around."

Joe doesn't talk about the legal side of his dual career all the time, but occasionally he wants a listener. Just a listener. I try not to say anything but *uh-huh* and *uh-uh*, though it's hard for me to keep quiet.

I got out some carrot sticks, put the sandwiches on plates, sat down, and looked expectant. Joe would talk when he was ready.

We both bit, chewed, and swallowed before he spoke. "Do you know anything about the Davidson killing?"

"Very little. We were out of town when it happened, and the newspaper accounts were rather vague. Or maybe they didn't match the gossip that I heard. When I mentioned Moe to Hogan, he said he hadn't been involved in the investigation. In fact, he sort of snapped me off. By then Hollis had confessed. So what happened?"

"On January fifteenth, Moe Davidson and his wife, Emma, were at their home in Indiana for the winter."

"Yeah—Moe used to stay here year-round, but after he and Emma got married, they began to split their time between her house and his."

"That's right. But on that day Moe got a call from a guy who lives near their place up here—his name is Harry Vandercool. Vandercool told Moe he'd seen a prowler over at their cottage. A group of homeless men were camping somewhere close by, and Vandercool was concerned because the house hadn't been closed up for the winter."

Joe looked up, frowning. "I'll have to ask Vandercool, but I think maybe Moe had been careless about getting the cottage winterized the previous year as well. This may have been a bone of contention between him and Vandercool, since Moe was no longer there during the winter, and Vandercool was afraid of frozen pipes and so forth."

"You mean, there goes the neighborhood? Did Vandercool think Moe was letting the place look shabby?"

"Something like that, maybe."

"If Moe had a year-round house, I guess he didn't need to put up shutters. But it's hard to believe any cottage owner around here could simply forget to drain the pipes and turn off the electricity. For one thing, there are so many people advertising that they're ready to do the job for them."

"At several hundred dollars a pop." Yes, opening and closing cottages is a popular job description in any resort community. Every painter, plumber, and handyman has clients who pay him to do this.

Joe went on. "I think Moe had winterized his own house the previous year, and Vandercool thought he was careless about the way he did it. Anyway, when Vandercool called Moe to report a prowler, Moe told Vandercool he'd come up and check on the situation. And sure enough, around noon the next day Vandercool heard a car driving in over at the Davidson house. Then he heard voices."

"Raised voices?"

"The statement doesn't indicate he heard a quarrel. I'll have to check to see how close Moe's house is to Vandercool. I don't know if Vandercool could have heard ordinary speech." Joe pulled a yellow legal pad over and made a note. "Vandercool decided to go over that afternoon and see Moe. I have an idea Vandercool wasn't too eager to do this."

"Moe was always off on some strange idea. He can't have been a fun neighbor."

"Probably not. So, about one thirty Vandercool looked out his window, and he saw someone coming toward his own house."

"Aha! Was it Royal Hollis?"

"Yes, though Vandercool said he didn't know his name at that time. But Hollis was barefoot."

"Barefoot? In January? In Michigan?"

"That was how Vandercool reacted. He was horrified. He went out and spoke to him. Hollis said that Moe had taken his shoes."

"That would be a really mean thing to do!"

"Vandercool gave Hollis some old shoes of his own. Then he went to Moe's house. When Vandercool got there, he was surprised to see a strange car, a Chevy with a Michigan plate, in the drive. Vandercool walked on, and behind the Chevy he discovered Chuck Davidson. He was leaning over his dad, and Moe was lying on his side. He appeared to be dead.

"Apparently Vandercool had never met Chuck, and when Chuck saw Vandercool he jumped up and said, 'Who are you?' I guess there was some confusion— 'What's wrong with Moe?' 'Have you called an ambulance?' and so forth—and Chuck explained he was Moe's son. He said he'd driven up with his dad and had gone out to buy gasoline. When he came back he discovered his dad lying there."

"I'm surprised Vandercool didn't know Chuck."

"I guess Chuck hadn't been around much in recent years, even though he lives in Grand Rapids."

"Yeah. Just sixty miles away. But I heard that neither Chuck nor Lorraine hung around with their dad much."

"Anyway, Chuck pulled out his cell phone but— naturally, since this is the lakeshore, where things are spotty—he didn't have any service. So he ran into the house and used the landline to call 9-1-1.

"Vandercool's statement says he first thought Moe had had a heart attack or something, but when the EMTs arrived they discovered a head injury. Moe was declared dead at the scene." Joe held up a packet of photographs.

"At least Ramsey got some pictures," I said.

"Yeah, and at least the body was still there when the State Police lab guys arrived."

"Did the autopsy find anything?"

"Not very much. They said Moe had died after being struck by a rounded object. Maybe a rock. And, yes, he could have fallen on something like that."

"Actually, Joe, there aren't too many rocks around here to fall on."

"Correct. Except that the Davidsons are like lots of families. They collect stones from the beach and bring them to the house."

"But nearly all the beach stones are small."

Joe dug through the evidence photos until he found one that showed a small, white, one-story house. "The Davidsons collected all sizes." He pointed to a cairn of rounded river rocks at the corner of the house.

"Those aren't out in the driveway," I said.

"True. I've made a note of that." Joe tapped his notepad, then spoke again. "As soon as the deputies talked to Vandercool and heard about the homeless guy he'd seen around Moe's house, they started out to find him. It wasn't hard."

"Hollis was still around?"

"Right. It looked as if several guys had been camping in a ramshackle cabin about a mile away, near the Interstate."

"I guess the highway has replaced the railroads of

earlier days. We've had similar people here in our neighborhood, and I've always assumed they got there from the Interstate."

"I don't know if anyone has studied that or not." Joe made another note. "But it sure seems that way. They hitchhike, rather than hopping freights the way those guys did seventy-five or a hundred years ago. And one of the sheriff's deputies was familiar with the cabin. I gather that he'd rousted homeless men from there in previous years."

Joe punched a finger into the air for emphasis. "And he'd rousted them at Moe's complaint."

"So Moe had a history of being at odds with the homeless guys."

"Right. Anyway, when Ramsey and his crew got to the cabin, they were surprised to find that Hollis was still there. In fact, there were signs that a couple of other guys had taken off hurriedly, but Hollis was hanging around. And he told the deputies that he hadn't hit Moe. He claimed Moe had hit *him*."

"Moe hit him? Not the other way around?"

"Right. Of course, they didn't believe him."

"Actually, knowing Moe, even as slightly as I did know him—well, I wouldn't be surprised if he punched someone. How aggressive is this Royal Hollis? Would he have punched Moe back?"

"I have no idea. But the deputies took Hollis away, and they recorded their interrogation at the sheriff's department."

"Did Hollis have a lawyer present?"

"No. He had waived his right to have one."

"Can he do that?"

"That's one of the questions I plan to raise. And since there are serious doubts—at least for me—about Hollis' competency—well, I think the sheriff's depart-

ment should have taken more precautions. I think
Clancy wanted to, but the sheriff overruled him."

Joe tapped on a DVD and some typed papers, then
picked up his sandwich. "I have a copy of the DVD and
a typed transcript. I'll look at it after lunch." He chuckled. "But the poor guy's first words nearly sent him up
for life."

I laughed, too. "I don't suppose he said, 'I'm not
homicidal.'"

Joe stopped with his sandwich halfway to his mouth
and stared at me. Then he laid the sandwich down, still
staring.

"Lee, how did you figure that out?"

It was my turn to stare. "You're not telling me that's
what he said?"

"How did you know?"

I sat back and rolled my eyes. "Remember? The old
man with the harmonica? Joe, you can't have forgotten
the guy who only wanted a bus ticket."

Chapter 7

I was sure Joe would remember. I certainly did.

In fact, at that moment I was having a vivid flash-back to the first day I saw this man, the person I now realized must have been Royal Hollis. It had been a day in late fall, two years earlier.

I'd been alone in our house, a house built more than a hundred years ago by my great-grandfather. The house sits in a secluded area, inside the city limits as far as water and sewer service goes, but in a neighborhood where the houses aren't close together. And the space between houses is filled with trees and shrubs and un-dergrowth.

I love our house, which is just an old white farm-house. But I come from the Texas branch of the family. I was raised in open country, with few trees around. I value trees, sometimes more than Michigan folks do, but I like to see the horizon.

So I sometimes find our neighborhood rather spooky. Joe indulges me by working year-round to keep the undergrowth from eating the house alive. Our property is fairly clear, except for a sort of privacy strip of trees and undergrowth between the house and Lake Shore Drive. But the sandy lane that serves as our driveway is kept in plain view. I like to see who's coming.

So on that autumn morning a knock on the front door caught me by surprise. I hadn't seen anybody walking up the road, and I hadn't heard a car drive up. Also, people who know us usually come to the back door. Who could it be?

The storm door was in place and locked, but I still opened the inside door only six or eight inches to look out.

Immediately, a loud, cheerful noise broke forth. Someone started playing a harmonica.

I opened the door a bit wider and began to laugh.

The man on the porch was not only playing, he was also performing a shuffling sort of dance. I call his motions a "sort of dance" because what his feet were doing didn't seem to have any pattern to it. Neither did the sounds from the harmonica. He was just moving around and making noises with a mouth organ.

He was an old guy; I'd have guessed his age at seventy-something. He wore raggedy clothes and had a raggedy beard and a torn ball cap. His gray hair was nearly to his shoulders, but it was neatly combed.

Despite his age, he was kicking up his heels like a lively young man. Lively, if not musically talented.

After about two minutes of this, he stopped playing. Then he took two steps back and said something so peculiar that it made his dancing and singing act seem close to normal.

"Hi, there," he said. "I'm not homicidal."

I'm afraid I laughed again. Not because I found his greeting funny. I didn't. I think I laughed because I was nervous.

So he went on talking. "I'm looking for some work," he said. "I could rake leaves—you can pay me what you want to. See, I need twenty dollars real bad."

I didn't speak, mainly because I didn't know what to say, and he went on talking. "Now, I'm not homicidal," he said again. "And ten dollars—or even five—that would help me a bunch."

"I'm sorry." I started to answer no, but he was still talking.

"I need a bus ticket, see? I came here looking for a job, but there don't seem to be any. So if I could buy me a bus ticket, I'd be on my way."

My impulse, of course, was to refuse. In this day and age we don't hire people we know nothing about to work around our homes. One of my Texas great-grandmothers, according to the family lore, had a steady stream of "tramps" calling at her back door and offering to chop wood in exchange for a meal. But today we call these wandering people "homeless," and we have agencies to house them in shelters. We tell ourselves they aren't truly needy. We shrink from personal contact with them—even with homeless people who promise not to kill us.

As if reading my mind, the man spoke again, repeating what seemed to be his motto: "I'm not homicidal." And he put his harmonica to his lips and played again. This time I could recognize the tune. It was "Home! Sweet Home!"

How could I resist? I had a home. Whatever his problem was, he didn't. And at least he was trying to be friendly and entertaining.

As soon as the tune ended, I spoke. "The garage is open and there's a leaf rake out there. If you'll rake for an hour, I'll contribute toward your bus ticket, but it won't be much because we don't keep money in the house. And I'll throw in a sandwich."

He gave me a grin. "Yes, ma'am. I'll do a lot for a sandwich. And I'm not homicidal."

So the non-homicidal drifter raked for an hour, and I made him two ham sandwiches, putting them in a sack and adding an apple and a dozen store-bought cookies. I dawdled about giving them to him, frankly, hoping Joe would show up before I had to come out from behind my locked doors and approach the old man. I even called Joe at his boat shop to ask him to come home, but he wasn't at the shop, and he had his cell phone turned off. I'd gotten myself into this situation, and I had to deal with it on my own.

The old man worked spryly, raking the leaves into piles and then stuffing them into bags he found in the garage. After an hour I got up enough nerve to carry his lunch outside, though I didn't go too near him. I set up a lawn chair with a folding tray beside it under a tree. I placed the sack lunch and a ten-dollar bill on the tray. I was still being cautious, but I told the old man his lunch was ready.

He washed his hands at the outdoor faucet, then sat in the lawn chair.

"This is a nice lunch," he said. "I thank you. It makes this a nice day." Then he tapped the ten-dollar bill. "And this helps me toward my ticket."

I felt rather guilty at that remark; ten dollars wasn't going to get him very far on down the road. I could have given him a bit more; my tale that we didn't have "money in the house" had been a code meaning we had nothing to steal. I could have anted up another ten.

"My husband is due any minute," I said. "He might have a suggestion on where you could find work."

Again I was covering my fanny. Telling the guy that I wasn't alone all the time.

"What kind of work were you looking for?" I asked.

"Oh, anything honest," the old man said.

Was I being played, just as I was playing him?

He spoke again. "See, I'm not homicidal."

Why did he keep saying that? I didn't understand exactly, but he ate, and I stood on the porch and talked uneasily about the weather—because Texas girls are taught to be friendly even to strangers. I was relieved when I heard a truck.

I looked down the drive. "Oh, here comes my husband," I said. "Good!"

And when I turned back to speak again to the old man, he was gone.

He was fading into the trees behind our house, lunch sack and all. But he had left in such a hurry that his ten-dollar bill was still on the tray.

"Wait a minute!" He didn't turn around. "You forgot your money!"

He disappeared into the undergrowth.

I was both shaking my head and laughing when Joe got out of his truck. "What's going on?" he asked.

I described my adventure with the homeless man. "I guess you scared him away," I said. "All I had to say was, 'Here comes my husband' and he disappeared into thin air."

Joe smiled, but he wasn't really amused, and I got that lecture I'd already been expecting—the one about being careful of strangers.

I gestured toward the heap of stuffed garbage bags. "Well, he did work on the leaves," I said. "I wouldn't normally hire somebody like that, but there was something about that harmonica I couldn't resist." I leaned toward Joe. "And he assured me—at least a dozen times—that he wasn't homicidal."

We put the ten-dollar bill on the little tray, weighed it down with a rock, then went in for our own lunch.

That afternoon we went out to do some shopping, and when we came back the money was gone.

The non-homicidal harmonica player never came to the door again, but once or twice I thought I saw him walking up a lane in the neighborhood, still wearing a ball cap with the bill half torn off. Whoever he was, he didn't bother us, even if we left the garage unlocked. Eventually I almost forgot the whole episode.

Now I reminded Joe about it. He shook his head. "I'd forgotten that. In fact, since I never saw the old guy with the harmonica, I had almost decided you imagined it. It's so unlike you to offer food and bus fare to some homeless guy."

"I guess it's my Texas great-grandmother's genes coming out. She was known for letting strangers sleep in the barn in exchange for chopping firewood."

"They probably marked the gate some way to tell other tramps this was a good place to ask for help."

"My grandmother thought they did. But nowadays— well, there are too many crazies around. No, if somebody really seemed to need help, I'd be more likely to call the Salvation Army shelter and tell 'em we needed a pickup."

"I don't think they offer that service. People have to get there on their own." Joe sighed deeply. "But that leads us back to that phone call."

"Yup. Made from the homeless shelter and assuring us that 'the wife' had something to do with Moe's death."

"Now that I've read up on the case, I guess I'd better make an effort to find out who made that call we got this morning."

"Do you think he was referring to Moe's wife? Emma?"

"Who knows? It could have been some other woman;

the caller probably didn't actually know Emma. It might have been Lorraine with the loud mouth. Or anybody. And even if he did mean Emma herself, there's probably nothing to the tip."

"After meeting Emma one time, I'm inclined to agree that any involvement by her is unlikely. She's just so very quiet. She almost hid in the corner while Chuck was showing me around the store. She let Chuck and Lorraine do all the talking."

"Besides, the investigation report indicates she wasn't even there."

"Wasn't there?"

Joe nodded. "Apparently Chuck met his dad someplace, and they came to the house up here together. Emma had dropped Moe off, then gone home. So it would be hard for Mrs. Davidson to have been involved in her husband's death."

"Oh. Well, what's the next step?"

"Maybe I can run by the shelter and see if they have any idea who made that phone call."

"Does it matter? If Emma Davidson wasn't there, why bother?"

"I'm not sure." Joe considered for a long minute before he said anything else. "I guess you could call it a hunch. Moe Davidson's death was investigated in such a superficial way—somehow I don't like to ignore that particular tip."

"Go for it," I said.

"I've got to see a judge at three o'clock. But maybe I'll have time to go to the shelter after that. I can't ignore a potential witness."

Chapter 8

I was at my office the next time I heard from Joe. At four fifteen he called and asked if I wanted to have dinner out in Holland that evening.

"Sure. What's the occasion?"

"I'm at the homeless shelter. The director says anybody who's familiar with the layout here could have wandered into the office and used the phone, especially in the morning, when most of the occupants are moving out and things are busy. So he recommends that I just ask people about Royal Hollis. And the best time would be as they check into the shelter tonight."

"Are you saying we're having dinner at the homeless shelter?"

"No, we could go out and eat after I talk to the clients. They finish serving by six thirty or so. I would just stay around on my own, but I need a little help from you. So my dinner invitation includes requesting a favor."

"What do you need?"

"A change of clothes. I'm wearing the wrong thing."

"The shelter has a dress code?"

"No." Joe laughed. "But I've got on my impress-the-judge suit. And that's not going to impress the shelter's clientele. They're pretty informal."

It was my turn to laugh. "I'll bring you some jeans."

"Not the ones with the hole in the knee or the brand-new ones, please. And a flannel shirt. But the shelter opens at five fifteen. The guys are lining up already."

"I'll hurry."

I made it by five o'clock, carrying Joe's clothes in an old gym bag. Joe snatched it from me and dashed into the men's room. By the time he came out I had introduced myself to the director—I noticed he also wore jeans and scuffed boots. I'd found time to change into jeans and a flannel shirt, too.

The director was a young, earnest guy. His nametag read DARREL. He explained that the shelter took only men—women and children were referred to a different shelter—and they could register for only one night at a time. Everyone left after breakfast the next morning.

"I don't know if anybody will be able to give your husband any information," he said. "But he can ask. And if you are going to wait for him, you can sit here in my office."

"Since I'm here, could you use some extra kitchen help? I might as well do a little work."

The earnest Darrel gave an earnest smile. "We can always use help. We have a paid person in charge of the kitchen, but we can use six or eight volunteers a night, and we rarely have that many."

Darrel led me to the kitchen and introduced me to the kitchen manager. He was small and scrawny, with hair shot with gray. His face was heavily lined, as if he'd had a hard life. I speculated that he was a former

client of the shelter. Darrel told me his name was Elkouri.

"So naturally we all call him Elk," he said. This was
obviously a joke; Elk was built more like a mouse than
a large horned beast of any type.

I offered to shake Elk's hand, but he avoided me by
picking up a tray of hamburger buns. He gave a little
cough, what I've heard described as a cigarette cough.
Hmmm. That was interesting. Our anonymous caller
that morning had coughed that way.

Elk looked at me suspiciously. "We work pretty hard
here, even the volunteers."

"I've got experience with food service, including
some at a shelter," I said. I didn't tell him I'd worked at
a shelter when I was doing a couple of years with the
Junior League of Dallas, one of the activities my first
husband had approved of for the former Miss Texas
competitor he saw as a trophy wife.

I tried to look eager. "What do you need me to do,
Elk? Wash dishes? Scrub floors? I'm pretty handy around
a kitchen."

Elk tipped his head back and squinted. "Can you lift
one of those big flat pans? Like the one with Tater Tots
in it?"

"Show me where the hot pads are, and I bet I can."

Three other volunteers had reported for work, and,
with Elk calling the shots, we got the food onto folding
tables and began to fill the plates as the men filed past.
The shelter had quite a crowd, at least seventy-five
men. Winter, naturally, draws the biggest crowds of
people needing a place to stay.

As I worked I saw Joe working, too. Now in his jeans
and flannel shirt, he went up and down the line of waiting men, questioning the diners. Some were obviously
giving him the brush, but he gave out some business

cards. After the line cleared he began to circulate among the tables.

The shelter's food looked more filling than either delicious or nutritious. That night's menu featured sloppy joes, Tater Tots, and frozen mixed vegetables. Dessert was sheet cake—unadorned and not very tasty-looking. Elk said the cakes had been donated by one of the supermarket bakeries. The food was served on paper plates and eaten with plastic utensils.

It was definitely not fancy, but it would keep a homeless man from starving.

After the food was served, Elk instructed the volunteers on how to put the leftovers away. Then we began the cleanup, scrubbing down the tables, washing up the pots and pans, mopping the floor. The clients drifted into another room, where there was a television set, or wandered up the stairs, apparently toward the dorms.

Elk offered all the volunteers dinner, but the other three declined. He told us we could leave, but Joe was still talking to one or two of the men, so I waited around, changing to dish drying duty. By the time Elk carefully rinsed and scoured his final serving pans, then put them into the hot soapy water, Joe was through with his interviews. He came over and picked up a dish towel, ready to help dry.

Elk glared at him. By then I'd realized that Elk glared at everybody.

"This woman of yours," he said. "She ain't afraid of hard work."

"I picked a good'un," Joe said. "And luckily, she picked me, too."

"Darrel says you're a lawyer. Whatcha askin' everbody about?"

"I've got a client who's in a lot of trouble. His name is Royal Hollis."

"Ha! I *guess* he's in trouble!"

"I'm hoping I can help him out."

I jumped in then. "Did you know him, Elk? He may have stayed here. He's the old guy with a harmonica."

Elk lowered his head until it was almost inside the giant pot he was scrubbing out. "Some people knew him," he said. "But Royal Hollis never come to the shelter."

Joe nodded. "It sounds as if he liked to camp on his own."

"That's how he got in trouble." Elk rinsed out the big cooking pot and handed it on to me.

Then he stood back and glared at us again. "I could give you some dinner."

Joe took a deep breath, and I knew he was going to say we had to leave. So I spoke quickly. "I'd love some of that sloppy joe, Elk. It smells just like my mom's."

"That sauce ain't canned," he said. "I make it myself."

Joe gave me a quizzical look, and I winked at him. By the time Elk had warmed some sloppy joe and fixed three plates—we got heavy crockery plates, not paper ones—we were through drying the pans, and the three of us sat down at the kitchen worktable.

Elk's sloppy joe turned out to be pretty good. The frozen vegetables left a lot to be desired, but I've definitely had worse meals. Heck, I've cooked and served worse meals.

We all ate for several minutes before I spoke. "Royal Hollis came by our house once," I said. "He raked some leaves for us. Seemed like a nice old guy. I was sure surprised when I heard they thought he killed someone."

"He's a kind of a loner," Elk said. "Or that's the scuttlebutt around this place."

"I'm sorry to hear that," Joe said. "I was hoping to find somebody who hung out with him, maybe who'd camped with him."

"Why would you want to talk to somebody like that?"

"The deputies didn't do much of an investigation, but when they picked Hollis up he was in a cabin at least a mile from where the killing took place. They did notice that more than one person had been staying there. I thought the other guys might know something that could help him."

"I guess they all split."

Joe nodded. "Probably Hollis came back after his run-in with Davidson and said he'd had some trouble, so the others took off. What I don't understand is why Hollis didn't take off with them."

"I guess he didn't know the guy was dead."

"Yeah, but if he told the others he had punched somebody, or shoved him down—or whatever happened—you'd think he would have known it was likely the sheriff would be there PDQ."

"Maybe Royal told them a different story."

"Like what?"

Elk sighed. "Well, the talk is that ol' Royal claimed the guy had shoved *him* down."

"That Moe Davidson struck Royal Hollis?"

Elk nodded seriously. "Now that's just Royal talkin'. And he didn't always make good sense. Or so I've heard."

I was careful not to look at Joe. Elk's story was a new version of what had happened when Moe Davidson was killed. If Moe had struck first, that might be the basis of a plea of self-defense for Royal. I considered that and decided—in my nonlawyer way—that it was unlikely. Moe had been the householder. All the prosecution had to say was that Moe was protecting his life and property.

But Elk was still talking. "What I always wondered was what that woman had to say."

I paused, my fork loaded with overcooked carrots and halfway to my mouth. When I spoke, I tried to sound innocent.

"Woman? What woman?"

Elk dropped his head nearly to his plate and didn't reply. "It's just scuttlebutt," he said. "Probably nothin' to it."

Joe chewed and swallowed. I could almost hear him thinking, I must not spook this guy.

"The sheriff didn't know that there had been a woman there," he said. "It might help Royal a lot if we knew there had been someone."

Elk kept looking at his plate. "Anything I heard was gossip," he said.

"I understand," Joe said. "Of course, it would have made sense for Mrs. Davidson to come up to the cottage with her husband."

Elk shrugged. "You want dessert?" he asked.

The conversation was over. Joe didn't ask another question, and I kept my mouth shut as well. We declined the sheet cake, told Elk his sloppy joe was delicious, thanked Darrel for his cooperation, and went out to the parking lot.

"You didn't get a fancy dinner out," Joe said.

"It might not have been fancy, but it was interesting."

"We could go to Russ' for pie and coffee."

"You're on."

Russ' is like a large-scale diner, with down-home food and good pie. I always like to go there, and I was eager to talk over Elk's comments and to find out if Joe had learned anything else interesting about Royal Hollis.

As soon as our order was on the table, I wanted to ask Joe a question. But he asked me one first. "How'd you figure out Elk was the guy who called us this morning?"

"I don't know that he is. But the caller this morning made a little noise—well, it could have been a cough like Elk's. I just thought you should talk to him. For someone who claimed that he never met Royal Hollis, he seemed to know a lot about him."

"Elk's the only person I talked to who admitted he'd ever heard of Hollis."

"Do you think he might testify?" I asked.

"I doubt it would do much good. But he's convinced that some woman was there at the house when Davidson died." Joe took a bite of apple pie and followed it with a sip of his coffee.

"Do you think it might have been Mrs. Davidson?"

"I don't know. But I guess I'd better try to track her down tomorrow."

"Do you think she'll be willing to talk to you?"

"I guess I'll find out."

Chocolate Chat

The Maya followed the Olmecs, settling on the Yucatán Peninsula and in what is today Guatemala. According to some accounts, the Mayan name for the cacao tree was simply "tree." They may have felt cacao was so important that it didn't need a specific name.

They believed that the cacao tree belonged to the gods, and its pods were gifts to humankind. Ancient drawings indicate that the pods were used in religious rituals.

Apparently the Maya originated chocolate as a drink. This was a bitter concoction, spiced with peppers and sometimes thickened with cornmeal. It was used for religious rituals, not just as an ordinary beverage.

The scientific name for the cacao tree, *Theobroma cacao,* means "food of the gods." The name was selected by Linnaeus, the Swedish botanist who came up with the method for naming plants. He named it after the Mayan belief that the trees belonged to the gods.

Images of cacao pods were carved into the walls of Mayan palaces and temples, and apparently were the symbols of life and fertility.

Chapter 9

At nine the next morning, Joe started calling Emma Davidson. At two o'clock that afternoon, they had not made contact.

He began with the Davidson house, talking to Chuck three separate times. Emma was out calling on friends, Chuck said. He had no idea when she would be back. Would she be home for lunch? Chuck had no idea about that either. And he had no idea exactly which friends Emma had intended to visit.

On the off chance that she might come home to eat lunch, Joe went by the Davidson house at twelve thirty. Lorraine opened the door. This time, Joe said, she didn't yell and swear at him, but she didn't invite him in either. The only information Joe got was that her stepmother was out, and Lorraine didn't know when she would be home.

"But," Joe had observed, "there are three cars in your driveway. One each for you, Chuck, and Emma."

"Some friend picked Emma up," Lorraine had said.

She did agree to give Joe's phone number to Emma if her stepmom should happen to check in.

I got all this secondhand, of course, when Joe met me for a late lunch and reported on his frustrating morning.

"Is Emma giving you the runaround?" I asked.

"Very likely. If she hasn't spoken to anybody about her husband's death yet, she probably still doesn't want to say anything."

"Did she talk to the sheriff's office after Moe died?"

"Not in any official way."

I grazed at my salad a minute before I went on. "Are you overreacting? Maybe Emma went shopping with her friend. If they went to Grand Rapids, they could easily spend the whole day at the mall."

Joe shook his head. "Chuck and Lorraine didn't have their stories quite straight. Chuck told me Emma had gone out to 'pay some calls on her Warner Pier friends.' But when I pointed out to Lorraine that Emma's car seemed to be in the driveway, she said someone had picked Emma up. So their stories don't match."

"One of them could have honestly been mistaken."

Joe spoke grimly. "I can attest to that. They're definitely mistaken if they think I'm going to give up."

No, I knew all the Davidsons were in for a surprise if they believed Joe would simply disappear because Emma was avoiding him. Joe doesn't yell and scream and beat on his chest, but he can wear down any opponent.

Joe smiled philosophically. "Let's think about something else while we're eating. How was your morning?"

I laughed. "That's not changing the subject. I spent most of the morning thinking about the Davidsons' building."

"You'd still like to get hold of it."

"Sure. I went over and talked to Tilda. She thinks there may be a good chance. But the guy I saw with her definitely has an interest."

"Chuck doesn't seem to object to you as a buyer."

"No, he's a realist. But I'm not going to pay more than the building is worth just to butter the Davidsons up. So it may be a lost cause. I don't like their asking price."

"Are you going to view the building again?"

"Tilda's coming over to show it for me at five o'clock."

"I'll stay out of the way."

We both laughed. Yes, even if Lorraine hadn't been rude to Joe that morning, the less contact they had, the better.

Life became more normal when I got back to the office. Dolly Jolly, who was in charge of making the chocolate while Aunt Nettie was in the South Seas, was working on the big clown figure that was to be the star of our exhibit for Clown Week.

The three-dimensional figure stood two feet tall, and Dolly had named him Warner Whacko.

Warner wore traditional clown whiteface—made of white chocolate, of course—with dark chocolate eyes and milk chocolate hair. His baggy suit was of white and milk chocolate in a Harlequin pattern, and his slippers were dark chocolate, with white chocolate pompons. He had a white chocolate ruff, edged in milk chocolate. This was the first time Aunt Nettie had turned a major display piece over to Dolly, and Dolly had produced a work of art. Clown Week visitors were going to ooh and aah as they passed our window.

Warner was simply for show, of course. The clowns we would be selling in the shop were much simpler in design. They were also solid chocolate. A chocolate piece as large as Warner would work only if it was partially hollow. But, like Warner, the smaller clowns also had Harlequin suits and white ruffs, as well as merry expressions on their white chocolate faces.

When I stopped to watch her, Dolly was adding eyelashes to the face of the big Warner.

"He's gorgeous!" I said.

"He's a lotta work!" Dolly yelled. Dolly is over six feet tall and big-boned, with a larynx to match her size. Even when she tries to whisper, her voice comes out as a shout.

"I wish I could make him more colorful!" she said.

"You could have dyed the white chocolate any color you like."

"Nettie didn't want to do that! She wanted him to look like chocolate!"

"I think she was right, Dolly. Warner might not have looked so subtle and sophisticated in bright colors."

"There's nothing sophisticated about a clown! Remember Moe and his squirt bottle?"

"Only too well. Hey, at five o'clock Tilda's going to show me that building. Do you want to come along?"

"I have an appointment for a haircut, but I could change it!"

"That's up to you. I won't commit to anything until you've looked the situation over."

Dolly leaned close to me, and I could tell she wanted to talk quietly. But being Dolly, she bellowed in my ear. "What are you going to do if the Davidson kids want an immediate commitment to buy?"

"I don't see why they should. The building just went on the market yesterday. I'll just tell them we have to wait until Aunt Nettie gets home. That will be less than a month."

But my stomach did a little dance as I walked back

to my office. I didn't want to commit to buying that building without consulting Aunt Nettie. I didn't have the authority to buy it in the name of TenHuis Chocolade. Joe and I didn't have the money to do it on our own, and getting a loan on my own hook might be a hassle. I could, I supposed, mortgage our home to get the money, but I really didn't want to do that, and I wasn't sure Joe would go along with it. He was already up to his ears in mortgage payments for the boat shop. His legal activities had grown so—well, active—that his time at the shop had suffered. Now the shop was barely breaking even.

No, I wanted to wait until Aunt Nettie came home to make a final decision on the purchase of the Clowning Around building.

But at five o'clock I learned that might not happen.

At that time Tilda was sitting in my visitor's chair, managing to look alternately sympathetic and excited. Her artificially red hair was standing on end, and the nap on her fake fur jacket seemed to be imitating it. Her cute little face was having a hard time taking the right expression at any given moment, because she had brought news—good and bad. Good for her, and bad for me.

"Lee, I was totally astonished. The phone call came out of nowhere. Yes, I showed the guy the building yesterday—you saw us. But I didn't expect him to make an offer! Not this quick."

Ecstasy took over her face for a moment. Then Tilda remembered to look concerned and sympathetic. I understood her mixed feelings. As a Realtor, Tilda represented the Davidson heirs. Her job was to get the most money for their property that she could. Doing that also increased her fee. But as a Warner Pier businesswoman, Tilda wanted to get along with the locals. Like me. She didn't want to sell some outsider a building I was interested in if it left me with hard feelings. A dissatisfied local customer could cause her a lot of problems.

"Did the caller make a good offer?" I asked.

Tilda nodded. "Above asking."

"And who is this guy?"

"His name is Philip Montague, and he represents a development company. I don't know any more than that. Montague made it clear he was acting for the company, not for himself."

I knew Tilda wouldn't tell me the amount of their offer until she had an okay from the Davidsons. Her face was still flashing between the exaltation brought on by getting a good offer and the sympathy she thought she should offer me.

I wasn't happy, but I didn't want to display my feelings. I tried to make my face deadpan. "Have you presented the offer to Emma, Chuck, and Lorraine?"

"Not yet."

"Is there any point in my looking at the building?"

"Of course, Lee! You may want to bid against these people."

"I doubt it." There was no point in making Tilda feel too sure of herself. "I'm not sure I would go as high as the asking price, much less above it. But I'd still like to see the building." I made a grimace I hoped looked like a grin. "I may want to crow over the final purchaser—tell him why he was a dumb bunny to spend real money on that property."

Tilda laughed nervously.

I stood up and reached for my jacket. "Let's go."

We had only to walk next door, of course, but it was closing time for the downtown businesses, so the street wasn't as empty as we might have expected. In fact, the people at the wine store on the other side of Clowning Around were outside on ladders, putting up plywood clowns—painted in garish colors—above their show windows. They're neighbors, so Tilda and I stopped to admire their decorations.

Then the out-of-town clowns—Kyle and Paige—came along. They were wearing their costumes and did a few handsprings for us. This caused cries of "Watch out!" from Tilda and me and the wine shop owners. A patch of ice is always a possibility on a Michigan sidewalk in February.

Finally Tilda unlocked the door, and the two of us went into Clowning Around.

Once again I was oppressed by the masses of clowns. They were on the shelves, on the floor, on the walls, and hanging from the ceiling. Big photos of groups of clowns were massed behind the cash register. I could hardly breathe for clowns. And I recalled that the back rooms—the rooms for storage and staff work—were just as bad.

I hadn't seen anybody working over there. I didn't know how Lorraine, Chuck, and Emma were going to have everything ready to open the store for Clown Week. But that was their problem. Looking at the building was my concern.

"I saw most of the main floor," I said. "How about starting the tour upstairs?"

Tilda led the way to the back of the building, where two closed doors were located side by side. "I can never remember which of these is the restroom and which the stairs," she said. She produced another key and tried the left-hand door. It opened readily and revealed a narrow staircase.

"I guess the building was originally set up so that the store operator could live above it," she said.

"There is a separate entrance to the upstairs off the alley, right?"

"Yes. Of course, I don't think Moe rented his upstairs much. He used it for storage."

"If his brain was as disorganized as this place, heaven knows what we'll find up there." I quit talking and followed Tilda upstairs. I didn't mention that the building was also spooky. I could swear ghosts were walking behind us, making the floor creak and causing drafts of the cold winter air to follow us.

The apartment was as big a mess as the downstairs. It was full of cardboard boxes and assorted stuff. Apparently that was simply the way Moe operated.

The area had other problems. The walls had patches of damp and peeling paint. The sinks had horrible brown stains from dripping water, and the appliances were old and dirty. If the apartment was to be rented, it would first require a complete renovation.

I pointed this out to Tilda. "The downstairs needs work, too," I said. "I definitely think their price is way too high."

"But, Lee, if you were changing this building into a modern, beautiful chocolate plant—with a workroom similar to the one you have now—you'd want a complete renovation anyway."

"If we could rent the upstairs out, it would help offset the cost of the work. But this place would need more than a coat of paint."

Tilda looked a bit dejected as we went back down the stairs. I didn't blame her. The place made me feel dejected. In fact, I felt more than dejected. I felt nervous. Scared. Jumpy.

Why? It was just a building that needed to be cleared out and cleaned up. It wasn't a haunted house or a torture chamber.

But the building not only looked spooky, it also sounded spooky. I kept hearing creaks, something almost like a door closing, and weird groans. I tried not to shudder.

Tilda turned on more lights in the workroom. Glaring light from bare bulbs beat down on us. It was a large open area—or would have been open if it weren't crowded with shelving, cardboard boxes, and heaps of clown paraphernalia.

"There is that little kitchen area," Tilda said. She pointed across the room.

I followed her. "Kitchen area" was a fancy name for a table with a Formica top and two metal folding chairs. An old refrigerator sat against the wall. An electric coffeepot was on the table. Water for the pot apparently came from a mop sink near the table. I will admit the sink was fairly clean, but it didn't look as if anybody had ever mopped. A couch, covered in once-fashionable plaid, was between us and the table. It was the only thing in the whole building that looked fairly comfortable.

As I approached the kitchen area, I heard that groaning again.

"What is that noise?" I asked.

"Something to do with the plumbing, I guess," Tilda said. She walked over to the mop sink, lowered her head into it, and put an ear near the faucets. "It is eerie, I admit."

I heard the groaning again and shuddered. "It gives me the willies. I'd almost think it was some sort of animal. But you're probably right about it being the plumbing."

I also went around the couch, but I couldn't get near the sink because Tilda had dropped to her knees and was looking at the drain. So I looked around the area, sweeping my eyes over the table, the chairs, the coffee-pot, and a heap of black fabric on the couch.

And the fabric moved.

"Oh, Tilda! There's something on the couch!" I'd barely managed not to scream.

"There's something everywhere in this place." Tilda stood up and turned around. And then she did scream. Because the heap of black fabric had moved again. Part of it slid onto the floor.

And it revealed a small, white hand. Someone was lying there.

My skin was crawling. On top of the strange sounds and strange boxes and strange mess, this was simply too creepy. But I took a deep breath, leaned over, and grabbed the black cloth. I yanked it away from the couch.

It revealed Emma Davidson, curled up and seemingly dead to the world.

Chapter 10

"Oh my God!" Tilda yelped out the words.

I dropped to my knees beside her. "Mrs. Davidson?" I shook her gently. "Wake up, Emma."

"I'd better call Chuck. He should know what to do."

"Call 9-1-1, Tilda. If Emma didn't wake up at the noise we've made, she's not asleep. She's unconscious. We need an ambulance."

I had made my words an order, and Tilda obeyed. She made the call. Still holding her cell phone, Tilda ran to the front door, ready to open it for the ambulance. "I'll call Chuck!" she said.

I sat on the floor beside Emma Davidson. She was barely breathing, but she *was* breathing. I didn't think she needed CPR, but what did I know? I'd had one first aid class.

Warner Pier has a volunteer ambulance service, but they react fairly rapidly. Or maybe they just don't have far to come. Anyway, they were there in less than ten minutes.

I was not happy to see that Greg Glossop was on the crew. Greg is the pharmacist who operates the drugstore that's part of the town's one supermarket. His nickname is Greg Gossip. The news about Emma Davidson would be all over town as soon as Greg could get to a phone.

I was even more unhappy when Greg examined the table, then dropped to his knees and looked under the couch and all around the area. "Aha!" he said. He pulled out a prescription container and held it above his head triumphantly. "Elavil! For depression. That can cause heart problems!"

His satisfied attitude made me angry. I was aware that if Emma had taken an overdose, knowing what drug was involved would help doctors treat her. But his smugness was annoying.

Tilda and I watched as the EMTs loaded Emma onto a gurney, rolled her out the front door, and lifted her into the ambulance. Before they closed the door Chuck pulled up, skidding into a parking place in front of the store. He yelled a few words of thanks to Tilda and me and assured us that Lorraine would meet him at the hospital. He climbed into the front of the ambulance, and it pulled out.

Tilda and I watched it go, siren shrieking. Then we each took deep breaths. My knees seemed to be knocking, and Tilda looked as shaky as I felt.

"Lock up the store," I said, "and let's go down to the Sidewalk Café. I'm buying. We both need a drink."

Joe found us there about twenty minutes later. He'd already heard about Emma.

"What was wrong with her?" he asked. "Heart attack?"

"She was barely breathing," I said. "And she was

unconscious. I guess it could have been her heart. Or a stroke."

I couldn't bring myself to tell him about Greg Gossip and the empty prescription bottle. I left that tale to Tilda, and naturally she told it. There was no point in trying to keep it quiet. And I wasn't even sure why I wanted to.

Joe ordered a beer. "I'm glad to hear they looked around for anything odd," he said.

"Why would you think there might be anything odd?" I asked.

"Oh, since her husband was killed . . ." Joe's voice trailed off. "I guess I'm just being suspicious. Well, Tilda, do you think Lee's a jinx?"

"In what way?"

"The first time she looks at the Clowning Around building, Lorraine goes berserk. The second time Emma Davidson may have OD'd."

Tilda laughed. "I kept a sharp eye on Lee. I think she was an innocent bystander. And now I've got to get home. My kids will be tearing up the house. Thanks for the drink, Lee. And I'll call you tomorrow to hear what you thought about the building—before the crisis hit."

"Let me know if you find out any more about the other bidder."

Tilda smiled, but she didn't say she would do that. I told Joe about the unexpected bidder. Then we found a table for dinner.

The Sidewalk Café, despite the implications of its name, isn't primarily an outdoor place. The name is a pun, because the restaurant is decorated with children's toys designed for sidewalk play—roller skates, marbles, jacks, jump ropes, and tricycles. Mock chalk drawings decorate the floor and walls. It's one of three restaurants operated by Joe's stepfather, Mike Herrera. One of the few Warner Pier restaurants that stay open all year long, it has good food of the casual sort: French dip sandwiches, beef stew, chicken strips, and hamburgers.

Joe and I go to the Sidewalk so often that we can order without looking at the menu, so we told the waitress what we wanted before we sat down. Then Joe looked at his watch. "I'd better give Belle Montgomery another call," he said. "I've spent the day calling first her and then Emma Davidson."

He pulled out his cell phone and punched some numbers. Immediately I heard a standard cell phone ring no more than twenty feet away. At first I thought this was a coincidence, but when I looked in the direction of the sound, I saw Belle sitting at a corner table.

I waved, Joe turned to see who was there, and we all laughed.

Joe went over to her table. I saw him gesturing, Belle shaking her head, then nodding and smiling. I beckoned. Joe waved to the waitress, pointing to our table. Belle picked up her wineglass, and they both came over.

"Your nice husband invited me to join you," Belle said.

"Of course. There's no point in eating dinner alone." I reminded myself that the crisis over Emma Davidson was not a suitable topic for discussion with an emotionally distraught person such as Belle. "Are you still at the Peach Street B and B?"

"Yes, but Sarajane can keep me only a few more days. I may go home then." She sipped her wine, then went on. "I wanted to talk to both of you, so this is lucky. I guess I wanted to try to convince you that I'm not complete white trash."

"We certainly didn't think that, Belle."

"Well, when someone tells you she never saw her father in her life . . ."

"Believe me," Joe said, "in our practice we run into families in much stranger situations than that. If I thought anything about it at all, I wondered if it had something to do with your father's mental state."

Belle nodded. "Yes, it did. He was serving in the army when my parents married. He was wounded—a head injury. When he came home, according to my mother, he wasn't the same person. She was afraid to be around him. Actually, she did take me to see him once or twice. In the military hospital. But I was too small to remember."

"Speaking as a defense lawyer," Joe said, "I might find that a help. His first attorney said the prosecutor was going to offer a plea deal. If we can show that your dad isn't competent—well, at least he might be in a different kind of confinement."

"A mental hospital rather than a prison?"

"Possibly."

"But apparently my father lived on his own for many years before he—well, took to the road. He held jobs, lived in regular houses. I guess he was pretty much on the edge—never held a job for long, never lived anywhere for more than a few months. But he wasn't homeless. Then about ten years ago he started this wandering way of life, with no fixed domicile."

Joe frowned. "I gather that your dad became one of the guys who like to camp on their own. He seems to have avoided homeless shelters."

"I don't suppose . . . No, it would be too much to hope for."

"We can hope for anything, Belle. What is it?"

Belle used her fork to draw a design on the butcher

paper that covered the table. "All that talk about a new investigation . . ."

"Yes?"

"Is there any chance at all that my dad could actually be innocent?"

Joe didn't answer immediately, but frowned and seemed to consider his reply. I kept out of it. I felt terribly sorry for Belle. She was grasping at straws. But the most surprising thing was the change in her attitude. When Joe had talked to her two days earlier I had felt sure that she thought her father had killed Moe Davidson. I had thought she was simply going through the motions when she offered to pay for his defense. Now she was allowing herself to think about his being innocent.

Was she in for a big disappointment?

"Belle," Joe said, "the last thing I want you to do is get your hopes up. Yes, I'm going to take a new look at the evidence, talk to the witnesses. But I wouldn't want you to expect a miracle."

Bell smiled wryly. "Miracles don't happen very often."

Joe nodded. "I'm glad you understand that. And now, I've been calling you all day so I can ask a question. Are you ready?"

"As ready as I'm likely to be."

"I wanted to tell you that I'm going over to the county seat to interview your dad tomorrow," Joe said. "If you want to go along, I'll be happy to give you a lift."

The waitress arrived just at that moment with Belle's dinner. We all sat silently until she had gone. Then Joe continued. "Of course, there's no particular reason for you to meet your dad at this moment. And you couldn't be present for his main interview."

Belle smiled. "You're offering me emotional support,

aren't you? A chance to meet my father without doing it on my own."

"I don't know that I would be much help emotionally," Joe said. "It would also be a chance for you to talk to your dad directly about his representation."

"His representation?"

"You said you were willing to pay for your dad's representation. I don't want to stand in the way of his making a change."

Belle was shaking her head. "I've changed my mind. No, whether I pay you or the State of Michigan does, I feel that you're the best person to represent my dad."

So that settled that question. When it came to the question of representing Royal Hollis, Joe was doing it. Unless Royal Hollis himself refused to have him.

We were all silent for a few minutes. I think we were absorbing the situation. Then I took a deep breath. "Well, as my Texas grandma would have said, let's have some pleasant dinner table conversation. Y'all can discuss business later. Belle, tell us about yourself."

"Myself?"

"Yes. Where are you from? What is your profession? Have you always lived in Michigan?"

Belle smiled. "I was born of poor, but honest, parents—or at least my mother was poor but honest. My dad may have simply been poor. And I've lived in Michigan most of my life."

When she was small, Belle said, she and her mother had lived with her grandparents. Her mother had remarried when Belle was five. Her stepfather was apparently a nice enough person, and Belle had grown up in Bay City, not far from Lake Huron. She had gone to college in Ohio, earning a degree in business. After college she had worked for an arts association in Saginaw, which is not far from Bay City, and had married one of

the group's board members. I deduced that he had
been some years older than she had been. They had no
children, and her husband had died two years ago. I
also deduced that she had inherited a bundle from him,
but of course Belle didn't say so.

"And now you know all there is to know about me,"
she concluded. Including the fact that she had an emotional hang-up about her father, I thought. But it wasn't
up to me to solve Belle's problems. She was on her own
there.

We were leaving the restaurant before Emma Davidson entered the conversation, and neither Joe nor I was
responsible for bringing her up.

Actually, our close friend Lindy Herrera dropped by
our table and introduced her into the conversation.

"What an experience you had with Emma Davidson," she said to me.

Belle gave a sort of gasp, and I realized that she
knew exactly who Emma Davidson was.

"It was startling," I said. "I hope she's better."

"What happened to Emma Davidson?" Belle asked.

I explained, trying to make the whole episode sound
almost casual. I left out the part about the pill bottle,
but Belle caught on right away.

"I don't suppose it could have been some sort of
overdose?" she asked.

"Maybe," I said.

We said good night then, and I drove off in my van,
leaving Joe to follow me home. And all the way to the
house I wondered about Emma. Then I wondered
about Belle. They were two troubled women.

But, I told myself firmly, they had to solve their own
problems. I was not a professional counselor, and I was
not even a close friend of either of them. Neither would
appreciate my taking more than a casual interest in

their woes. I resolved to put all their problems out of my mind. I even resolved not to think about the Clowning Around building that night.

This lasted until Joe and I went in our back door. The message light on the answering machine was flashing. Joe punched the PLAY button.

The impersonal voice of the electronic guy who takes our messages spoke. "Wednesday. Ten oh six p.m.," he said.

Next we heard a whispery little voice. "Mr. Woodyard? This is Emma Davidson. I got your phone number from the telephone book. Please call me. I need to talk to you in the worst way."

Chapter 11

"Well, darn!" Joe said. "I left my cell phone number. Why did she call this one?"

We chewed that question over until we got in bed, and then for twenty minutes afterward. Which proved, I guess, that we had become an old married couple.

But it *was* a puzzle. All day long Joe had called Emma Davidson, and each time he had left his cell phone number and asked that she call it. But when she did finally call, she looked our home number up in the phone book and called our house. Why?

The most obvious explanation, I maintained, was that Chuck and Lorraine were trying to keep her from calling Joe and therefore had not passed the cell number on to her.

"But that implies they're controlling her actions," Joe said. "That's hard to visualize. She's a grown woman."

"The one time I saw her, she didn't exactly act assertive."

"Maybe not. Everybody says Emma is naturally quiet. Being quiet, however, is a long way from being a . . . a *prisoner*."

"Elder abuse does occur," I said.

We were concerned enough that I called the Davidson house to check on Emma. Lorraine answered and told me that Emma had been admitted to the hospital in Holland and would be there at least overnight. She thanked me for calling 9-1-1.

"Emma's been a worry to Chuck and me," she said. Her voice sounded slurred and whiny. "She doesn't seem to want to get over our dad's death."

"It's very soon after her loss." I didn't add that it might take years to come to terms with a death like Moe's. I couldn't resist asking another question. "Were you and your dad close?"

"We hadn't been in recent years," Lorraine said. "He could be a real bastard, as I'm sure you're aware. And he and Chuck went at it over money. But it had nothing to do with Emma! She's a nice lady. Chuck likes her, and so do I. We're really upset over what's happened to her."

She didn't sound upset, but I left it at that.

At eleven o'clock Joe turned over and shut his eyes. He has that wonderful knack of putting whatever concerns him out of his mind and going to sleep quickly. My mind doesn't function that way. I picked up a book and tried to get into a mind-set that would help me doze off. I was far from sleepy.

I felt uneasy, as if I had forgotten something. What? What could it be?

I put my book down and went over the day's activities. I couldn't remember anything I'd forgotten to do at the office. I hadn't heard from Aunt Nettie, so I hadn't forgotten any of her instructions. The purchase of the Clowning Around building was hanging fire, of course, but I had done all I could do about that for the moment, and I honestly thought I had put it out of my mind for the night. What was bothering me?

I finally growled in annoyance and picked up my book again. I wasn't accomplishing anything by trying to remember. I lay down and immersed myself in an old Agatha Christie novel I'd picked up at the library sale. That seemed to do the trick. After twenty minutes I felt quite dozy and reached for the bedside lamp. Lying in the dark, I felt even closer to sleep.

And just as I reached the verge of never-never land, I remembered.

I sat straight up in bed. "Joe!"

"Uh?" he murmured, but he didn't say anything. I turned the light back on, and he didn't stir. Should I wake him up?

I decided that would be mean. I might not be right.

I was now wide awake. I got up, went to the answering machine, and played Emma's message again. Actually, I didn't listen to what the message said. I listened to the voice saying it.

Whisper, whisper. It sounded right, but could I be sure?

No, I couldn't. But it was possible.

Emma Davidson's whispery little voice sounded a lot like the person who had called the police station ten days earlier—the one who had been so amazed to learn that Royal Hollis had been arrested in the killing of Moe Davidson.

Could Emma have been the person who called?

How could I check? What was the phone number for that call? Had I written it down? Could I remember it?

All I was sure of was the area code: 765. A check of the map in the front of the phone book showed me that number was for central Indiana. Emma Davidson lived in Indiana. But did she live in *central* Indiana? I didn't know. I didn't even know the name of the town she lived in.

I eyed the computer. I could go online and figure it out. Finally I decided that identifying Emma's hometown could wait for morning. Emma was safe in the hospital. The question my subconscious had been working on had been answered. Time to go to bed. This time I dropped off as soon as I lay down.

Six hours later, after I had made the coffee and put the toaster out as a breakfast table centerpiece, I told Joe about my midnight inspiration.

"Do you think I should tell Sheriff Ramsey?"

"I don't think he'll have an interest. I seem to recall he came by here to tell me that he wouldn't help with further investigations into the Davidson case."

"That's the way I recall it, too. And I can't be sure it was Emma's voice."

Joe nodded. We both sighed. Then we spoke, almost in unison. "Hogan! We need Hogan!"

Yes, Hogan—our friend and my uncle by marriage—would be the perfect person to advise us about this. Hogan was a levelheaded police officer and a perceptive detective. He would know if the anonymous call made to the police station was likely to mean anything—if it had been made by Emma Davidson. He would know if we should tell anyone in authority, and he would know who that person was.

I spread butter on my toast with vicious slashes of my knife and bit into the bread savagely. I was frustrated. "Well," I said, "if the authorities aren't going to question Emma Davidson, maybe you can."

Joe nodded slowly. "Yes, that's what I was trying to do yesterday. I wanted to question her in light of what we learned at the homeless shelter, when Elk gave us some strong hints. But I can't do it today. First, her doctor may not want her to have visitors. Second, I have to go to the jail and interview Royal Hollis. Which is going to be a different sort of challenge."

"Maybe Royal won't have his harmonica along," I said.

"A harmonica! Just what you need for the clown show."

It took me a minute to realize what he meant. "Oh no!" I said. "The hospital stunt! That's this morning! I was hoping to forget."

"Nope. You're stuck, Ms. Chamber of Commerce." Joe waggled his hands beside his ears. "The sick kiddies are going to love you."

Yes, one of the tourism committee's promotional stunts for Warner Pier Clown Week was to visit a hospital in Holland, where we were to entertain the patients, particularly the children, by wearing clown outfits and doing clown tricks. Naturally, the television news and the newspaper had been alerted to our plans.

Yes, I had a clown costume. I had borrowed it from the Warner Pier High School drama department, courtesy of my friend Maggie McNutt, speech and drama teacher. She wasn't charging me, but I knew I'd be on the hook for a nice donation to Maggie's scholarship fund.

"So you get a nice visit to a jail," I said, "and I have to dress up and scare sick children. Who's in for the hardest day?"

"You are," Joe said. "I'll face a whole prison full of inmates before I take on sick kids. They terrify me. But you're the one who agreed to serve on the tourism committee. And now I've got to be on my way."

He gave me a nice good-bye kiss. "If you run into

Chuck or Lorraine," he said, "it might be best not to mention that phone call."

"I'll just ask about Emma. She's probably still in the hospital."

The visit to the children's ward went all right. My borrowed costume was half red and half white, with big floppy ruffles around the neck, wrists, and ankles. It had obviously been made for a guy, but it was baggy enough to fit a woman who's nearly six feet tall. In fact, I put it on over my regular clothes. It fastened in the front with a strip of Velcro.

The costume came with a small white felt hat, and Maggie had pinned a giant floppy red bow on top of that. I borrowed a pair of Joe's tennis shoes to give myself big clown feet. Actually, it takes a pretty big foot to hold me up, and a pair of my own shoes would probably have filled the bill.

I drew the line at wearing clownish makeup, so I settled for bright red lips, drawn extra big.

About a dozen of us went to the hospital, with Kyle and Paige, our professional clowns, leading the group. Someone took a group photo before we started performing, of course. We were all dressed in cheerful clown costumes suitable for children, except for one tramp clown. That guy—or maybe gal—came in too late for the photo. He had on such thick makeup, including teardrops falling from his left eye, that I couldn't tell which Chamber of Commerce member he was. He—or she—was a silent clown, so I couldn't guess from the voice either.

To my relief, the local newspaper and television reporters and photographers showed up, along with a newsman/photographer from Grand Rapids, and a guy with a camera who said he was a stringer for the *Chicago Tribune*. The large papers might not use anything on Clown Week, but we had tried. And that was what the hospital event was all about, of course. We were happy to entertain the kids, but we were the tourism committee from the Warner Pier Chamber of Commerce. Our purpose was to get publicity for our winter promotion. Everybody understood that.

Kyle and Paige were the big hits, naturally. They actually knew what they were doing. In fact, they pleased the hospital administration so much I overheard discussion about their coming back for a separate gig. I had ignored Joe's suggestion about bringing a harmonica, but I did take my guitar. I had rarely played it since I'd dropped out of pageant competition, but "There Was an Old Lady Who Swallowed a Fly" and "Itsy Bitsy Spider" seemed to go over well.

Shortly after one o'clock, I finally got around to going to the reception desk to ask about Emma Davidson. I knew Chuck and Lorraine weren't visiting that afternoon, because they'd been working at Clowning Around when I left for the hospital.

The volunteer checked the list of patients carefully, the way hospital folks are required to do because of patient privacy rules, but she finally gave me Emma's room number.

That surprised me a bit. If the doctors thought that Emma had attempted suicide, I would have expected some restrictions on her visitors. But apparently there were none.

I took the elevator up to the fifth floor and trotted down the hall. Emma's room was a long way from the elevator, but she was fairly near a nurses' station. Did the hospital have a psychiatric unit? It seemed to be large enough to support one.

Emma's door was shut. I rapped softly. No one hollered for me to come in. Should I give up? I decided I should be a bit more aggressive. I pushed the door open a few inches and spoke through the crack.

"Mrs. Davidson?"

I heard a grunting noise. That seemed odd.

I pushed the door open a couple of feet, and I stuck in my head—still with the silly bow on top.

A clown. To my astonishment I was facing a clown. That tall clown in a hobo outfit with a grin painted from ear to ear and tears painted on his cheek. The one I hadn't been able to identify.

He was standing beside the bed. Somebody was lying in that bed. Feet were kicking. The grunting noise was coming from the bed.

I couldn't see who was in the bed because the clown was holding a pillow over the person's face.

I shrieked.

Chapter 12

After I shrieked, I shouted, "Help!"

Then all hell broke loose.

The hobo clown dropped the pillow and charged at me. He yanked the door open and knocked me aside as if I were a rag doll. I was suddenly on my fanny on the floor. I scrambled to my feet and ran to the bedside. Emma Davidson was looking around wildly.

"Keep breathing!" I was still yelling. "I'll catch the guy!"

I ran back to the door and got all tangled up with a nurse who was coming into the room. I yelled again. "She's alive! I'll try to catch the clown!"

When I got into the hall, I frantically looked both ways. No sign of a clown. A woman in navy blue scrubs was standing behind the nurses' station, her mouth agape.

"Which way did he go?"

Silently, she pointed toward the elevators. The door to the stairwell next to them was closing.

I pounded down the hall, my giant shoes slapping with every step, and yanked that door open. I ran out onto the landing. Concrete stairs led down, and I took them. Down I went, feet thudding, round and round. I held the handrail, terrified that Joe's shoes would trip me up.

There was movement below me, but I couldn't see exactly who was there. I followed anyway. A door opened and slammed shut. Had the noise come from the second floor or the first?

When I got to the level marked 2, I swung the door open and ran out into a hall, barreling into another person in scrubs. This one was a man.

I yelled, "Did a clam run out this door? I mean—a *clown*! Did a clown run out this door?"

The man laughed. "Not a clam or even an oyster. And you're the only clown. Is this a Keystone Kops act?"

I ran back into the stairwell and thudded down another flight, then ran back out of the stairwell and onto the first floor hall. There I stopped and looked both ways. Everyone I could see wore ordinary street clothes or scrubs. There was no clown—dressed as a hobo or dressed as anything else. I had lost him.

I punched the elevator button. I was panting. I wasn't going to climb all those stairs. Going down them had been bad enough.

When I got back to the fifth floor, of course, things were worse than bad. I hurried to Emma's room. She was sitting up by then, but she looked dazed. A nurse was standing over her bed and glared at me.

"This clown business is ridiculous," the nurse said. "I'm going to file a complaint about the public information office setting this up. The hospital should never have become a party to such a stupid publicity stunt.

You and that other clown have disturbed the entire floor."

I realized that I was the only witness to the attack on Emma, and no one else had any reason to believe it had even happened.

Emma might have believed it, but the nurse wouldn't let me talk to her, so I didn't know if she backed up my story or not. It was entirely possible that she had been either asleep or unconscious. She certainly hadn't seemed alert at the moment. She might not know what had happened. I had a strong feeling that no one had asked her.

I stood quietly and let the nurse rave on, but every time she paused, I asked the same question. "Have you called the police?"

Additional people appeared to care for Emma, and the nurse and I moved out into the hall. An administrator came. She was angry, too. I kept demanding the police. Finally, a hefty young guy in a security service uniform appeared. I turned to him, and for the tenth time I demanded the police.

I repeated the story that I had witnessed an attack on Emma Davidson. I threatened to tell Emma's family. I generally made myself so annoying that they eventually did call the police. I think they hoped the police would arrest me.

And they nearly did. Unfortunately, or maybe fortunately, one of the officers who took the call knew Joe. Or knew of Joe. He was a young guy with Dutch blond hair and a nametag that read VANDERBERG.

Officer Vanderberg immediately pointed out to the assembled hospital group that my husband was representing "the man who killed Mrs. Davidson's husband."

I gave an angry sniff. "Joe was named by the judge,"

I said. "He didn't ask for the job. And Royal Hollis hasn't been tried yet."

The second cop didn't introduce himself, but he had a nametag that read BUSH. He assured everyone that I was pulling some publicity stunt designed to help Royal Hollis. I denied this. We quickly reached an impasse. Nobody even asked me if I knew the hobo clown. And, of course, I couldn't identify him. Or her.

Officer Vanderberg recommended that the hospital drop the whole thing. "That's the way to fight a publicity stunt," he said. "Don't let 'em get any publicity with it."

I didn't shut up. "If I warn you Mrs. Davidson is in danger, and you don't do anything, and somebody kills her, you're going to be the ones—the hospital and the police department—who are getting publicity. And it's going to be lousy."

At that point silence fell, and everybody around me took a deep breath. They all stared at something behind me.

When I turned to see what was going on, I was looking straight at Emma Davidson. She was on her bed and was being pushed out of her room.

The hospital administration representative spoke firmly. "Mrs. Davidson is being moved to another room, and only family members will know where she is. She will not be in any danger."

Emma Davidson didn't seem to hear her. She was beckoning. Was she beckoning to me? I took a tentative step in her direction. This caused the security guy to jump in front of me.

"Let me talk to her," Mrs. Davidson said in her whispery voice. "Please!"

The security guy stayed with me, but he allowed me to move two steps closer. Emma ignored him. She looked straight at me.

"Thank you, Mrs. Woodyard. Thank you." She wiped her eyes. "Even now Moe is trying to hurt me."

Oh dear. Because her attacker was dressed as a clown, she thought her dead husband was after her. Was she mentally unbalanced? Or just momentarily confused from the stress of being attacked? I wanted to pat her hand, but I was afraid the security officer would pull a pistol on me if I touched her.

I could see two things about Emma Davidson. First, there were tears in her eyes. Second, her face was covered with red speckles. That's when I did reach out and pat her hand.

"It'll be all right," I said. "The hospital is taking responsibility for keeping you safe."

I turned my head and glared at the administrator. "And I'm sure your doctor will explain that red speckling on your face."

I heard Officer Vanderberg take a deep breath. Maybe he was smart enough to know that sort of speckling can be caused by asphyxiation. On a previous occasion I had unfortunately learned firsthand that victims of strangulation are nearly always covered with tiny red dots, almost like a thousand pinpricks. They're hard to see on a dark person, of course, but Emma was fair enough for them to stand out.

At that point I touched my head and realized I was wearing a hat with an enormous bow pinned to the top. I snatched it off, feeling like a fool. I could hardly blame the hospital staff and law enforcement officials for also thinking I was an idiot. I clamped my jaw shut and vowed to keep quiet.

So they let me leave. Nothing more was said about causing a breach of the peace, disturbing a whole floor of patients, or any other crimes I might have committed.

It was one of the most ludicrous and humiliating events in a life that has been filled with ludicrous and humiliating events.

Accompanied by the two cops, I collected my coat, guitar, and other belongings from the public information director's office. My escorts did a bit of eye popping when I yanked open the Velcro down the front of the clown suit, but they hid any disappointment they felt when they saw flannel-lined jeans and a TenHuis T-shirt underneath. The public information director didn't seem to have heard anything about the fiasco on the fifth floor, and she gushed at me about how wonderful the Warner Pier clowns had been, and how much all the children had loved them. I said thanks while I took off Joe's tennis shoes and put on my winter boots.

The policemen escorted me to my van. I didn't say anything, but as I was unlocking the door, Vanderberg spoke. "Hey, were you one of the people who found the murdered guy at the Dorinda nursing home a couple of years ago?"

"My husband and I did. It wasn't fun."

"Then you're related to Hogan Jones in some way."

"He married my aunt. I have nothing to do with law enforcement." I got in the van and started the motor. Then I lowered the window. "But believe me, I'll know how to raise a stink if anything happens to Emma Davidson."

I resisted the temptation to run over Officer Bush's foot as I drove away. He had said less, but acted worse, bringing up the publicity stunt idea. The rat.

The cops watched me until I moved on. I thought they might watch me until I crossed the city limits, but they let me drive away on my own.

I did head for those city limits, until I saw a FOR SALE sign, and the realty name on it was the same com-

pany Tilda VanAust worked for. That reminded me
about the Holland company—one Tilda didn't seem to
know much about—that had made an offer for the
Clowning Around store: P.M. Development. The man
who had called Tilda had been named Philip Montague.

I flipped a U-turn at the next intersection and headed
for the Holland Chamber of Commerce. They would at
least let me look at a phone book. I could find out
where the P.M. Development office was, and the chamber staff might even have some information on Philip
Montague.

At the Holland chamber, the pleasant young woman
behind the desk said that Philip Montague was not a
chamber member, and P.M. Development also didn't
belong as a company. I did find a Philip Montague under the business listings in the phone book, but there
was no clue about what sort of business he was in. I
checked the yellow pages for "Development Compa-
nies" and drew a blank.

By then my search had intrigued the chamber staffer.
"Just a minute," she said. "It seems as if his name
showed up on a list of membership prospects."

She whipped out a file and found him. Again there
was no information except an address, the same one
listed in the telephone book.

"A mystery man," I said. "But I guess I can go by
this address and see what's there."

The young woman leaned over the counter that sep-
arated us. "Be careful," she said. "There's an X by his
name."

"An X?"

"Yes. That's our membership director's code for 'forget this one.' It may just mean that he was unfriendly
or uninterested in joining the chamber. But sometimes

she uses it to mean the whole thing seems fishy or that someone came on too strong."

Hmmm.

I took the magnetic TenHuis Chocolade sign off my van, so that my identity wouldn't be obvious. Then I drove toward the address listed in the telephone book.

Philip Montague's neighborhood was in an older part of Holland, near the downtown, but was a residential area, not a business district. That doesn't mean anything, I told myself. Lots of people work from home. I drove on.

The neighborhood was a perfectly respectable one, as far as a person from Warner Pier could tell, but Philip Montague's house somehow didn't look too respectable.

Holland, after all, was founded by Dutch immigrants, and it has that traditional scrubbed look that most people associate with the Netherlands. The flowerbeds always look neat, the houses are freshly painted, and old cars are rarely parked on the front lawn. Everywhere in Holland I expect to see old women in winged caps and wooden shoes on their knees scrubbing the sidewalk.

Montague's house didn't fit the Holland pattern. It needed paint, and the hedge was overgrown. The sidewalk had too much snow on it to be scrubbed, even by an old lady on her knees.

It wasn't deserted, however. Two men wearing heavy hooded jackets were moving a chest of drawers through the front door. A white van was parked in the driveway, but there was no business sign on its side.

As I passed, one of the men turned his head toward the street. The hood shadowed his features but his face was aimed straight in my direction.

Chocolate Chat

The Toltecs followed the Maya, and later the Aztecs came south to formerly Mayan territory from their original home in Mexico. Both peoples used cacao in their religious ceremonies.

Many are familiar with the Aztec legend of Quetzalcoatl, the great leader who sailed away on a raft but promised to return one day. Surprisingly, this was originally a Toltec legend, but became part of the Aztec culture.

This legend had, of course, dramatic effects on world history. When the Spanish arrived in vessels strange to the Aztecs of the early sixteenth century, the Aztecs believed their ordained leader had arrived to reestablish his kingdom. By the time they realized they were instead facing an invasion, they had pretty much lost the war. The result—which might have occurred in any case—was European domination of South and Central America.

The cacao tree, however, conquered the Spanish, in a sense. The conquerors took the seeds back to Europe, and for a hundred years in European history only the Spanish had chocolate.

Chapter 13

All I could see was a pair of bushy black eyebrows. I circled the block and drove by again, slowly. The second time the men had gone inside.

No sign identifying it as a business marked the house. I couldn't think of a single sensible reason to go to the door, so I once more headed for the city limits.

As soon as I was back at my office, I called the Warner Pier Chamber of Commerce office to see if the secretary could help me identify the hobo clown.

Somehow I wasn't surprised to learn that she couldn't.

"I don't think any of our chamber clowns are wearing hobo costumes," she said. "Of course, that's a traditional clown outfit, but our logo for the promotion is a clown in a colorful, baggy suit, and we encouraged everyone to dress like that."

She had been the photographer for the event, and she checked all her photos. The hobo clown wasn't in any of them.

"I remember seeing him," she said, "but I never

talked to him. The costume covered the person so completely I have no idea who was in it."

I hung up and decided it was time to indulge in my daily chocolates. Every TenHuis employee is allotted two truffles or bonbons each working day, and I always eat my allotment.

We were pushing some leftover Christmas flavors, so I first ate a gingerbread truffle ("milk chocolate inside and out, flavored with ginger and dusted with natural cane sugar"). I next soothed myself with one of my very favorite truffles, cinnamon ("milk chocolate filling flavored with cinnamon, enrobed with dark chocolate and finished with a dusting of cinnamon"). Yum. I ate each of them slowly and savored every bit.

I'd barely swallowed the last nibble when the phone rang. My caller ID told me it was Joe.

Considering the way the day had gone so far, I wasn't sure I wanted to talk to him. But I answered. "Hi."

"Can't I let you out for a minute without your getting in trouble?"

Whew. He obviously had heard about my adventures at the hospital, but he sounded more amused than annoyed.

"Who blabbed?" I asked.

"Our stand-in police chief. Somebody from Holland called Clancy."

"I suppose he scolded you as if it were your problem."

"I'm sure his version was garbled. You can't possibly have chased a clown through a hospital. Not one you believed might be a murderer."

I considered his question. "I hadn't thought of it in that light, but I suppose that's one interpretation. However, it's not the interpretation the Holland police put on it."

"What happened?"

I described the events at the hospital. "As you see,

according to the hospital and law enforcement authorities, the whole thing was just a publicity stunt. The clown didn't even exist, even though two of the nurses also saw him. So he couldn't have been dangerous at all."

"I'm glad you're all right. I'm on my way back from Dorinda. I'll be there in half an hour." Joe hung up.

Until then, I guess, I had felt that the hospital chase was over. Now I saw that the repercussions were still echoing. I also saw that I'd better get my side of the story out to the public before the hospital and Clancy Pike got their side out. When that happened, my already flaky reputation was going to crumble like a fresh French pastry.

So I called Tilda VanAust.

Tilda was my contact with the Davidson family. I could ask her if I should talk to them directly.

Luckily, Tilda was in her office, and she hadn't heard anything about the hospital chase yet. I poured out the story, leaving out the part about Emma saying that Moe had come back from the grave to attack her.

"So, Tilda, should I try to talk to Chuck or Lorraine? They've probably heard from the hospital by now. Heaven knows what they've been told."

"Oh my! I'll have to call them, Lee. But I know you or Joe would never do anything so—well, weird—as a publicity stunt. But Chuck and Lorraine don't know you guys as well as I do."

"I don't care what they think about Joe and me. My concern is that someone tried to smother Emma Davidson. I'm convinced that's what I saw. I want to make sure that she's safe."

Tilda assured me that she understood and that she would talk to the Davidsons immediately. I hung up. Then I went back to our workshop and told Dolly I needed to talk to her. I took her into the break room and repeated the whole story of my adventure to her. And I just happened to do it within earshot of one of the chocolate ladies, Nadine Vanderhill. Nadine isn't exactly a gossip, but she always wants to know what's going on. If anyone asked, she'd tell my side of the story.

After twenty minutes I went back to my desk, confident that I'd done as much damage control as I could.

By the time Joe got to my office, I was tired of the whole thing. I told him that I'd answer any questions he had, but I'd rather hear about his meeting with Royal Hollis.

Joe grinned at me. "My only question is, How do you get into these messes?"

"I sure didn't do it on purpose. But when you innocently peek in the door of a hospital room and find the person you've come to visit struggling for her life . . ." Tears stung my eyes. "Oh gosh, Joe. I'm afraid I'm going to cry."

"Hey! There's no need for that. Though I will mention that I believe your whole story, and I told that big guy over at the police station that I did."

I gave him a hug, and I got one back. Right there in my glass-sided office.

"Let's go home," he said. "I can't tell you about Royal Hollis in a place this public."

We went home. Joe built a fire. We opened a bottle of wine. I dug out some crackers and cheese. We sat on the couch and snuggled up.

"Gee," I said, "I wish we had time for a session like this one every night."

"It's too bad it takes a crisis to get us to pay some attention to each other."

"Aw, come on. Things aren't that bad. I got some pretty effective attention a couple of nights ago."

Joe laughed, and I raised my glass. "Cheers! And, now: Is Royal Hollis crazy?"

"I'm afraid not. But I'm no psychologist."

"You know, Joe, if he was the guy who raked leaves for us once, he didn't strike me as crazy. Not an ordinary person, certainly, but not crazy."

"I think you're right. He's coming out of deep left field. But he ought to be able to aid in his defense. The way the law requires."

"Does that mean he has no defense?"

"I worried about that one all the way home." Joe sipped his wine and seemed to go into a trance. I let him be for three or four minutes. Then he spoke. "He just can't tell a story in a normal way."

"I remember how he talked when he was here."

"Then you probably understand. He's simply not looking at the world the way most of us do. But when I got the story out of him, it was a completely different tale from the one the sheriff got."

"Oh? What does he say happened?"

"He admits he'd been prowling around the Davidson house. He kept saying, 'I never went inside.' As if that was a defense. But he did go into the garage, and once or twice he apparently lit a fire in the charcoal grill. Inside the garage."

"Yikes! He's lucky he didn't burn the place down. Or asphyxiate himself."

"He said, 'I opened the window a crack.' So he's aware that was a danger. You know, Lee, I think everything he did at the house was just to keep warm."

"Living outdoors like he did, with no shelter except an old shack, and considering that Moe hadn't put his shutters on, I think that in his place I would have broken into the house."

"Well, Royal did have alternatives. If he could get to Holland, he could have gone to a shelter."

"But getting there is not easy. Thirty miles to hitch-hike. Or walk."

"But he did break into one thing—the hot tub." Joe laughed. "And I think he's sort of proud of that. 'A man's got to keep clean.' Or so he told me. But that's not the part of the story that surprised me."

"Oh? What did he have to say?"

"All along everybody involved in this case has told basically the same story. Moe came to the cottage and discovered Royal in the hot tub. Moe confronted Royal. They mixed it up."

"Of course, Moe was the householder. He had the right to order Royal off his property."

"Correct. But all the stories feature a confrontation between the two men. It includes Royal shoving Moe down."

"And Moe doesn't get up."

"Yes, that's the story that's been told by everyone. By Chuck, who witnessed the quarrel. By the neighbor, who came on the scene a few minutes later. By Sheriff Burt Ramsey and by Clancy Pike, in his former role as sheriff's deputy. They weren't witnesses, but they got a story out of Royal. And that's the story they say Royal told. But Royal told me a different story today."

"What? What kind of story?"

"Royal said he knew he was in the wrong, and that when Moe showed up, he didn't argue with him. 'It was his house.' That's what Royal told me. He claimed that he tried to run away. Of course, Royal can't run much. Moe caught up with him immediately. And Moe shoved Royal down. Not the other way around."

"Joe, I don't know about the law, but Moe had the right to use force to get Royal off his property. Or am I misunderstanding the law?"

"No. Michigan is a 'stand-your-ground' state. Moe had the right to protect his property. And Royal says Moe did that. He shoved Royal down. But the rest of

Royal's story is different. Royal says that he got up immediately, and Emma—Emma!—ran up and began to lambaste Moe for shoving Royal."

"Emma? Lambasting Moe? But she's so meek and mild. And she wasn't even supposed to be there!"

"Yes, that's the mysterious part. First, no one else says Emma was there. Second, if she was there, it's hard to picture her having the nerve to stand up for Royal. And apparently Moe didn't take it well. He turned on Emma. They began to quarrel."

"What did Royal do?"

"Royal got up and took to the woods. He ran into the woods, and incidentally he says he left his shoes behind. He continued to hear Emma and Moe yelling at each other. He swears he didn't come back. But he had shoes when he was arrested."

Joe sat quietly a minute or two, then spoke again. "Of course, Vandercool—the neighbor—says he gave him a pair of shoes. Could Royal be trying not to tell that? He might have been afraid it would get Vandercool in trouble for helping him."

Joe got up and rearranged one of the fireplace logs. Then he stood before the fire, toasting the backs of his legs, and he gave me a long look.

"Lee, I wish I could believe that Royal didn't kill Moe at all."

That possibility was so remote we didn't really discuss it.

But Emma's role remained open to question. Royal claimed that Emma was there. But Chuck and Emma had both said she wasn't. Moe's neighbor, Harry Vandercool, hadn't reported seeing Emma at the Davidson house the day Moe died. Clancy, the sheriff's deputy who had investigated the case, had not indicated that Emma had been there.

But did Royal know Emma? Could he have mistaken someone else, such as Lorraine, for her?

"And speaking of Emma," Joe said, "I never did get to talk to her."

I thought about Emma. She called our house and left a message, but when Joe tried to call her back, Lorraine and Chuck said she was unavailable. Then Tilda and I found her unconscious—apparently after a suicide attempt. And now I was convinced someone had tried to kill her.

Finally I spoke. "Emma's whole story about her overdose doesn't work, you know. If you want to talk to someone before you commit suicide, you don't quit trying to reach them. Emma would have kept calling you."

Joe nodded. "Right. And as for the attack on Emma you witnessed this afternoon, that doesn't make sense either. If someone is trying to commit suicide, and you want them to die, then you don't interfere and try to smother them the next day. Most killers would just wait and see if the suicidal impulse returns."

"That seems like a more practical solution."

I got a simple supper together, and we tried to talk about something else while we ate it on our laps in front of the fire. But I was still thinking about Moe Davidson's death and the new questions about how it had happened, and I'm sure Joe was, too.

We had worked our way to ice cream by the time Joe went back to the subject.

"I guess the next thing to do is talk to Moe's neighbor," he said. "Harry Vandercool. I'll call and see if I can meet him tomorrow."

Chapter 14

The name Harry Vandercool seemed familiar to me, but I couldn't place him. Neither could Joe. That might mean nothing in a larger community, but in a town of twenty-five hundred, it's a little odd.

Joe looked him up online. He didn't find out much. So we looked at the address in the phone book, and I figured out the name of someone I knew slightly who lived nearby. I called her. She didn't know Harry Vandercool either, she said, but she knew who he was. Vandercool was one of the army of retirees who had moved to Warner Pier in recent years.

"He had some sort of business in Holland," my informant said. "Retail, I think. Maybe."

"Does he go to a church? Or belong to any clubs?"

"Not that I know of. I don't think we've ever met. Not formally. He was at the property owners' association meeting."

Joe really likes to know some background about a

witness before he interviews him, but he gave up and called Harry Vandercool cold.

Vandercool readily agreed to talk to him. He suggested that Joe come to his house the next morning. Then Joe got a surprised look on his face. "Lee? I'm sure she would come if she doesn't have something already scheduled."

Joe listened. Then he grinned. "Oh! Well, I'm sure she'd be glad to give you an update on the chocolate business in southwest Michigan. Let me ask her."

Joe took the phone away from the side of his head and looked at me. "Are you available to go calling at ten o'clock tomorrow morning?"

"I guess so. But why?"

"It seems Harry Vandercool had Vandercool's Chocolate in Grand Rapids until he retired."

"Oh! He's *that* Vandercool! I'll be glad to talk to him."

Joe confirmed the time and hung up. We both laughed. "I've never met Mr. Vandercool," I said. "I didn't know his first name, but Aunt Nettie has spoken of him."

"Vandercool says you bought a cooling tunnel he sold when he retired."

"We're still using it."

"He says we should come to his house. 'That way we can look at the situation on the ground, so to speak.'"

"Sure. You can see how long it took him to walk over to Moe's and other details like that."

Harry Vandercool's house was in a wooded area south of Warner Pier, off Lake Shore Drive. He was, like us, on the inland side. Lakefront property is extremely valuable these days, but ordinary people can manage to live in the area if they don't insist on a lake view.

Harry was a bit farther away from the lakeshore

than we are, maybe half a mile, on a lot with plenty of trees. His property was nice and neat. His house was painted white, with black shutters. His walks and even his driveway were bare of snow. And he had a real concrete walk and drive; none of this gravel stuff Joe and I use. There was a folksy Welcome sign beside the front door.

Harry Vandercool was clearly a man who would be bothered by a cottage that looked abandoned and neglected—especially right next door. I immediately saw why he had noticed something was wrong at Moe and Emma's house and why he had called to tell them about it. This was a man who wanted the neighborhood kept up.

Yet his house sat alone, surrounded by trees. And since it wasn't on a main road, no one except Harry and his callers would ever see it. The Davidson cottage wasn't even visible from the Vandercool house. Although most of the trees were without leaves in winter, a large plot of evergreens lay between the two properties. The bushy trees completely blocked the view from one to the other.

So I wondered just how Harry Vandercool had known there had been a prowler at the Davidson house. He wouldn't have just casually noticed. He would have had to go over and look.

Had Moe and Emma asked him to keep an eye on things? Or had he taken the job on himself?

As soon as Joe parked his truck in the Vandercool drive, I saw a man come out the front door and start down the steps, accompanied by a small black dog. This had to be Harry Vandercool.

Vandercool was a small man, the kind of man who makes me feel like a giantess. I guessed his age at around seventy. He had thin white hair and a colorless face and pale blue eyes. I still didn't remember meeting him before, but I might have. He was so ordinary I could have stumbled over him daily and never noticed. The dog wasn't even very noticeable. Just a short-haired black dog of no particular breed. He didn't bark or jump on us, though he frisked about at the sight of strangers. When Joe knelt to greet him, he stood quietly to be petted, arching his neck.

Mr. Vandercool told us the little dog was named Java. "Because he's the color of black coffee," he said.

Mr. Vandercool gestured toward the house. "Come in, come in," he said. "I've made some coffee. And I have some TenHuis chocolates!" He smiled proudly.

Oh dear. He was a customer—a local customer—and I didn't remember him.

But Mr. Vandercool was shaking his forefinger at me. "I usually shop in South Haven," he said, "so I got these truffles at the supermarket there. I'm sure yours are fresher."

"Oh, we deliver down there every other week," I said. "Their chocolates ought to be fine. And I appreciate a chocolate expert seeking TenHuis out."

Mr. Vandercool's living room matched the outside of his house. It was neat as a pin, with very few decorative items on the walls and tables. It was masculine, but traditional—no overstuffed sectionals or square cornered leather chairs. I was a little surprised by the floral fabric on the camelback couch, until I saw the picture on the mantelpiece. It was Mr. Vandercool standing beside a lady of a suitable age. The picture screamed "anniversary." The room screamed "widower."

Java's bed was next to Vandercool's chair. As soon as we were in the house, Vandercool said, "Go to your bed, Java," and the little dog obediently sat in his special spot.

Mr. Vandercool served coffee—remembering to offer cream and sugar—and put out a plate of truffles and bonbons. I took a blackberry truffle ("dark chocolate filling flavored with genuine Michigan berries, enrobed with dark chocolate, and decorated with a purple swirl"). Joe went for a mocha truffle ("dark chocolate interior and coating, trimmed with white stripes"). Our host then sat down on the flowered couch, took a deep breath, and began speaking before Joe could formulate a question.

"I'll always have a deep sense of guilt about the death of Moe Davidson," he said. "I mean, what did it matter if that poor homeless man tried to get warm? It wasn't worth dying over."

"Calling friends about a problem at their home is a neighborly act," I said. "You had no way of foreseeing . . ."

Mr. Vandercool was shaking his head. "I didn't do it to be neighborly. I did it to point out Moe Davidson's dereliction of duty. I wasn't a good neighbor. I was a know-it-all. And Moe knew that. I think he came up here mad—mad at me—and that anger probably figured in the situation with Royal Hollis. So I am partially responsible for what happened."

"Mr. Vandercool," Joe said, "you're raising some basic questions about human relations. How much are we responsible for our fellow man? That one is way beyond me. All I can do is gather the facts about this case."

Vandercool nodded. "I understand. The law isn't interested in why I did something, but in what I did. But I do want you to understand that I feel a lot of sympathy for both Moe and Royal Hollis in this—this stupid situation. It should never have led to anyone's death."

"Just what did happen? From your point of view."

Mr. Vandercool took a deep breath. "Emma did ask me to keep an eye on things when she and Moe left in October. She assured me that they'd be back to close the house properly in a week. But they never came."

He continued his story. He walked Java twice a day, and one of their favorite strolls led by the Davidson house. "There's a path between the two houses. It leads through the evergreens. And Moe and Emma didn't mind us going that way."

Because of this he saw the house nearly every day, so he was quite sure the Davidsons hadn't come back to put up shutters, drain the pipes, and do the other things necessary to winterize a house.

"Of course, it's a year-round house," he said. "As long as the furnace was working, it probably wasn't going to damage anything, but it's just, well, a careless way to manage things."

Mr. Vandercool would definitely not have approved of doing anything in a careless way.

November and December went by. Freezing weather set in. Snow fell, and on his walks Mr. Vandercool began to notice footprints that were not his own.

Finally, on a day early in January he came upon Royal Hollis in back of the house. The Davidson house had an unattached garage, and Hollis was standing near its door.

"Did he startle you?" Joe asked.

"Not really. He was around this neighborhood quite a bit."

"So you knew who he was?"

"I didn't know his name—not his full name. But he would come by and play his harmonica, and sometimes I had a little chore for him." Mr. Vandercool smiled. "He had a lively personality, you know. You couldn't get mad at him." His smile went away. "Or *I* couldn't. Maybe I encouraged him to stay around in the neighborhood."

Mr. Vandercool was determined to feel guilty about Moe's death, I saw.

"But he wasn't doing any harm," Vandercool said. "Not that day. He was doing just what I was doing— walking around the house. I didn't see him again."

It wasn't until about a week later that Mr. Vandercool noticed that the latch on the hot tub was broken. When he touched the lid, it lifted easily.

"I blame Moe," he said. "You're not supposed to put temptation in people's paths. You shouldn't leave money out, or wave an expensive cell phone around on a public conveyance, or just swallow any story that someone tells you. So I thought that Moe was—well, asking for it. The tub should have been properly emptied and locked."

That's when he called Moe and Emma at their Indiana house. Moe had sounded angry, but when Vandercool offered to call the sheriff and report a prowler, he said no. He said he'd be up the next Saturday to drain the pipes and put up the shutters. He'd look for any damage himself.

So Vandercool hadn't been surprised when he heard a car the next weekend. "It drove in around noon," he said. "Of course, I can't see over there. Moe planted those evergreens years before I moved here."

Huh. So it was Moe who hadn't wanted anyone to look at his house.

"Did you go over to talk to Moe?" Joe asked.

Vandercool sighed. "I started to. But sound carries so out here—well, I heard yelling. I thought it would be better to stay away for a while."

"Did you think Moe was yelling at Royal Hollis?"

"No! To tell the truth, I assumed he was yelling at

Emma. He could be awfully rude to her. But I went out on the porch. I was really surprised when Hollis ran into my yard."

"Hollis ran into your yard?"

Vandercool nodded vigorously. "He ran toward me down the path that connects my lot with the Davidsons'. He was half-dressed."

"Half-dressed?"

"Yes. He had on his overalls, and he was carrying his shirt and coat. But he didn't even have his shoes."

"He was barefoot?"

Another nod. "It was pretty obvious that Moe caught him actually in the hot tub. Moe must have yelled at him, and they must have fought. I guess that's when Royal Hollis hit Moe. Killed him."

"What did Hollis say to you?"

"He said, 'I left my shoes. I gotta go back and get 'em.' But I tried to talk him out of that. I thought it would just cause more trouble. I told him he could have a pair of mine. But he kept moving as if he was going back over to Moe's. I ran into my mudroom and grabbed up a pair of tennis shoes. I shoved them at him; then I went to get two pairs of socks. He sat down on the porch steps and put them on."

Vandercool turned to me, looking almost as if he were going to cry. "The shoes were too small, but the temperature was way below freezing. He had to have shoes! I didn't know what else to do."

I patted his hand. "That was a kind act, Mr. Vandercool."

He grimaced. "Anyway, Hollis put the shoes on and before I could stop him he took off through the woods."

"Did he go toward the Davidsons'?" Joe asked.

"No, he ran off toward the Interstate." Vandercool sighed. "I was afraid to face Moe. I admit it. But I decided I had to try to get Hollis' shoes back. So I waited, oh, maybe fifteen minutes, and then I went over there. I walked down the path, and when I came out on the Davidsons' side of the bushes, I saw Chuck kneeling on the driveway. It took me a minute to see that he was kneeling beside Moe. And Moe was dead."

Chapter 15

I felt that Mr. Vandercool seemed to have reached an emotional stopping place. Joe apparently realized that, too, and he spoke.

"How about a little break? Maybe this would be a good time to walk over toward the Davidsons' so I can get an idea of the layout."

The older man nodded and turned to his dog. "Java! Walkee."

Java jumped to his feet and scurried across the room to get his leash. As Mr. Vandercool snapped it onto the little dog's collar, he smiled apologetically. "Since my wife died, Java and I are partners."

I looked at the gray on Java's snout and hoped that Mr. Vandercool wouldn't be left alone.

We three humans put on our jackets and boots, and we started on our expedition. The path between the Vandercool house and the Davidson place led through the evergreens on the Davidson side. The path wasn't wide, but Mr. Vandercool had obviously trimmed back some branches to make it easy to get through, and the surface of the snow was trampled down. The only really narrow place was the final gap through the evergreens.

When we came out on the other side we were perhaps a hundred feet from the Davidson house. The house was nondescript. Two cars were parked in the drive. I could see heat vapor coming out of a roof vent.

The house was quite ordinary—just a white frame structure of no particular architectural style. Because we live in a quaint little town filled with historic houses, all Warner Pier people are interested in architecture. I mentally placed the construction of that one in the mid-1950s. Midcentury modern, it's called. Personally, I would have labeled it "midcentury boring."

Mr. Vandercool stopped as soon as he came through the evergreens, and Joe and I stood on either side of him.

"I see that the drive is quite close to the evergreens," Joe said. "Just where was Moe's body?"

"Right where that blue car is," Mr. Vandercool said. "I guess it's Lorraine's. Chuck's Chevy was parked farther back."

"Where was Moe's car?" Joe asked.

There was a long pause. Mr. Vandercool turned around, frowning. "I can't remember. It doesn't seem to me . . . Honestly, I don't remember it being there at all."

Why had Joe asked about Moe's car? According to Chuck's story, Moe's car had never been at the house at all. Moe, presumably driven by Emma, had met his son someplace between their Indiana home and this house. Chuck had dropped Moe at the house, then gone out to get gas. When Chuck got back, he witnessed the struggle between his dad and Royal Hollis.

But Elk Elkouri claimed that Emma had been at the

house. So did Hollis. Were they dragging Emma in as a distraction? Or had Emma really been there?

My heart began to pound. Emma Davidson might be able to tell the real, true story of what happened.

Then I told myself to calm down. If Emma told the real, true story, it might make things worse for Royal Hollis. I couldn't allow myself—or Joe—or Royal Hollis—to hope.

I was still standing there in a mental fog when I heard the voice of a woman—a whiny voice.

"And what do we have here?"

Lorraine—bleached hair, brassy makeup, and all—was standing on the small back porch of the Davidson house. She called out, "Hi! Chuck told me I owe you an apology."

"I don't want to take Java over there," Harry Vandercool said quietly. "It tends to cause trouble. I found out yesterday that Lorraine's not exactly a dog lover."

He waved at Lorraine in a pseudofriendly way, then turned around and went back down the path toward his own house.

Joe and I walked toward Lorraine, tramping through the snow. Unlike their neighbor, the Davidsons hadn't cleared a path except quite close to the house. Joe and I walked over to the start of the path, then stopped.

Lorraine's makeup was as vivid and inexpert as it had been at Clowning Around. She looked at Joe and spoke again. "Chuck says I was obnoxious the other day when you came in the store."

"My appearance must have been quite unexpected," Joe said. "If I'd known that you were there, I wouldn't have come over. So maybe I owe you an apology, too. Shall we call it even?"

"Sure." Lorraine waved her hand, and I saw that it

held a glass. "Do you folks want to come in for a drink?"

"No, thanks," Joe said. "I've got to finish talking to Mr. Vandercool and meet with some other witnesses."

Lorraine's eyes weren't quite focused. "I know it's not even noon yet," she said, "but it's so damn lonely out here. Since my mom died, I haven't even wanted to see the place. This stupid house always reeked of anger. At least Chuck and the old man aren't both here to yammer at each other. And me."

"Chuck didn't get along with your dad?" Joe asked.

"They always fought about money. Now Chuck says we have to stay around until the house is officially on the market. And we have to try to get all that clown crap sold this week. We'll never have a better chance than at the idiotic Clown Week."

I decided to ignore that crack and jump into the conversation. "How is Emma doing?"

"The doctors are keeping her a couple more days."

"As long as they're being careful that clown doesn't threaten her again."

"If there really was a clown. They've called in a psychiatrist. That'll mean more drugs." Lorraine shrugged and waved her glass around. "Forget the drugs! What Emma needs is some of this stuff. That'd loosen her up."

That seemed to end the conversation. Joe and I said good-bye and Lorraine assured us she'd tell Chuck we'd been by. She didn't explain why he needed to know.

Then we went back to the Vandercool house. Mr. Vandercool and his little dog were standing on the porch.

"Why did Lorraine think she needed to apologize?" he asked.

"She and I had a little run-in the other day," Joe said. "But you had some questions for Lee, didn't you?"

For a moment I couldn't imagine what he was talking about, but then I remembered that Mr. Vandercool had wanted to know about the chocolate business.

"Oh," I said. "I haven't reported on the state of chocolate in west Michigan, Mr. Vandercool. Did you have a specific question?"

We went back inside, and he asked a few questions. Who had closed? Who had added to their line? What stores had added staff? None of it was too complicated.

After we'd covered the subject pretty well Joe began to make motions as if he was ready to go. He thanked Mr. Vandercool effusively for his cooperation. Then, as he was sliding his arms into the sleeves of his jacket, he spoke very casually.

"Have you remembered anything more about Moe's car, Mr. Vandercool?"

"Moe's car? You mean on the day he was killed?"

"Yes. When we were over there, you said you weren't sure Moe's car had been in the drive. I guess it was the car Emma is currently driving—the one that's over in the drive now."

"Yes, that's the car. A Toyota sedan."

"Was it over at Moe's house that day?"

"I don't think it was." Mr. Vandercool slowly shook his head. "No, now that I think of it, I'm sure there was only one car in the drive. I assumed that Chuck had driven his dad over, maybe come to help him close up. But, no! That can't be right."

"Why not?"

"Because—well, I thought I heard Moe yelling at Emma earlier."

"Yelling at her? You mean calling her name?"

Mr. Vandercool looked so embarrassed, I thought he

was going to blush. "I hate to sound like a nosy neighbor."

Joe grinned. "Go ahead."

"Moe had quite a mouth on him. He talked to Emma awfully rough sometimes. I could hear him. My wife wouldn't have stood for it. Of course, sometimes Moe talked rough to other people, too. I guess he did it to everybody."

"So did you hear him yelling at Emma *specifically*, or did you just assume it was Emma?"

"I guess I just assumed, now that you mention it."

"But when you went over, she wasn't there."

Mr. Vandercool nodded, and we left. As soon as we were in the truck, I spoke. "And what is the story on the car? Do you think Elk was right? Emma was there that morning and cut out before the sheriff's deputies got there? Could she have witnessed Moe's death?"

"It's possible, but I'm not counting on it. And an eyewitness account from her might do Royal more harm than good. But before we leave, I want to ask Lorraine another question."

Joe parked his truck in the Davidsons' drive and went to the door—the back door, since that had been the one Lorraine came out of to speak to us. I waited in the truck. In a moment the brassy blonde came to the door. She poked her head out, and she and Joe spoke for a few minutes. She didn't yell at him.

Joe was still wearing his deadpan lawyer face when he got back in the truck.

"Did she know if Emma was there that morning?" I asked.

"I didn't ask her that. I just wanted to know if Emma still wanted to talk to me. Lorraine said she doesn't know."

"I doubt it's come up, with Emma in the hospital."

"Whether she wants to talk to me or not, I sure want to talk to her." Joe was silent as we drove back to our house so I could pick up my van.

As he stopped to let me out of the truck, I spoke again. "Will you have to get permission from Emma's psychiatrist before you can talk to her?"

"It's a weird situation. She hasn't been committed, as far as I know. She was trying to reach me before this suicide attempt happened. It might ease her mind if she finally could tell me whatever she wanted to tell. Or it might push her over the edge again." Joe sighed. "I don't know which way to jump. But for the rest of today, I have to jump on something entirely different."

"What's that?"

"Finances. My salary. The agency is facing a budget crisis."

"I thought you faced that last fall."

"We did. But this Royal Hollis business has complicated things. The Fox Foundation president heard about my appointment in the Hollis case, and he wants to know what I'm up to. Webb called me yesterday."

Webb Bartlett is a close friend of Joe's who serves as president of the board for the nonprofit legal association Joe works for. Webb serves as liaison with major donors, such as the Fox Foundation.

"The foundation board is meeting today, so Webb and I have to be available to answer questions."

"You have to assure them you haven't gotten the agency involved in a criminal case."

"Yeah." Like most people reared in west Michigan, Joe pronounces "yeah" as if it were a Dutch word. He went on. "And they need to know that I haven't lost my mind. And as you know, I'm not too positive on that point, because I may definitely be crazy to have taken this case. Anyway, Webb and I have to be in Grand Rapids for their meeting."

"Gosh! You need to hurry."

"True. Their business meeting starts at two. I'll probably have to turn my cell off most of the afternoon. I'll call you when we're on our way back."

He gave me a quick kiss, and I got out of the truck and waved him off. Then I went in the house. I called the office to check in, assuring Dolly I *would* come in to work sometime that day. Then I made myself a sandwich and got a Diet Coke out of the refrigerator. I was ready to head back out the kitchen door when the telephone rang.

"Nuts," I said. "I'm on my way. If I stop to answer the phone it'll just hold up the parade."

But the phone rang again, and I picked it up. "Hello?"

"Is Mr. Woodyard there?"

It was a little whispery voice. I could barely hear it.

Oh no! I thought. Here we go again.

Chapter 16

"This is Lee Woodyard. Is this Mrs. Davidson?"

"Yes." Her voice was weaker and more whispery than ever. "I must talk to your husband."

"He wants to talk to you, too, Mrs. Davidson. Where are you?"

"I'm still in the hospital. They won't let me out. Can I . . . Can I call him?"

"I'll try to reach him and have him call you. What is your phone number?"

There was a long pause. "I don't know."

"What is your room number?"

"I'm not sure. They follow me if I leave the room, so I stay inside."

"Is the number written on the phone?"

She didn't answer, but I could hear her breathing softly.

"It ought to be on the telephone, Mrs. Davidson."

"There are numbers, but I can't read all of them."

"Tell me what they are. Please."

More silence. Oh Lordy! After all the time this woman had spent calling Joe, and all the time he had spent calling her, was she going to get away again?

"There are two I can't read. Then there's a four. And a three. Does that mean anything?"

"We'll make it mean something. Joe has been trying to reach you. I'll find him, and he'll try again."

"It may be hopeless. Moe may come back." I heard a little noise. Surely it wasn't a sob. "Or was that a dream?" She whispered the final words, then the line went dead.

I punched the number of Joe's cell phone immediately. He hadn't had nearly enough time to get to Grand Rapids; surely he hadn't turned his phone off yet. But he didn't pick up. I left a message on his voice mail.

Well, as my Texas grandma always said, there's more than one way to skin a cat. (I never knew why anyone would want to do that, but that's what she always said.) I decided to call Webb Bartlett—Joe's friend, his boss, and his companion for this important meeting in Grand Rapids.

First I called Webb's cell phone. No answer. Then I called his office. Darned if it wasn't closed. His secretary must've been at lunch, and I didn't know her cell number. I called the poverty law agency; Webb is often there, though his office is elsewhere. They hadn't seen Joe at all. Webb had been by earlier to pick up some papers, I was told, and he was now on his way to Grand Rapids.

Finally I told the secretary there that it was desperately important that I reach Joe. "It's a genuine emergency," I said.

She sighed. "I understand, Lee, but he's on a trip about a genuine emergency of his own, and it would take a miracle to reach him."

But miracles do happen sometimes, I reminded myself. I had to keep trying. However, there was nothing to do right at that moment.

I decided that there was no point in my moping around the kitchen telephone, so I put on my winter jacket and went to the office. I'd barely walked in when Joe called.

"Hi," he said. "Andrea says you've broken a leg."

It took me a moment to reply, so he spoke again. "Or was it some other emergency?"

"It's not a painful emergency, Joe. The effusive Emma Davidson called again. I mean, elusive! The elusive Emma Davidson called."

"Did she leave a message?"

"A few numbers, but they didn't make sense to her or to me. She said she's still in the hospital, but she doesn't know what room. She seemed kind of dopey."

Joe sighed. "Damn."

"That sums it up. She also said it was important for her to talk to you."

"Seems as if I've heard that before. But I simply can't dodge this meeting today."

"I understand. Is there anything I can do to help?"

"I hate to make you skip your own work to do mine."

"Oh, you know I hate to miss anything. I can work anytime. Like tonight."

Another sigh. "I hate to ask you, but if you could try to find her in that hospital and talk to her, it would really help."

"I'll be glad to."

Joe apologized again and said good-bye. And I went to poor, long-suffering Dolly Jolly and told her I had to do an errand for Joe. "I'm terribly sorry, Dolly. I'll stay late tonight and get the payroll done."

THE CHOCOLATE CLOWN CORPSE   139

Dolly, as usual, shouted her reply. "It's all right, Lee! I know you wouldn't do this if it wasn't important! By the way, you had a message!"

"What about?"

"That Montgomery woman called! She wants to talk to Joe, too!"

"Did she say why?"

"Nope! Just said something about leaving for home."

"Hmmm. Well, I'll tell Joe when I see him."

I left for Holland humming. And all the way I tried to understand just why I was so pleased and excited about going there. I finally decided that I simply like being in the thick of things. I'm just a nosy woman. So live with it, I told myself.

Of course, I wasn't sure I could do anything. I didn't know how to find Emma Davidson's room. She was likely to be in the psychiatric ward, and I knew that that sort of area is normally closed to the public. I wouldn't be able to simply walk in, the way I had walked into the room she had been in earlier. But I had to give the direct approach a try.

So I parked in the hospital parking lot, took three deep breaths to pump up my confidence, and walked into the hospital. I went straight to the volunteer at the desk, the one charged with giving out information to visitors.

"Emma Davidson, please," I said.

The volunteer, a gray-haired woman, consulted her computer screen. "Yes, here she is—oh. I'm sorry. We don't have a patient by that name."

"That's a disappointment. Her son told me she was here."

The volunteer looked flustered. "I can't give out any information."

I leaned over confidentially. "Could you suggest a

room number where she might receive mail? I'd like to
send a card at least."

She looked flustered again as she consulted the
screen. "I am sorry. I'm not allowed to give out any
information."

"I'm sure her son would give it to me, but I hate to
bother him."

"I'm sorry."

I looked disappointed and went away, but just as far
as the hospital coffee bar. There I bought a cup of cap-
puccino, found a table, and plotted. And hoped I didn't
run into one of the security guards who had tossed me
out earlier.

The first plan I considered was going into the hospital gift shop, buying the largest stuffed animal they
had, and asking them to deliver it to Emma Davidson.
I was sure they'd take it up to her, and I could follow
the teddy bear.

Yes, that might work. But it would draw attention to
me. The volunteer in the gift shop was sure to remember an almost six foot tall blonde, even in Holland,
Michigan, where tall blondes are standard issue.

I filed that as a fallback plan and decided to work on
the numbers Emma had given me: four and three. I'd
begin by exploring.

I finished my coffee and took the elevator to the second floor.

This hospital wasn't the size of Methodist or St.
Luke's, the facilities in the Houston medical complex
where I'd visited relatives once upon a time, but it was
too large to simply walk up and down the halls checking all the rooms—unless I wanted to spend all day
doing that. I decided to start by assuming that the
phone numbers were likely to have some relationship
to the room numbers. Four and three.

The second floor housed the maternity ward. I already knew that, since I'd visited new moms there a few times, but I'd never noticed the pattern of room numbers.

I walked along casually until I saw an empty room—no bed, no patient, no name on the door. But it did have a telephone. I went in.

Hurrah! The phone number contained the final two numbers of the room number. I felt a thrill of pleasure and pumped my fist.

Then I wandered on down the hall. There was a room 0243 on that floor, of course. But the young woman in the bed was surrounded by family, and all of them were cooing at a new family member. In Spanish. Definitely not Emma Davidson. I went up the stairs to the third floor. No luck there either. So I climbed to the fourth. I did notice that there were restrooms near the elevator on each floor.

For nearly twenty minutes I wandered the halls, looking as inconspicuous as an ultratall woman can look. Finally I came to room 0643. Aha! There was no patient name on the door, and the door was firmly closed, unlike the doors of the empty rooms I'd seen elsewhere. Their doors had been standing open.

The room was also in full view of the nurses' station. I waited until one nurse at the station sat down to work on some papers, and the other picked up the telephone. Then I peeked inside room 0643. I saw a short, plump lady sitting in what hospitals pass off as an easy chair. She was near the room's closet, wrapped in a hospital blanket and looking worried.

"Mrs. Davidson." I spoke softly.

"Oh! Mrs. Woodyard! I'm so glad to see a friendly face." Tears welled in her eyes and ran down her cheeks.

I went in, closed the door behind myself, and knelt by her side. "I'm so glad to find you, Mrs. Davidson. What can I do to help you?"

"Get me out of here!"

Oh gee! That was one thing I wasn't prepared to do. I was sure Emma Davidson was receiving mental treatment. If she left the hospital and then committed suicide— I wasn't going to be part of that. "But Mrs. Davidson—"

She clutched my hand. "Mrs. Woodyard, I'm not crazy. I did not attempt suicide. These doctors—even Chuck and Lorraine—everyone thinks I tried to kill myself. I did not!"

"Then what happened? Tilda VanAust and I found you unconscious."

"I don't know what happened. The last thing I remember is eating lunch—Lorraine gave me a Bloody Mary. I didn't want to drink it, but she insisted. Kept saying 'a little booze' would relax me. Then I woke up in this hospital, with the doctors poking at me. But this morning I quit taking all the pills they keep giving me, and I'm feeling better all the time."

She made a dismissive gesture. "That's not the main problem. I'll get hold of my own doctor, back in Indiana, and he'll tell these strange doctors that I'm not suicidal. But I can't ease my mind until I talk to your husband."

"Unfortunately, Joe is in Grand Rapids this afternoon. It will be evening before he can get back."

She dropped her head to her hands. "They may have killed me by then! I'm so frightened! Since Moe attacked me—I mean the clown with the pillow—you're the only person I can trust!"

I was almost sorry I had come. Her feelings seemed almost irrational, and I might be making things worse.

But I couldn't honestly tell Mrs. Davidson that the danger was just in her imagination. After all, I'd witnessed the attack by the strange hobo clown. I believed she was actually in danger.

Then I heard a noise at the door. Someone was coming. Emma grabbed my hand. "Get in the closet," she said. "Quick."

While she talked, she swung the closet door open. I jumped inside and closed the door, leaving just a narrow crack.

I was able to see the nurse who came in. He was a large man, wearing navy scrubs, of course, just like ones the nurses at the desk had on. He had black hair, the type that's too black. It was obviously dyed. His eyebrows also were a deep black, though their color looked more natural. And he seemed familiar. Why? The phony color of his hair was so distinctive I thought I'd remember where I'd seen him, but I didn't. Who could he be?

"How're you doin'?" he asked. "Ready for your meds?"

His voice was deep and resonant.

Emma leaned her head back and half closed her eyes. "I guess so," she said. Her voice sounded much weaker than it had when she'd been talking to me. But I was surprised by her remark; she'd just told me she wasn't taking her medication.

The big man handed her a small paper cup, and I was surprised to see Emma take the pill in it docilely. The man then tucked her into bed, urging her to take a nice nap. Emma lay back, again with no argument, and the nurse left.

And the moment he was out the door I knew where I'd seen those black eyebrows. They were on the forehead of the man who had been unloading furniture at the address of P.M. Development, the company that had bid on the Clowning Around building.

Quite a coincidence. Could this be a nurse? Suddenly I doubted it.

I came out of that closet like a Texas prairie dog that had just discovered a rattler coming in the opposite end of its burrow.

Chocolate Chat

The pre-European peoples of South and Central America associated drinking cacao with sexual prowess, and also associated it with wealth. The drink was not for commoners. Only kings and nobles drank it.

This may have been primarily because it was incredibly expensive. In fact, it didn't just cost money. It *was* money.

The wealthy used cacao beans to buy things. One often-quoted passage from early Spanish explorers reports that a hundred beans could buy a slave; ten beans, the services of a prostitute; and four beans, a rabbit. One early European praised use of the beans this way because cacao beans could not be hoarded or buried by the miserly. The beans would sprout or rot.

At that time cacao would not have been used for cooking, only for drinking. In fact, such a use might have been considered sacrilege. So if you yearned for a plate of turkey mole, you would have been out of luck.

Chapter 17

I was sure the nurse was a fake and that he had given Emma poison. I had to get help for her, quick.

Emma was motioning for me to stay where I was. "Sometimes they come back," she said. That time she whispered intentionally.

Then she picked up her plastic water glass from the bedside table and spit the pill into it.

"I just get so groggy on that stuff," she said. "I took Xanax for a week or so, right after Moe died. I quit then because I hated the way it made me feel. I'm not starting it up again, even if the doctors think I should be on it."

I stood there, staring at Emma. I'd just witnessed another attempt on her life. I ought to scream the hospital down, to call the cops, to raise Cain until someone did something—something!—to protect her.

But what could I do? I'd tried the screaming and yelling act the day before and almost got arrested. The hospital had made a perfunctory attempt to keep Emma safe by changing her room and limiting access to her, but the guy whose eyebrows and hair didn't match had shown how easy it was to get around their efforts. So had I, for that matter. I'd just waited until the nurse was on the phone and walked right in.

I could think of only one place where Emma would be safe.

I pulled out my cell phone and called Sarajane Harding. Luckily, she answered.

"Sarajane," I said, "is your spare room available?"

She hesitated, then spoke softly. "Yes."

"If I'm lucky, you'll have a tenant for it in an hour or so."

"Fine." Now Sarajane sounded resolved. "I'll turn up the heat in there."

I hung up and turned to Emma. "Mrs. Davidson, I'm about to kidnap you. I hope you'll go willingly."

"Mrs. Woodyard, that is exactly what I want."

"Okay. Do you have any clothes?"

"They're folded in the dresser drawer."

"If you'll put them on . . . Oh, but we don't want the hospital to know you're about to make a break for it."

"I'll dress in the bathroom, in case the nurse looks in."

"Good. After you're dressed, climb under the covers and pretend to be asleep. And promise me you won't eat or drink anything."

"Oh?" Her voice quavered.

I took the plastic cup with the pill she had spit out. I stuffed two tissues in on top of the pill and put the whole thing inside one of the disposable gloves from that container found on every hospital room's wall. I knotted the end and put it in my purse.

"Eat or drink nothing, except water from the tap. In a clean cup," I said. "I'm going to figure out some way to get you out of here."

As I headed for the door, I paused. "It may take me a while. But I'll be back."

I peeked out the door. Yes, I was right. The nurses on this floor were all wearing scrubs in the same color, navy blue. The fake nurse had apparently checked that out and made sure he matched. Each department must be color-coordinated.

A woman passed carrying a dustpan and a roll of paper towels. Housekeeping, I noted, was wearing purple.

I checked the ceiling for cameras. There was one near the elevators. I was sure they were mounted near the outside doors as well.

Again I waited until the nurse was distracted by the phone. Then I scooted for the stairs. I went down five floors, double checking the location of the restrooms on each floor. Then I went down one more floor. Aha! Every hospital I'd ever been in had relegated radiology to the basement, and this one was no exception.

Everyone in radiology was wearing scrubs in a color I call puke green. As I watched, one staffer headed for the elevator, pushing an empty wheelchair and carrying a clipboard. Nearby was a "family" restroom. Good.

Then I located an inconspicuous door that led to the basement parking lot. I'd been carrying my heavy winter jacket. I put it on, went out, and got into my van.

Luckily, the hospital is only a few blocks from a Target store. I found the scrubs department and bought a puke green shirt and pants in the largest size and a purple set in medium. I included footies and a head cover in both colors. Then I went to the office supply department and bought a clipboard. Luckily I had enough cash to pay for all this. I sure didn't want to use a credit card for the cops to check on later.

I had another stroke of good fortune: this Target had a family restroom. I locked myself in for privacy. Then

I took a small tube of hand lotion from my purse, rubbed it on my eyelashes, and ruthlessly took my mascara off. I used the hand soap and some rough paper towels to scrub the rest of the makeup off my face. When I looked in the mirror, my eyes had disappeared, and my face was completely blah.

Joe says he's amazed at how much makeup it takes for me to look as if I'm not wearing any. My false face doesn't seem to bother him; he never complains about the time I take to try to look as good as I can.

But I hate an overly made-up look. I'm sure it's a hangover from my days in beauty—I mean, scholarship—pageant competition, when I had to use stage makeup and look glamorous. I'd rather look—well, classic. So I keep my makeup and hairstyle simple. But Joe's right. It takes a certain amount of makeup to look as if I'm not wearing any.

The one thing I usually won't give up is mascara. Without it, my blond eyelashes simply disappear. I have no eyes. But for a kidnapping, that was exactly the look I wanted.

After my makeup was gone, I brushed my hair into a raggedy-looking bun and fastened it up with a rubber band I found in the bottom of my purse. I looked in the mirror. Perfect. I looked absolutely awful.

I put the puke green scrubs on over my jeans and T-shirt, then put on my winter jacket and pulled up the hood. I usually leave the hood tucked inside and wear a knit cap.

As soon as I was back in the van, I called Joe's cell phone. He didn't answer, of course, so I left a message. "I'm trading my van for your truck. I assume you have a key so you can drive the van home. I'll explain later."

I found his truck in a lot near his office and was able to leave my van only two spaces down.

Then I went back to the hospital, pulled into the underground section of the parking lot, parked as close to that inconspicuous door as I could, and went inside. I didn't look at the cameras, but I tried not to look sneaky either.

In the basement family restroom, I added my jacket to the Target sack. I checked the wastebasket. Yes, the custodial staff had stashed several extra plastic bags in the bottom. I took two of them.

Then I stood in the hall outside Radiology, looking at my watch to pretend I was waiting to meet someone. When everybody in Radiology was busy, I scooped up a wheelchair, a hospital blanket, and a washcloth. I plunked the Target sack and the washcloth in the seat of the wheelchair, and draped a hospital blanket over them. Holding my clipboard officiously, I took the elevator to the sixth floor.

Just fifty-nine minutes after I'd left Emma Davidson alone, I was back to pick her up.

The only bad moment came when I got to her room. She didn't recognize the new me. I startled her so much she nearly fell off the bed.

When Emma did realize who I was, she began to laugh. She seemed excited and amused by the whole adventure.

"I've written a note," she said. "I'll leave it on my pillow, as if I'm eloping. It explains that I'm going of my own volition. It doesn't mention you. It just says I asked a friend to pick me up."

I laughed, too. The situation really was ridiculous. I motioned to the wheelchair.

"You'll have to sit on my jacket," I said. "And if you know any prayers, say them. We're not doing anything illegal—I'm sure you have a perfect right to leave the hospital if you want to. But I'd rather not have a big confrontation."

My heart nearly failed as we left Emma's room and heard one of the nurses call out from the central station, "Where are you going?"

I waved my clipboard. "Radiology. I'll bring her right back."

Luckily, the nursing station phone rang just then. The nurse looked at me closely, but she turned away and answered the phone. Emma and I cut out for the elevator. We went down two floors, to the fourth floor.

As soon as we had locked ourselves in the family restroom near that elevator, I gave Emma the purple scrubs. She was still laughing as she pulled them on over her clothes. I handed her the plastic trash bags and the washcloth as props.

She left the restroom first and walked casually—at least I told her to walk casually—toward the elevator. I followed in one minute, still carrying my Target sack.

To my horror, I saw that a skinny man in navy scrubs was approaching Emma. I cringed as he spoke to her. "Could I have some spray cleaner?"

For a moment I thought Emma was going to blurt out a confession. The poor woman was so shy to begin with; she wasn't designed to go on the run.

But she merely looked at him and blinked. *"Qué?"* she said.

The hospital staffer got a long-suffering look on his face. "Never mind," he said. "I'll find it." He walked off down the hall.

The elevator came. Emma and I got on without looking at each other and descended to the basement.

We kept our distance in the basement, too. I went into the family restroom—for what I hoped was the final time in that sort of facility—and put my jacket on. I covered my head with the hood, then went out the door without a direct glance at Emma. A sidelong glance showed me that she was energetically wiping a handrail with that silly washcloth.

My hand was shaking as I opened the door of the truck, started the motor, and pulled it around to the door. Emma came out as soon as the truck stopped.

Then we hit a snag. She was short, and the darn truck is tall. I thought I was going to have to get out, go around, and give her a boost.

And behind her, coming down the basement hall, I could see two guys in security uniforms.

Just as I thought all was lost, Emma got a foot inside the truck, found the handhold, and hauled herself in.

"Hang on!" I said. "We're not waiting to buckle up."

And I drove off—still trying to look casual. The security guys stopped outside the door and looked all around. They did not seem to notice Joe's truck.

"Whew!" I said. "I'm not cut out for a life of crime."

"Maybe not," Emma said. "But you seem to be good at it." Her voice was noticeably stronger, but she still sounded whispery. "I do appreciate your help."

"We're not home yet. The heater should get warmed up in a minute. We shouldn't freeze before we're out of Holland."

"Should we leave Holland? I need to go to a hotel, I guess, and if we leave Holland, it'll be hard to find one."

"Oh! I was going to take you someplace else."

"Not your house! I don't want to be any trouble. And it would be awfully easy for somebody to find me there."

"No, not my house. First, let's get out of town. Then I'll explain what I had in mind."

"All right." Emma still sounded timid. "I just don't want to go to my house. I don't want to involve Chuck and Lorraine. Not that Lorraine would notice. She's in a stupor most of the time. The poor thing."

I drove us south to Saugatuck and pulled off at the first exit, then parked outside a fast-food joint. I left the motor running and turned around to face Emma.

"First," I said, "you haven't been declared incompetent or otherwise ordered to seek treatment, have you?"

"Oh no!"

"If not, I don't think anyone can insist that you stay in the hospital. As a competent adult, you can refuse treatment. So you're not doing anything illegal by leaving the hospital."

Emma smiled.

"And if a friend asks me to take her someplace," I said, "I don't think I'm doing anything illegal if I give her a ride."

"That's a load off my mind."

"But you mustn't do anything that's dangerous to yourself, Emma! I couldn't stand that."

"Oh no! I don't want to hurt myself. I'm trying *not* to get hurt."

"I have one question. When I chased off the guy with the pillow, you said one thing I didn't understand."

"What was that?"

"Something about 'Moe is still trying to hurt me.' What did you mean? Did he physically abuse you?"

Emma sighed deeply. "Oh, Moe never *hit* me."

"Someone told me he yelled at you."

"Sometimes. It's just that—well, no matter what I did, he wasn't happy with it. I couldn't please him, no matter how hard I tried." She sighed again. "I know that clown wasn't Moe. I really do. I was just so frightened because he looked just like Moe. His clown makeup was registered, you know. I don't understand how a different person could wear it."

Then she straightened up in her seat. "I'm trying to buck up and be stronger about facing my problems. Except, if I could only talk to your husband. I need to do that first."

"He should be available this evening. But here's my suggestion for right now. My aunt and I have a friend named Sarajane Harding, and Sarajane runs a bed and breakfast inn. She has one room, however, a nice guest room, that's very quiet and private. It's right next to her personal apartment. I called her, and she says you can use that room. It's not exactly a hideout, but I don't think anyone would come looking for you there."

Emma smiled even more broadly. "That sounds wonderful. Could your husband come to see me there?"

"Yes. I'll call him as soon as we get you installed."

She seemed content with that plan. I didn't go on to explain just why Sarajane had this "quiet and private" room.

Sarajane is herself a former abused wife, and she works with the underground railroad that aids abused women who are trying to escape their tormentors. She specializes in women in so much danger that they need new identities and completely new lives. Aunt Nettie and I have occasionally been able to help these women with temporary jobs. Our husbands, both Hogan and Joe, pretend they don't know about Sarajane's activities. Some of the things she's involved in, such as fake ID cards, aren't quite legal, and Hogan is, after all, a police chief. As a former city official, Joe also tries not to know what's going on.

By the time we got to Warner Pier, the winter darkness had closed in, and I felt safe going straight to Sarajane's. Once I had delivered Emma to her new landlady, I went into the kitchen and pulled out my cell phone. I wanted to call Joe and try to explain what I'd been up to. I wasn't at all sure he was going to approve.

I was almost glad when he didn't answer. The situation was so complicated that I needed to make a few notes before I talked to him. There was a stick-on memo pad on Sarajane's refrigerator, and I grabbed a sheet, ready to outline my afternoon.

Then someone spoke behind me, and I nearly jumped out of my scrubs.

"Oh, hi, Lee. Have you quit the chocolate company and gone in for something medical?"

I whirled around and found myself facing Belle Montgomery.

What the heck was she doing there?

"Oh golly!" I said. "You left a message. I thought you went home."

"No, the message was supposed to be that I wasn't going home. Why? Shouldn't I be here?"

No, she shouldn't. The daughter of the man accused of killing Moe Davidson should not be in the same bed and breakfast inn with Moe's widow. It was all wrong. A potential scene to end all scenes.

How could I get her out of the kitchen and keep her out?

I reached for Belle's arm. "Let's go into the living room," I said.

"I was going to go out to dinner. If you're on your own—would you like to go along?"

"I need to reach Joe."

"Where has he been today? I've been trying to catch him."

"An emergency came up . . ." I tugged at Belle's arm again, but the darn woman just stood there.

Belle laughed. "Lee, you haven't answered my question. What are you doing in those scrubs?"

"It's a long story." I tugged again. "Come in by the fire, and I'll tell you."

I'd succeeded in moving her only one or two steps when the door to the pantry hall opened, and Emma and Sarajane came in. Sarajane was talking enthusiastically, and Emma was whispering replies. They stopped when they saw Belle and me.

"Oh," Sarajane said. "Belle. I thought you went out to dinner."

"I was just leaving." She stared pointedly at Emma. Silence grew. Sarajane and I looked at each other.

Finally Sarajane spoke. "This is Emma. She's just arrived. She's a personal guest of mine. Emma, this is Belle."

Belle was still staring. "Emma, you seem familiar. Have we met?"

Oh heavens! Belle must have seen Emma's picture in the newspaper or on TV.

Emma whispered. "I don't think so."

Belle turned to me. "Lee, I wanted to tell you and Joe about a decision I've made."

I devoutly hoped that her decision was a vow of silence. But no such luck. She went on.

"I'm coming out of the closet about my family. I'm telling everyone." She took a deep breath and turned toward Emma and Sarajane. She spoke proudly. "Yes, my father is Royal Hollis, the homeless man who has been arrested in the death of Moe Davidson."

Chapter 18

Sarajane and I both gasped so hard we inhaled nearly every molecule of air in that kitchen. What a time for Belle to decide to come clean.

Sheriff Ramsey, Chuck, and Lorraine had been yelling, "Git a rope," every time Royal had been mentioned. How was Emma going to react? Hysteria? Sobs? Anger? Fear?

I didn't know what to expect, but "My goodness" was definitely not on my list.

Because that was what Emma said. She took a step toward Belle, and her expression became quite sympathetic. "My goodness," she said. She followed that with, "Oh my."

Then Sarajane took control of the situation. "Dinner," she said. "Emma, you and I need to have a little conference before dinner." She grabbed Emma's arm with a grip of steel, and she steered her back into her secluded bedroom. If Emma had resisted, I firmly be-

lieve Sarajane would have put her in a judo hold and
thrown her through the door.

I took my cue from Sarajane, though I didn't use a
judo hold either.

"Belle," I said, "I want to hear about how you
reached that decision. Let's go out to dinner together."

I got Belle into the living room. Then she stopped
dead and turned to face me. "Was that Mrs. Davidson?
She looks like the picture I saw in the paper."

"Yes, Belle."

"So she came here? Am I going to have to leave?"

"I don't think so. Frankly, she wanted a few days of
solitude, so I'd appreciate your not mentioning that
she's here. To anyone."

"Does Joe know what's going on?"

"No, Joe hasn't talked to her. He had a crisis with his
regular job and has been in Grand Rapids all day. With
his cell phone turned off. I was just going to call him
again."

I yanked my phone out of my pocket and called Joe.
He didn't answer, but I left a message, and he called me
back before I could ditch those puke green scrubs.

"What are you up to?" he asked. "I'm on my way
back from Grand Rapids, and I just got a phone call
from Clancy Pike saying that you kidnapped Emma
Davidson this afternoon."

I think that the presence of Belle Montgomery was
the only thing that kept me from losing it completely. I
had thought I could handle things calmly, but that
comment nearly pushed me right over the edge. I did
not want to deal with Clancy Pike. And I didn't want
to explain the events of the afternoon over a cell phone
in front of Belle.

I couldn't ask for sympathy, so I attacked. "Listen,"
I said, "I'm going to my office. I'll ask Belle to go with

me. And you'd better show up there within an hour ready to listen. And Clancy's story isn't exactly true."

I hung up and turned to Belle. "Joe's going to meet us at my office. I suggest that you and I leave. Stay here while I check with Sarajane."

I called Sarajane out of Emma's room, afraid that she might change her mind about letting Emma stay. But she didn't seem to care.

"Oh, it'll be all right," she said. "Emma's reaction to Belle's announcement was rather—well, unexpected, but she doesn't seem angry. I don't think they'll have a knock-down-drag-out. In fact, she seems to feel sympathetic toward Belle."

"I'll take Emma to my house if you're uneasy."

"No. I've had women here who were hard for me to understand before. None of them ever attacked me."

I leaned close. "The hospital was afraid that Emma would harm herself."

"Not in my house." Sarajane's voice was firm. "Not herself. Not anybody else."

She patted my shoulder and went back to Emma. I heard her speaking. "Now, Emma, do you have any prescriptions with you? Any over-the-counter drugs?"

I decided I had to trust Sarajane. She had a lot of experience with desperate people.

But how about Belle? Could I trust her? Would she be willing to keep her mouth shut? Or would she start telling the world that Emma was at Sarajane's?

I wanted to take Belle away with me so I could keep an eye on her. There was no reason Belle shouldn't shout Emma's whereabouts from the rooftops. And that might be disastrous with someone wandering around trying to kill her.

If I could keep Belle with me until Joe came, maybe I could keep her quiet. Maybe. It might be a challenge.

I went back to the living room resolved to meet that challenge.

"Belle, do you like pizza?"

"I'm not very hungry."

"Neither am I, but we need to eat. I also need to go to my office if the genius ladies who make our chocolate are going to get paid tomorrow. And I asked Joe to meet us there." I took a deep breath to signify that I was changing the subject. "So, in the few days you've been in Warner Pier, have you been introduced to the Dock Street Pizza Place?"

"Actually, yes."

"Then you know about one of our local treasures. What do you like on your pizza?"

She was vague about her pizza preferences, so I called in an order for what Joe would want: an extra large pizza with pepperoni and mushrooms. I also asked for three side salads and an order of garlic bread. I took ten minutes to remove my incriminating scrubs—just in case the cops should come looking for me—and to put on minimal makeup. Belle and I went by to pick up the pizzas and took them to the office. I turned on the lights in the retail shop, so Joe would know we were there, and took Belle back to our break room. There were soft drinks in the refrigerator and an oven for the pizza and bread. I stowed the pizza and bread away and got two sodas. Then I sat down and took a deep breath.

Belle hadn't said much on the way to the office, but I could almost hear her brain clicking. She had been thinking madly. I expected her to start talking as soon as we were settled in the kitchen, and she didn't disappoint me. "Lee, just what is going on?"

Luckily, the trip for pizza and to the office had given me time to consider what to tell her. And I'd decided to request a delay—just until Joe got there.

"Belle, I've gotten myself into an extremely complicated situation. I need to tell Joe about it—I haven't done anything illegal, but I may need a lawyer! He should be here in another half hour. Would you mind waiting, so I can tell you both at the same time?"

Belle looked at me narrowly. "I guess that's all right."

Was the crisis over? That would be a lot to hope for.

Too much to hope for, actually. Belle popped open her can of Diet Coke, then spoke again. "Is this Mrs. Davidson okay?"

I decided I'd better level with her.

"I can't swear she isn't disturbed," I said. "But I've been with her most of the afternoon, and she seemed pretty sensible to me."

"Didn't I hear that she attempted suicide?"

"That's what we all thought, but she says she didn't. There's only one thing I feel sure of: She's safer there at Sarajane's than she would be at the hospital. Or at her home. So I appreciate your not saying anything about her until the situation is a little more claptrap."

Belle looked stunned, and it took me a moment to realize what I'd said. Claptrap?

"Not claptrap!" I yelped the words. "Clear-cut. Until the situation is more clear-cut!"

Belle's expression changed from stunned to amused. Then to highly amused. Then to laughter. I began to laugh, too. The pair of us sat there, clutching our Diet Cokes and roaring.

And just as our hilarity reached a peak, we heard someone pounding on the front door.

We stopped laughing instantly. Belle frowned. "Is it Joe?" she asked.

"He probably hasn't had time to get here. Besides, he has a key. I guess I'll have to answer it to find out."

Of course, I'd check carefully before I opened the

front door. I peeked around the edge of the shade, and there was plenty of light outside for me to see who was there.

"Dadgum," I said. "It's Chuck Davidson."

I wanted to pretend I wasn't there. But that wasn't going to work. The light was on, both in the back room and in the shop. And I'd twitched the blind. Chuck was already calling my name. I just had to brazen it out.

I sighed and opened the door, prepared either to have a fight or to lie my head off.

"Come in, Chuck. What's up?"

"Oh, Lee! Has Emma contacted you?"

"No." At least that was true. I'd contacted her. "Isn't she still in the hospital?"

"She's gone! Lorraine and I don't know where she is. Are you sure she didn't call you?"

"She called the house trying to reach Joe, but he wasn't there. Why should she call me?"

"She seems to have some big thing—well, since the episode at the hospital, when the two of you say the strange guy was in her room, she seems to think you're a friend."

"I hope I am. I'm sure she needs one."

Chuck paced up and down the shop for a moment. He looked frantic, and I almost expected him to start wringing his hands. I felt sorry for him.

"Personally, I need all the friends I can get, all the time," I said. "Where do you think Emma has gone?"

"We don't know. Hospital security is looking everywhere. She left a note, said she was leaving the hospital, and that she'd called a friend to pick her up."

"I see."

"That hospital was clearly negligent! I'm going to sue the . . . Well, anyway, I thought she might have contacted you."

"Emma lived in Warner Pier for at least two years. She probably has lots of friends here, people she knows better than she knows me."

"Lorraine and I can't think of any she's mentioned, Lee. She's so shy. Apparently she just stayed home. And my dad—well, he didn't encourage her to get out and do things, meet people. All her friends are back in Indiana."

"There's been time for one of her Indiana friends to drive up for her."

"I can't imagine that. Lee, I'm worried about her. I'm afraid she's had a complete mental breakdown."

"What does Lorraine think?"

"Oh, Lorraine." Chuck's voice was filled with disgust. "Lorraine has her own problems. I can only worry about one of them at a time, and today it's Emma's turn. Honestly! When my dad married Emma, I hoped he'd finally decided to act like a normal person. But, no! He just made her crazy, too."

I began to sympathize with Chuck. He did seem to be the only normal person in the Davidson family. I couldn't tell him where Emma was, of course, because she'd asked me not to. But maybe I could talk to her. Chuck—and Lorraine, too—did deserve some reassurance about her safety.

Chuck kept on talking. "Clancy Pike thinks you might have helped her leave the hospital, Lee."

I'm sure my voice was cold. "Joe and I have had our run-ins with the stand-in chief. He's suspicious of us because of my connection with Hogan Jones, the real police chief. Hogan doesn't get along with the sheriff, and the sheriff is the former boss of Clancy Pike. But if Clancy suspected me of doing something illegal, I think he'd be over here pounding on the door."

"He was at the hospital, looking at the security film."

"Hmm. Well, he'll see me on it. After Emma called and couldn't reach Joe, Joe asked me to go by the hospital and see if I could talk to her."

"Then you did see her!"

"The hospital wouldn't admit she was there, and I didn't know her room number."

Chuck deflated. "Oh. At least they made some effort to guard her privacy. But, Lee, poor Emma has really lost it. All this stuff about someone trying to kill her . . ."

Chuck had pushed me too far.

"Wait a minute! Chuck, you're forgetting that I was there. I saw the clown holding the pillow over her face. That was a genuine attack. I guarantee it."

We stared at each other for a long moment. Then I spoke. "Emma actually is in danger, Chuck. I can't judge her mental state, but that attack really happened."

For a moment I thought Chuck was going to hit me. He got red in the face, clenched his jaw, and squinched his eyes.

Then he turned and opened the door. "Whatever!" He stepped outside and yelled back over his shoulder, "I tried to talk to you!" He left.

"Whew!" I said.

But what had Chuck meant by his final remark? What was he going to do? He was obviously putting pressure on Clancy and the hospital to find Emma. By siccing Clancy on me, he could cause me a lot of trouble, and he could cause Joe even more.

I heard a voice behind me. "Lee?"

I jumped and whirled around. "Belle! Honestly! I was so annoyed with Chuck that I almost forgot you were there."

She was frowning. "Lee, I can't blame Chuck for being worried about Emma. Why didn't you at least tell him that she's safe?"

"Because Emma asked me not to."

"And you keep your word?"

"I try to."

I wanted to explain to Belle that I try not to say I'll do something unless I feel sure I can keep my word. In this particular situation, I was beginning to think I'd spoken too soon. But if I told Chuck she was safe, he'd know I was in touch with her, and Emma had asked me not to tell him anything.

"The predicament with Emma has a lot of fortifications that I hadn't foreseen," I said. "I mean, ramifications!"

Belle still looked as if she doubted my decision. But before I could argue it out with her, there was a loud knock on the street door.

After I'd jumped a foot off the floor, I peeked out. "Thank goodness! It's Joe," I said.

I unlocked the door and let him in. As soon as I had locked the door behind him, I grabbed him around the neck. He hugged me back.

"This has been one heck of an afternoon," I said.

"And it's not over yet," he said. "A Warner Pier police car is right behind me."

Chapter 19

"Oh no! Joe, I've got to talk to you before I talk to Clancy Pike!"

"We haven't got time," Joe said.

"But I don't know what to tell Clancy."

"When in doubt, keep your mouth shut."

Joe opened the door and, sure enough, Clancy Pike stood on the sidewalk outside.

His warm winter cap with the earflaps fastened on top hid his bald head, but he pulled the hat off very politely. I thought he was going to bow. Somehow his courteous behavior made him even more threatening. There was just so much of him. It was like having an extremely docile lion in the house. I kept waiting for him to pounce.

"Hello there, Joe. Lee. May I talk to you for a moment?"

"Come on in," Joe said. "I was getting worried about that car following me. Finally I realized it was you guys."

"Sorry. We didn't mean to make you nervous. We just didn't see any reason to pull you over before you got wherever you were headed."

Pike came in, and with him was Jerry Cherry, one of the Warner Pier patrolmen. Belle Montgomery had followed us into the shop, and Joe introduced them.

"You're Royal Hollis' daughter?" Clancy looked at her narrowly.

She held her chin up. "That's right."

I jumped into the conversation. "Have you found Emma?"

Clancy shook his head. "We hoped you had heard from her. How'd you know she was missing?"

"Chuck came by. He's in a real snit."

"He's concerned, of course. That's why we were hoping she'd contacted you or Joe."

I was terribly tempted to make some neutral comment, such as "I can't help you," that avoided a literal untruth. But if you're going to lie, do it. I firmed my resolve and spoke.

"Sorry. I don't know a thing about Emma."

"You were at the hospital."

"Smile!" I said. "You're on *Candid Camera*!"

Clancy nodded, but he didn't find my wisecrack funny. "Yep. The cameras caught you going in about two o'clock and leaving after three. Why were you there?"

I repeated my story about Emma calling Joe and his asking me to find out what she wanted. "But I couldn't pry the room number out of the hospital volunteer. So I had a cup of coffee in the snack bar. Then I walked around the hospital awhile, but I didn't get any inspiration about how to find Mrs. Davidson, so I left and did some errands." I could only hope they wouldn't check the cameras at Target and catch me buying scrubs.

I rushed on. "But I'm a little confused. I mean, Emma hasn't been declared incompetent or anything, has she?"

Clancy shook his head.

"Then if she wants to leave the hospital, she can, right?"

"That's correct. But you claimed earlier that someone tried to kill her."

"The hobo clown! I still think he was trying to smother her."

"If we felt sure she *had* left the hospital on her own, then that would settle everything. But as long as there's a possibility that she's in danger or that someone forced her to leave against her will, we have to keep looking for her, just to be sure she's safe."

Clancy looked at me significantly, and so did Jerry Cherry. They clearly expected some reaction from me.

The temptation to say "I'll get Emma to call you" was really strong. I looked at Joe. He was standing behind Clancy. And he crossed his eyes. I wasn't sure what he meant by that, but I decided I'd better keep quiet.

"She called earlier," I evaded. "But not after I got back to Warner Pier."

"When did you get to Warner Pier?'

"Oh, maybe five, five thirty."

"Did you go home?"

My imagination failed me. I hadn't gone home. I had gone to Sarajane's. But I couldn't reveal that. There was a pause.

Then Belle Montgomery spoke. "Lee is trying not to embarrass me, Chief Pike. I needed someone to hold my hand. I've been staying at the Peach Street B and B, and I had earlier left a whiny message asking Joe to call me. Lee came out there to reassure me. Then she even invited me to come here for some pizza."

She turned to me. "I checked on the pizza in the oven, by the way. I turned it back to one seventy-five."

She'd saved my neck, and I would gladly have hugged hers in gratitude. I restrained myself and simply nodded. Clancy nodded, too. Still completely deadpan, he wrote in his notebook.

Then he spoke again. "Could I ask a favor, Mrs. Woodyard? May I use your men's room?"

The question was obviously designed by Clancy to allow him to get a look around the place. I didn't care if he looked under the cooling tunnel and into the milk chocolate vat and on every shelf of the storage closet. There wasn't anything there he couldn't see.

"Our facilities are unisex," I said. "But you're welcome to use them. Joe, could you show Clancy the way? And I'll get everybody some chocolate."

I grabbed three four-piece boxes off the shelf. I could tell what was in each by the wrappings. First I gave Belle a box of champagne truffles ("dark chocolate interior enrobed with white chocolate and embellished with dark chocolate stripes"). I gave Jerry four chocolate malt truffles ("milk chocolate filling flavored with malt in a milk chocolate shell dusted with more malt"). For Clancy I picked out Kahlúa truffles ("milk chocolate filling, flavored with coffee liqueur, enrobed with milk chocolate, and trimmed with dark chocolate stripes").

None of them turned them down. I doubted I could bribe Warner Pier's cops with chocolate, but I felt that Clancy and Jerry's acceptances were good signs. At least Clancy thanked me very politely when he came back from the restroom.

As soon as the street door shut behind Clancy and Jerry, I turned to Belle and started to tell her how much I appreciated her helping me cover up. But Joe put a finger to his lips.

"Now, where's that pizza?" he asked loudly.

The three of us went to the back of the building. As soon as we were in the break room I began to applaud. "Yay, Belle! You saved my skin."

"I want to hear the whole story," Joe said, "but could we get the pizza out of the oven first?"

So Joe and Belle heard about my initiation as a kidnapper through mouthfuls of pizza and salad. I think I was overly excited; I hadn't been hungry earlier, but now I was starving.

Joe ate, too, but he managed to do it with his deadpan lawyer face on.

Belle's eyes got bigger and bigger. When I reached the part when Emma said "Qué?" Joe burst out laughing.

I stopped to catch my breath, and Belle spoke. "So, what is Mrs. Davidson doing out at Sarajane's? I mean, why did you take her there?"

I dropped my eyes and poked my salad with my fork. Joe was silent as well. Then we peeked at each other, and Joe laughed.

"This is when I get as tactful as Clancy and visit the men's room," he said.

He left while I explained that Sarajane was highly experienced in helping women who were in danger. "I hope you'll help us keep her secret," I said.

"Of course!" Belle nodded enthusiastically. "In fact, a friend in Saginaw was a volunteer at a women's shelter, and she told me women who were in extreme danger were always a problem for that organization."

Belle took a bite of salad, then spoke again. "I'm surprised that Emma hadn't taken advantage of Sarajane's facilities earlier. It's easy to visualize her husband beating her. He was probably one of the biggest jerks I ever met in my life."

I started to agree. Then the full impact of what Belle had said came through. She had met Moe?

But when? How? When Belle had come into the shop two days earlier, she had acted as if this was her first visit to Warner Pier. So how had she known Moe?

I hope I didn't gape, since my mouth was full of salad greens, but I certainly stared. If Belle had known Moe, why hadn't she told me? Why hadn't she told Joe?

Joe picked that moment to reappear. He slid into his chair and spoke casually. "How'd you meet Moe?" Then he stabbed his own salad and took a bite. But he kept looking at Belle.

A long silence fell.

"Oh," Belle said. "I blew it."

Joe nodded. "You blew it if you wanted us to continue to think that this was your first visit to Warner Pier."

"I could have met Moe someplace else."

"True. Did you?"

"No." Belle stared at her plate. "Over the Columbus Day weekend my dad got picked up for panhandling in Saginaw. He wasn't ever charged with anything, didn't have to stand trial, but the police released him to a homeless shelter there. I knew the director, and he'd given me advice about how to look for my father. Unfortunately, my dad left before the director could tell me that he'd turned up. But my dad had said something about heading for the Warner Pier area. So I came over here looking for him."

"How did Moe figure into the story?"

"I went to the police station to ask where a homeless man might hang out. The chief—I guess it was your uncle, Lee—told me there was an area where hitchhikers camped. He told me that the fellow at the clown shop lived near there. I went to the shop to ask if Moe had seen any homeless men in the area."

"I doubt you got any help."

"That Moe was awful! He swore at me. Told me those guys were a—well, a blot on his neighborhood. Called them bums! He said he'd be glad to kill one of them if he got the chance." Tears were welling in her eyes. "It wasn't fair! My dad is like he is because of wounds he received serving his country!

"Then this Moe guy told me I must be a complete slut if that's the kind of family I came from. Finally, well, I gave him as good as I got. We had quite a slanging match. He ordered me out of his store."

I patted Belle's hand. "I'm sorry, Belle. But I'm glad to hear you told Moe off."

Joe's eyes narrowed. "Did you say this happened on Columbus Day?"

"Yes."

Joe nodded and took another slice of pizza.

"I know, I know! Just a couple of months before Moe was killed." Belle spoke angrily. "Maybe our fight added to Moe's anger. Was he still mad? Was that one reason he attacked my dad, one reason Moe was killed? I've asked myself that a hundred times."

"Why didn't you want us to know you'd been in Warner Pier before?" I asked.

"It was a humiliating experience."

That was true. But was it a good reason for not telling Joe and me she'd been looking for her dad in Warner Pier previously? Frankly, it sounded sort of thin. But Joe didn't seem inclined to cross-examine her, so I also decided to let it drop. For the moment.

I chewed and swallowed, then spoke. "So. What do we do next?"

"Well, as you pointed out to Clancy," Joe said, "since

Emma hasn't been declared incompetent or otherwise required to stay in the hospital, you didn't do anything illegal by breaking her out. In fact, I think you were pretty clever about it."

"But, Joe, I understand why Clancy—and Chuck and Lorraine—are looking for her. And I don't think they're going to quit. I certainly don't want them to trace her to Sarajane's. And they might do that." I sighed. "And Emma is still determined to talk to you."

"Yes, I need to have a one-on-one meeting with her," he said. "But maybe it should wait for morning."

"Joe, people are looking for her."

"Yeah, I'm afraid we need to do something about that. She needs to call someone and tell them she's all right."

"But we don't want them to trace the call. A throw-away phone?"

"Maybe. But a pay phone would be easier."

"Are there any left in Warner Pier?"

"Surely there's one at the train station in Holland."

"That's thirty miles! How about the Shell station?"

Joe grinned. "They do have a pay phone, left over from the days when truckers used them. That would be a logical place for one of us to stop, in case the local cops are keeping an eye on anybody."

"I need gas, too," Belle said. "I could go along."

That's what we settled on. I gathered up my payroll materials—those ladies still had to be paid. Joe moved my van around to the alley, and Belle and I got in it. Then he took his truck and both of our vehicles pulled out at the same time—one headed northwest and the other southeast.

Joe went to his boat shop and went inside for ten minutes. I took Belle to Sarajane's. We wrapped Emma in a winter jacket with a hood, then loaded her into my van. I drove to the Shell station, followed by Belle in her own car, and we both pulled up to gas pumps. Our timing was perfect. Joe pulled into the station and parked in a way that blocked the view of our actions with his pickup.

Then he politely pumped gas for both Belle and me. Meanwhile, with visibility limited, Emma went into the station—it isn't one of those giant truck stops—and went to the pay phone. It's located in the area where coffee and snacks are available, with two booths where drivers can eat.

Joe had written out a script for Emma to read, just to be sure that she didn't let anything slip. I went with her to be sure she followed it.

Emma called her own house. Luckily, nobody answered, and she was able to leave a recorded message. "Chuck, Lorraine, it's Emma. I didn't want you to worry, but I decided to leave the hospital. I've gone to stay with a friend. I'll call soon. I'm perfectly safe."

She hung up and turned to me. "Now, all I have to do is tell Joe what happened. Since he's Royal Hollis' lawyer, I'm sure he can tell me how to handle things."

"Aren't you tired, Emma? He could talk to you in the morning."

She shook her head vigorously. "No! I've been trying to get this done for a week, and I'm not waiting any longer!"

I was sure Joe was tired, too, but he had to speak for himself. And as I expected, he agreed to go back to Sarajane's and let Emma get whatever was bothering her off her chest.

The surprise came when Emma asked me to go along. And the next surprise came when Joe endorsed her suggestion. Why would he want me to sit in on a discussion of a client's case?

We left my van at the station, and Emma rode with Belle. As soon as we were in Joe's truck I quizzed him. "Why am I here, Joe?"

"I know you'd rather be working on your payroll . . ."

"Ha! Working on a payroll isn't exactly thrilling."

"I guess not. But you seem to soothe Emma. She trusts you." He laughed. "Especially after you busted her out of the hospital. Plus, I can tell you're dying to know what she's going to say."

"That's true. I was expecting a detailed report as soon as you got home."

It was only eight thirty when we got to Sarajane's. Bless her heart, she let us have the room off the parlor that we'd used for Joe's conference with Belle a few days earlier.

Belle was dying of curiosity, just like me, but she said she was going to bed. Sarajane delivered a pot of coffee to us. She also said good night.

Naturally, after days of trying to talk to Joe, Emma found it hard to begin. Joe didn't help her. He just busied around, getting out a big legal pad for notes and fixing a cup of coffee. Then he took a pen in his hand and looked at her expectantly.

Emma sighed deeply and spoke. "The truth is, Royal Hollis didn't kill Moe. I did."

Chapter 20

H uh?
      Emma's statement was crazy, but as she made
it she seemed perfectly calm and rational.

I tried to take it in. It wasn't easy. Although Joe and
I had touched on the possibility that Royal hadn't killed
Moe, that had simply been wishful thinking. Everyone's assumption had been that he had done it. Royal
had even confessed.

Or had he?

Joe had never been happy with Royal's confession,
true. But I had thought that was because Joe didn't
think Royal was competent. He doubted that Royal understood what was going on, and he didn't think Royal
grasped the implications of the story he told the sheriff's deputies.

Plus, Joe didn't think Royal intended to hurt Moe. If
he had hit Moe, it was because Moe struck him first.

In addition, the sheriff kept urging a serious legal
charge on the prosecutor. Joe thought Royal Hollis was

being accused of a more serious crime than he committed—murder rather than manslaughter. These things had nothing to do with the truth of the homeless man's confession.

Even after Elk told us that a woman had been present when Moe and Hollis tangled, it had not occurred to me that Royal might not have committed the crime at all. I had just considered the missing woman a possible witness. Now Emma was making the possibility of Hollis' innocence a probability.

Emma's confession was going to make Burt Ramsey feel like an idiot.

Then it hit me. Burt Ramsey wasn't going to like feeling like an idiot. Instead of freeing Royal from all charges, Emma's claim was going to cause a whole bunch of trouble. And in the end it might not help Royal Hollis.

"Oh my gosh!" I said.

I may have reacted with excitement, but Joe maintained professional decorum. "That's hard to believe, Emma. Why don't you tell us the whole story?"

Her hands were shaking, but Emma kept speaking calmly.

"I'm not saying I intended to kill Moe. But I did it. I was so upset with him—well, I struck him in anger. And he died. It was entirely my fault."

"Why were you angry with him?"

"Oh, it was just the end of a whole lot of things—and some of them were my fault. I think I'd finally just had enough."

She looked at Joe imploringly. All he did was nod. This was enough encouragement, I guess, because Emma kept talking.

"Maybe I'm just dumb, but Moe had fooled me completely. When we first met, I mean. He was so active in the community, served on committees, and donated a lot of money to projects that made the town better. And personally he was, well, a good guy. He was always cheerful and considerate." She blinked hard. "Then we got married, and the real Moe came out."

"I knew Moe well enough to know he liked to have his own way," Joe said.

"He sure did. Like—well, the first shock I had was how disappointed Moe was to learn that all my money was tied up! He didn't even try to hide the way he felt about that. Jack—that was my first husband—knew I was a pushover. Everything he left me is in trust, and I can only use the income." Her voice rose. "And Moe's capital was gone before we married. He gave it all away!"

Joe shook his head. "I always wondered where Moe got his money."

"Verita! His first wife. It came from her. They lived simply, but Moe gave away every cent she had."

"Moe did own the Clowning Around building. And his house."

"They're both mortgaged to the maximum. Moe had nothing but his social security. He was broke all the time. He could always come up with a clown event to go to or a charitable campaign to give to. Or a city council candidate to back. Anything to get his picture in the paper. It took everything he had."

"You were supporting the two of you?"

"Mainly. My income isn't all that large, and Moe wanted to own two houses and give—give generously— to every project that came along." She sighed deeply. "Then there were other problems. After we were married, his whole personality changed."

I doubted that. Moe had always been a jerk, but Emma simply hadn't seen it until after they were married.

"Moe began to be rude," she said. "To me. And he wasn't, well, provident. Like not closing the house up properly. He made me leave so suddenly in October that there was still food in the refrigerator up here. He wanted me to sell my house in Indiana! Or mortgage it. He yelled at me because I wouldn't do that. My whole life got to be a nightmare."

"What happened the day Moe died?" Joe asked.

Emma dropped her head to her hands for a moment. "That awful day," she said. "Moe was so angry when Harry Vandercool called him. Of course, he did his happy act for Harry—thanked him effusively and promised to come right up and take care of the situation. But—oh!—Moe was really mad. He snarled and yelled at me all evening. Like it was my fault! And then Chuck called and wanted to see him. Moe was already mad at Chuck, though he would never tell me exactly why. It was something about money Moe had given to some organization—but that had nothing to do with Chuck. Moe talked so ugly to him—I was ashamed of him. But Chuck insisted on seeing him. He said he'd meet us at the house up here. I remember Moe said, 'He claims he can explain.' That whole thing made Moe have another fit. It was a nightmare."

Emma stirred her cup of coffee and sighed deeply. "I guess one reason I went up to the cottage with Moe was that I thought I might be able to keep him from fighting with Chuck. I was so ashamed of myself for being married to Moe. I guess that's when I made up my mind I was going to ask him to leave my house. But I thought I ought to see a lawyer first. And we did need to check on the Michigan house. So we left early and got here around noon.

"As soon as we parked in the drive, we saw that poor man in the hot tub. The way Moe acted was simply horrible! He jumped out of the car, screaming at him. I jumped out, too, and I tried to get Moe to stop yelling. Poor Mr. Hollis climbed out of the hot tub. He was trying to put his clothes on. And he was wet, of course! He couldn't get them on."

She fished a wadded-up Kleenex out of her purse. "I felt so sorry for him! And Moe was awful. I grabbed his arm. I tried to tell him to calm down. That only made things worse. Moe shoved me aside. He went up on the deck. Mr. Hollis was trying to get away. He tried to put his underwear on, and he fell down."

"Did Moe hit him?"

"No. Moe was just yelling. Mr. Hollis got back up on his feet. He moved away and backed down the stairs. He fell in the snow. Then Moe got hold of the poor man's shoes! It was wintertime. I'm sure he had only one pair of shoes. There was snow and ice everywhere. Mr. Hollis tried to get the shoes back. That's when they began to struggle."

"Over the shoes."

"Yes! I was so angry with Moe."

"Why?"

She blinked. "Why?"

"After all, Royal Hollis was on your property."

"Moe's property! Not mine."

"But at the least Hollis was trespassing. In the eyes of the law he was definitely in the wrong. Why were you angry with Moe? Why not with Royal Hollis?"

"Because Moe had no compassion! He was cruel! I couldn't bear it!" She wiped her eyes again. "That's why I hit him."

"You hit Moe?"

"Yes! I caught him completely off guard. He had his back to me."

"Did you use a weapon?"

"No, no! Just my hands. I ran at him, and I hit him in the middle of the back with both hands. He went down—ass over teakettle!"

For a moment Emma looked triumphant. "But I didn't mean to *hurt* Moe! I just wanted him to let that poor man go. I didn't mean to kill him."

Joe frowned. "I don't see how shoving him—even a hard shove—could kill him, Mrs. Davidson."

She looked up sharply. "Moe hit his head! As he went down he whacked his head on the steps to the deck. He was bleeding. And he just lay there."

Mrs. Davidson mopped her eyes; her Kleenex was sodden. Joe looked solemn, and I must have been bug-eyed. This story was perfectly believable—but also a complete surprise. None of us spoke for at least a full minute.

Then Joe pulled a handkerchief out of his breast pocket, and put it on the table in front of Emma.

"Thank you," she said. She blew her nose. "Mr. Hollis ran away."

"Did you call an ambulance for Moe?" Joe asked.

"Chuck said he would take care of him."

"Chuck was present for all this?"

"Oh, no. He drove up just as Mr. Hollis ran off. I told him what had happened. I also told him I was going to get a divorce." Emma patted her eyes again with Joe's handkerchief. "Moe was still lying there, but he was moving. It never occurred to me that he was seriously hurt. Honestly, I thought he was just trying to get sympathy. Chuck told me it would be best if I just left and went home. He said he'd calm his dad down and call me that evening."

Emma blew her nose again. "But that evening Chuck came to see me instead. He drove down to tell me Moe was dead."

There was nothing to say. I patted Emma's hand. Her tears were still running, and she was holding her head in both hands. It was several minutes before she looked up at Joe.

"And now," she said, "now you're wondering why I didn't call the police right that minute."

"What did you do?"

"I listened to Chuck! He convinced me that I shouldn't do that. He said that the police thought Moe's death was an accident. That he fell on the stairs and hit his head. He said that I was perfectly justified—those are the words he used, 'perfectly justified'—in trying to stop his dad from attacking Mr. Hollis. He said legally I didn't need to come forward, explain what had happened, to stand trial. I hadn't meant to injure Moe, and his death was just an accident. And he said that's what the police thought. So there was no point in my confessing."

She mopped her eyes again. "I was a coward! I let Chuck convince me." She took two deep breaths before she spoke again. "I had no idea anyone had been arrested for Moe's death."

"Emma," I said, "did you call the police station a couple of weeks ago?"

"Yes. Someone said it was the chocolate company."

"It was me."

Emma nodded. "I thought it must have been. That's when I found out that poor Mr. Hollis was being accused of killing Moe. Of course, I immediately told Chuck I was going to come forward."

"And he tried to stop you?" I asked.

"He said I had it all wrong. That I didn't shove Moe down. That it was Royal who hit him." She twisted her hands together. "And that's just not right!"

Joe frowned. And I'm sure I did, too. Joe was the first

one to speak. "Emma, let me think about all this for a moment."

"I'll do anything you say to make the situation right."

Joe didn't answer. He stared at his yellow pad and drew a picture of a boat on it. He was probably wishing he had never left his boat shop. I was certainly wishing I were back in TenHuis Chocolade because Emma's problem was a real doozy.

Mostly because she'd handled it all wrong.

I don't know a lot about law, but I did—unfortunately—know a lot about Sheriff Burt Ramsey. And Sheriff Burt Ramsey had a culprit all lined up for the death of Moe Davidson. Ramsey would be happy to send Royal Hollis to prison and forget him. Ramsey wasn't going to want the widow of the victim turning up and trying to plead guilty. Not a widow who had been under treatment—even briefly—for mental issues. That was going to be a complicated case. Because, let's face it, Emma might not have shoved Moe. She might well have just imagined that she shoved him—or I was ready to predict that that would be Ramsey's theory of the case.

Joe finally spoke. "Emma, the first thing you need is your own lawyer."

"I was hoping you could help me handle this matter."

"I'm representing Royal Hollis. Your interests could well be adverse to his. Do you see what I mean?"

"But I want to help him go free!"

"I understand that. However, you need a different lawyer to make sure you don't wind up being treated unfairly yourself."

"But that's the reason I wanted to talk to you, Mr. Woodyard! Because you represent Mr. Hollis. Can't you just call me as a witness?"

The discussion went on for ten minutes. Emma was completely focused on unburdening her conscience. She didn't seem to see the implications. After all, her story was so nutty that once she told it, any judge in Michigan might commit her to a mental hospital with a clear conscience.

In the end she agreed to let Joe contact his former mentor, Mac McKay, and get him to recommend several lawyers to her. Mac is a former Warner County attorney, Joe explained. Joe had been an intern for him, back when he was a law student at the University of Michigan.

"Mac knows everybody in the legal world in this part of the state," Joe said. "He doesn't practice anymore, but anybody he recommends will do a good job for you."

"I guess that's the best I can do," Emma said. "It's just that you and Lee have been so kind to me. And Lee saved my life! And I just can't die until I've done my duty."

By then it was nearly eleven o'clock, and Joe and I went home. We had to stop by the Shell station to pick up my van. All my payroll records were still in the passenger's seat. Seeing them there made me more tired than ever.

The payroll took me an hour and a half. Joe helped by writing the names on the pay envelopes. And as soon as I stuffed the last envelope he got us each a bowl of ice cream.

I ate mine, then asked him an important question. "Joe, is anybody going to believe Emma?"

"I think it's unlikely. I'm having trouble doing it myself."

"The problem is that she's so meek and mild. But Hogan tells me that even the meek and mild can kill if they're pushed hard enough."

"True. To me there are important questions. Whatever happened on the day Moe died, does Emma *believe* that she killed him? And if she does believe it, is her belief rational?"

"I spent quite a lot of time with her today, and she seemed perfectly rational to me. But right at this point a large proportion of the population seems to think I'm not rational myself, because nobody believes I saw someone try to kill her."

"Emma sure backs you up." Joe squeezed my hand and grinned at me. "And I believe you."

"You'd better. But the fact that you have to tell me you believe me means you have doubts."

"I'm sure you saw the clown in her room, Lee. I'm sure you interpreted his actions as a threat against Emma."

"Yeah, yeah. But people who didn't see him leaning on that pillow, who didn't see her kicking . . ."

I choked up and quit talking.

Joe moved his chair close to mine and put his arms around me. He didn't say anything either. He just held me.

"Thanks," I said. "Thanks for believing my not very believable story."

Joe hugged me tighter. "Actually, we're faced with several unbelievable stories."

"Emma's and mine. Who else?"

"Maybe 'contradictory' would be the best word. Emma says she shoved Moe down, then left in the family car."

"The only unbelievable part of that is that she could shove him hard enough to kill him. And that's not impossible."

"Yes, just unbelievable. Then there's Chuck's version, the statement he made."

I sat up. "I've never heard Chuck's story, except in a general way. What does he say happened?"

"He doesn't mention Emma. He says he and his dad drove to the cottage in Chuck's car. He was inside when his dad confronted Royal Hollis. Chuck heard the altercation and ran out to find Hollis heading for the woods and his dad lying on the drive, dead or dying."

"That's completely different from Emma's story. What is Hollis' story?"

Joe shook his head. "It's rather confused, I'm afraid. It boils down to 'he took my shoes.' But he denies hitting Moe."

"His story matches Harry Vandercool's, I guess."

"Yeah. Mr. Vandercool says Hollis took off for the woods at least fifteen minutes before he went over and found Chuck kneeling beside Moe's body."

"So Hollis did have time to double back and tangle with Moe again. But, Joe, none of these stories explains why anyone felt it necessary to try to kill Emma, the way the clown and the fake nurse did. A second crime of violence in the same family just can't be unrelated."

"I guess it could be, but I'm like you. I don't believe it. But we know Chuck wasn't the clown who tried to smother Emma. He and Lorraine claim they were working at the shop all day."

"Right. I saw them as I left for Holland, and later on Dolly Jolly talked to them. And I'll take her word anytime."

Joe and I sat side by side, considering for at least a full minute. Then Joe squeezed my hand and stood up.

"I give up," he said. "No more thinking about it tonight. Let's go to bed." He waggled his eyebrows at me.

I waggled mine back. "Sounds like a good idea."

We left the dishes on the table, and we didn't listen to the messages on the phone, and we didn't read the mail, or do any of the other routine things that bedtime usually involves. We locked the back door and threw the bedspread on the floor, but that was all.

Joe apparently set the alarm before he went to sleep, because it went off at six thirty.

"It's not morning already, is it?" I asked.

"I'm afraid so. I'm going to get in the shower. You don't need to get up yet."

I rolled over and buried my head under the pillow as Joe left the bedroom. But I was edging into consciousness. The thought of the dirty ice cream dishes began to prey on my mind. I got up, put on a robe, and went out to the dining room to organize things. The day was guaranteed to be a doozy.

After I moved the ice cream dishes to the sink, I glanced through the mail. Nothing but ads. The local newspaper, the *Warner Pier Weekly Gazette*, had also been delivered the previous day. When I picked it up, a flier for Walmart fell out. I glanced at it.

And on the back page was an ad for men's hair color.

I felt as if I'd been struck by lightning. I grabbed up the ad and ran to the bathroom. I banged on the door, yelling.

"Joe! Joe! I know who tried to kill Emma!"

Chocolate Chat

In ancient days chocolate was given to Aztec warriors to encourage battle success. It was sometimes compressed into wafers so it would be easy to carry while traveling.

But it was also linked to love. Scientists believe this is because it contains phenylethylamine. This chemical is an endorphin, and endorphins produce feelings of happiness or even euphoria. Like being in love, naturally.

The famed eighteenth-century courtesan Madame du Barry reportedly plied her lovers with chocolate, and a heart-shaped box of chocolates is the dream of many teenaged girls. But only if it comes from someone special.

Legendary lover Casanova supposedly recommended chocolate over champagne as an "elixir of love," and as late as 1905 a British magazine urged women to be cautious in indulging in romances, chocolate, and novels, warning that such things could lead to moral downfall.

Chapter 21

Joe opened the bathroom door enough to get his head out. He had wrapped a towel around his waist, but his hair was dripping. "What's wrong?"

"Nothing! I mean, I figured out who it was!"

"Is the house on fire?"

"No! But I've got to share this news!"

"Lee! There's a draft, and I'm freezing. Either come in or stay out, okay?"

"Sorry!" I went in and shut the door behind myself. "But I really want to tell you!"

Joe turned back to the sink. He picked up a hand towel. "What brought this on?"

"An ad for men's hair color. It fell out of the *Gazette*."

"And you rushed in here to tell me there's no need for me to get gray hair?"

"No! When I saw the ad I recognized the man who tried to poison Emma."

"He was in the ad?"

"Don't tease!" I quickly recapped the scene in the

hospital room, when a large man in scrubs came in and gave Emma a pill. "Which she only pretended to take," I said.

"And you thought it was some sort of poison."

"Well, not at that moment. I would have jumped out and yelled if I had thought that. But Emma had quit taking the medication they had her on, so she just pretended to take the pill. After the guy was gone she spit it into a paper cup. I stuck a couple of Kleenex in the top to keep it from falling out and wrapped it in a rubber glove."

"Have you still got it?"

"It's in my purse. My main concern at that moment was getting Emma out of the hospital. But I got a good look at the guy who brought it in, and he seemed familiar."

"When you saw him while you were hiding in the closet."

"Yes. He had home-dyed black hair."

"Home-dyed? How could you tell?"

"Because I've hung around beauty shops a lot. I know what professionally colored black hair looks like and what home-dyed black hair looks like. If somebody does it at home, either a man or a woman, they nearly always mess it up. Hair colored in those dark shades by an amateur looks harsh. And dull. And lifeless."

"Dead hair?"

"Right."

"But Lee, how many hundreds of men in Holland dye their hair? And most of them probably do it at home. How would that tell you who the guy was?"

"There's more to the story, Joe. Do you remember that I told you about seeing that man from P.M. Development? The one Tilda showed the Clowning Around shop to? He had odd coloring."

"He had dyed black hair?"

"No! He had prematurely gray hair—almost white."

"You've lost me here. How does a guy with white hair equal a guy with black hair?"

"Because they both had black eyebrows. The guy at the development company had white hair but heavy black eyebrows."

"Like a skunk?"

"Not striped. But the contrast between the hair and the eyebrows was very noticeable. So if a guy with white hair and dark eyebrows wanted to look different— say for a security camera—what would he do?"

Joe grinned. "He might bleach his eyebrows."

"You're right! He might. But it would be much easier to buy some hair dye at Walmart and color the white hair black. And as soon as he was finished with his need for black hair, he could wash the dye out."

"It's that easy?"

"Yes. If you use the right product. When I was in high school I played a fortune-teller in a skit, and my friends and I decided I needed black hair. I couldn't afford a professional job, so they helped me color it. We bought something at the drugstore. And the day after the skit I washed it out."

"It's interesting to think of you as an exotic brunette."

"It took all the water in the hot water tank to get the black color out, and then I still had a couple of green streaks. But it can be done."

"That's not much to go on, Lee."

"I feel sure the so-called nurse was the man from the development company. And he gave Emma the pill I think was poisonous."

"But we don't know that it was."

"Right. Some law officer will have to get the pill analyzed. And that means I've got to tell somebody this whole story."

Joe rewrapped his bath towel around his waist. Then he began to rub his hair with the smaller towel. He was looking at me steadily.

"Lots of luck finding the right person to tell," he said.

"I know," I said. "I guess that could be a problem."

I watched Joe until he finished toweling his hair. He ran a comb through it.

I sighed. "You have great hair."

"Thanks. I don't plan to color it anytime soon, either professionally or at home."

"Good. I'll make coffee."

I went into the kitchen and began to fix breakfast. Watching Joe do his hair might be a fun way to start the day—love those shoulders!—but the task I needed to accomplish was going to be a challenge.

After the fiasco when I chased the clown through the hospital, leaving three law enforcement organizations convinced that I had made up the whole adventure as a publicity stunt, I needed to keep a low profile. But instead, what had I done? I'd kidnapped a patient from the hospital, and I believed I'd witnessed a new attempt on her life. And the potential victim now claimed to be a murderer herself. The whole thing was a confused mess.

I could tell the world about the episode in the hospital—take an ad out in the *Chicago Tribune* and go on *Good Morning America*—and still nobody in a responsible position was likely to believe that anybody had tried to kill Emma. And they also would never believe that I had identified that person.

I put coffee and water in the coffeepot and plugged it in. I got out the toaster. I put last night's ice cream debris in the dishwasher. In other words, I tried to get on with life. But none of this routine helped me figure out how to handle my problem.

My problem was telling some law enforcement officer that I was convinced that the man I'd seen at P.M. Development was the one who had come into Emma's room. I also had to convince someone he had tried to kill her. And that he could well have been the clown who tried to suffocate her earlier. He was the right size.

My first impulse had been to ask Joe how I should handle it. His skills would be useful in accomplishing this, while mine weren't much help. But as I had watched him towel his hair dry I had realized I couldn't bug him about it.

Joe had his own problem, a different problem. He had to get legal help for Emma. That had to be his first responsibility, not only to Emma, but to his own client.

If Emma told her story right, his client—Royal Hollis—might be completely exonerated. If she told it wrong, Joe might wind up accused of getting a witness to lie. My dad, a Texas fisherman, describes an unpredictable person as "about as stable as a bass boat in a high wind on a big lake." That might apply to Emma.

Whether Emma was mentally unstable was beyond me, but she could certainly be made to appear unstable. And she was certainly easy to influence. By her own account it hadn't been hard for Chuck to convince her she should withhold her story about shoving Moe.

If I thought law enforcement wasn't going to believe me . . . Well, my problem was nothing compared with the one Emma had. And Emma's problem was Joe's problem. I needed to handle this one myself.

But if I wanted to tell some law enforcement officer who Emma's attacker had been, which cop should I tell?

Hospital security? I shook my head. They wouldn't have the authority to do anything about it. The Holland police force? I shook my head harder at the idea of talking to the two guys who had tossed me out of the hospital. I wanted to talk to a detective, not some mere patrolman. And if I wandered into the Holland Police Headquarters and asked to see a detective—well, I'd have to start from go and explain the whole situation. It would take hours. That would be a last resort.

No, Clancy Pike was the best. Clancy scared me, but at least he knew who I was, and he knew the background of Emma, Moe, Moe's kids, and Moe's death. He wasn't likely to actually bite me. And if the Holland police were needed, Clancy would surely be able to refer me to someone in Holland who could help.

So when Joe sat down at the breakfast table, I took a deep breath and spoke. "I'll try to talk to Clancy Pike as soon as he can see me."

Joe blinked a couple of times. "About the guy with the dyed hair? If you wait until afternoon, I might be able to go with you."

"No. First, I've just got to do it myself. Second, you need to concentrate on Emma and her story."

"I need to help my client, Royal Hollis. And today that means I have to help Emma make her story credible. So she needs a lawyer to look out for her interests. If nobody believes her, she won't help Hollis at all."

Yes, my problem was quite different from Joe's, even though both involved Emma. We didn't discuss it further. What else was there to say?

As soon as Joe had eaten a piece of toast, he got on the phone. I could hear him talking to his mentor, Mac McKay, as I loaded the dishwasher. By the time I got out of the shower, he'd left.

I was on my own.

I put on an outfit that made me feel authoritative—a black wool skirt and sweater with knee-high boots. No flannel-lined jeans today. I added a silver chain belt and a red scarf. I combed my hair into a businesslike bun. I put the TenHuis paychecks into a manila envelope and headed for the office. As soon as I got the checks passed out, I'd call Clancy Pike.

And this time he wasn't going to intimidate me. I was determined.

After I'd handled the office details, I called and arranged an appointment with Clancy for ten thirty. Then I got out my notepad and made an outline of what I needed to tell him. This was not going to be a good time for a tangled tongue or confused thoughts.

I was in the Warner Pier police station at ten twenty-five. Clancy Pike, naturally, didn't show until ten forty. I suspected this was a ploy to make me nervous, so I stiffened my spine and vowed not to let that work. I said hello when Clancy walked into the station, but I remained seated in the visitor's area until he called me into his office.

When I closed the door behind me, Clancy raised his eyebrows nearly to the top of his forehead, or where his forehead would have ended if he hadn't completely shaved his head.

He gestured toward a chair. "I'm sure you'll be happy to learn that Mrs. Davidson called home last night."

"Oh! Yes, I am happy to hear that."

His voice was completely lacking in irony as he continued. "She said a friend picked her up, and that she's fine."

"That's wonderful."

"Yes. Of course, we'd rather talk to her face to face." He stared at me, his face completely blank. "Now, what can I do for you?"

It was my turn. I started with a deep breath.

"I realized something important this morning, and law enforcement needs to know about it. But I don't want to be irregular—I mean, irresponsible!—I don't want to be irresponsible about making accusations."

So much for not getting my tongue tangled.

Clancy nodded.

"First," I said, "I have a confession to make. Not to a crime. But yesterday I did find the hospital room occupied by Emma Davidson."

"How did you do that?"

"She had called our house and left her phone number for Joe, and I used that number to find her room. Emma begged for Joe to come talk to her. But he was out of town and couldn't get there. So he asked me to visit her."

I continued the story, up to the point that the man with dyed hair came in and gave Emma a pill.

"And this morning I realized who that man was. I think his name is Philip Montague. He is the man from P.M. Development, the man whose company is bidding on the Clowning Around property next door to us. I saw him over there with the Realtor."

Clancy looked skeptical, and I couldn't blame him. "He didn't just resemble that man?" he asked.

"I believe it was the same man."

"And you thought he gave Mrs. Davidson something harmful?"

"Right. And I have it here in my purse."

I produced the rubber glove containing the paper cup with the pill.

That's where we began. And half an hour later, that's about where we ended. Of course, Clancy had only my word that the pill was the same one the fake nurse had given Emma. Cops put great importance on what they call "chain of custody," proof that evidence was passed from one person to another. I had no chain of custody at all. Clancy knew this better than I did, and we didn't discuss it.

But Clancy asked lots of questions, ending with "Do you have any idea why this P.M. Development guy would try to harm Emma Davidson?"

"No idea at all. I only saw him two other times—once walking by him and the second time driving by him in a car. I know nothing about him, and I know of no connection he has with Emma or with the Davidson family. It's crazy! But I am convinced that's who it was. And I am convinced he tried to harm Mrs. Davidson."

I shut up then. If I said any more, I'd be admitting that I helped Emma leave the hospital. I wasn't ready to do that.

I hadn't expected my interview with Clancy Pike to be friendly, and it hadn't been. But he hadn't yelled at me, and I hadn't yelled at him. I hadn't broken down and cried. And he didn't hold me for further questioning, though he was frowning as I got up to leave.

"This is a Holland PD case," he said, "and I'm not sure how I fit in."

"I know! But I thought you would know somebody up there, could tell somebody who needs to know what's going on. Or refer me to somebody I could talk to. Maybe then the Holland police wouldn't think I was an idiot before I even opened my mouth. I know you can't just rush out and arrest that developer, simply because I think it's the same man. But what if he really is the same guy? What if he kills Emma? I just can't stand by and pretend I didn't notice he dyed his hair."

Clancy asked me not to say anything to anybody

about all this, and I assured him I wouldn't. Then I left, feeling that for the moment I had done what I could about the P.M. Development man.

When I got back to the office, Dolly Jolly was holding down the cash register, and the rest of the place was all but empty. It was lunch hour on payday, after all, and everyone had gone to the bank. In fact, Dolly was ready to go, too.

I shooed her out the door, then helped myself to a tiramisu truffle ("layers of white and milk chocolate filling enrobed in dark chocolate and embellished with milk chocolate stripes").

But Dolly was barely out the door when Kyle and Paige Walters walked in.

It took me a moment to recognize them, because it was the first time I had seen them in ordinary clothes, not costumes. We greeted each other enthusiastically, and they bought a pound of chocolates as a gift for their mother.

"I hope y'all have some fun entertaining the tourists in Warner Pier," I said.

"Oh sure," Paige said. "We always have fun. This is a crazy way to make a living, and we sure wouldn't do it if we didn't enjoy it."

"I wish we had some money," Kyle said. "We'd look at buying the clown store and sticking around."

"Actually," I said, "it would be a good business for professional clowns. Of course, you'd have to have an efficient manager for the times you were on the road."

Paige smiled. "But aren't you interested in the building?"

"If we ever want to expand, it would be an ideal location. But if the bidding gets too high, we're out of it. And we're not the only people looking at it."

I handed their box of assorted truffles over. "I hope your mom likes these. And now how about a sample for yourselves?"

Paige picked a dark chocolate cheesecake truffle ("white cream cheese–flavored filling covered with dark chocolate and trimmed with a dot of white chocolate"). Kyle went for ginger wasabi, one of the spiciest truffles we offer ("dark chocolate filling seasoned with ginger and horseradish, enrobed in dark chocolate and embellished with crystallized ginger").

"Tonight's the big night!" Kyle said as they went out the door. "See you there!"

For a moment I felt quite blank. Tonight? Then I realized what he was talking about.

"Oh my gosh! Tonight's the big opening of the winter promotion. I've got to dress up like a clown!"

I fought the impulse to bang my head against the display cabinet. Then I grunted, groaned, and spoke again. "I believe I'll cut my suspenders and go straight up!"

Chapter 22

One of the advantages of being born into a rural Texas family is that you grow up hearing colorful expressions. And the one about cutting my suspenders was one of my grandmother's favorites. It really summed up how I felt at that moment.

The Clown Week opening was the final straw, the limit, the absolute end. I wanted to worry about Emma and how to keep her safe, about Royal Hollis and his possible innocence, about how Joe was going to deal with those problems. The last thing I wanted to do or even think about was that opening event for Clown Week. But it was coming in a few hours.

Clowns were going to be wandering all over Warner Pier. The big sled ride was going to be swooping from the high school down to Dock Street. Skaters were going to be gliding over the ice. Horses were going to be pulling sleighs down our streets.

And tourists—we hoped—were going to be going in and out of our shops spending money.

I had helped plan the event. I had helped promote it. Now I had to finish it up and try to make it go off well. But it was the last thing I wanted to think about.

It was a wonderful idea, but I didn't want it to be tonight.

I wanted to think about the P.M. Development guy trying to kill Emma and why the heck he would want to do that. I wanted to think about why Emma had confessed to killing her husband and wonder if it could be true. I wanted to think about why the stories of Chuck, Royal Hollis, and Emma were so different from one another.

A community promotional project, normally so important to me as a Warner Pier merchant, was simply of no interest.

But I had to think about it. So I did. I looked over my notes on the opening and tried to figure out what my responsibilities were. And when I really analyzed it, I didn't have too much to do. My biggest responsibility was to show up by four o'clock with chocolates for the "Top Banana" warming room and opening reception at Warner Point High School. I didn't have to be dressed in my clown outfit until five o'clock, when the reception would begin.

Stop panicking, I told myself.

I quickly made out an order sheet for four party trays, to be loaded with molded chocolate clowns and a variety of truffles. Luckily, the chocolates could come from our regular stock; we didn't have to mold or decorate anything special. Thanks to Dolly and the ladies in the back, I could be confident that at three forty-five the trays, securely covered with plastic wrap and in big flat boxes, would be ready for me to take to the party.

These would be added to other donations from merchants—both "in kind," like my chocolates, and financial. Moe Davidson had usually been first in line to support this sort of project. This made me think of the tale Emma had told us the night before, including the bit about Moe giving away the money he had inherited from his first wife and how mad that made Chuck. I could certainly understand Chuck's feelings, especially if Moe did this just for personal publicity, not out of genuine kindness or concern for his community.

As I took my order blanks back to the workroom, I met Nadine Vanderhill, one of the geniuses who make our bonbons and truffles. If I refer to them as "the hairnet ladies," no disrespect is intended. We'd be out of business in an hour without their abilities and hard work.

Nadine has two additional impressive skills. First, she's lived in Warner Pier all her life, and she knows everything about everybody. But her second skill is truly singular. She doesn't tell everything she knows, unless someone with a good reason asks. I'd already used Nadine to try to tell my side of the hospital chase episode. Now I decided to pump Nadine for information.

"Hey, Nadine," I said. "What do you know about the Davidson family?"

"You mean Moe and his group?"

"Yeah. I guess he grew up here."

"Oh yeah. Moe and I went to school together. But his first wife, Verita, she was a summer person. I think she was from Chicago. They got married right out of high school. I don't think her family was very happy about it."

I laughed. "Do these 'mixed' marriages ever work?"

Nadine laughed, too. "You mean, how our mothers tell us not to date the summer guys? Well, it's not quite the same the other way around. The local guys can get away with dating and marrying summer girls. But they usually move away from Warner Pier."

"But Moe and Verita stayed."

"Yeah. He worked here and there. Sales work. Never was a big success at anything. He was too interested in that clown stuff to concentrate on a job, and I guess he wasn't a good enough clown to make a living at it. Verita worked in Holland, some office job. She raised the kids, and Chuck and Lorraine left Warner Pier as soon as they could. Then Verita died. She had cancer. Her mother had the same thing."

"Was her family wealthy?"

"Not so much. I mean, they weren't one of these ultrarich summer families. Comfortable, I guess you'd say. I think her father was an insurance salesman. Something like that. She inherited that house where Moe and Emma lived. I guess she left some money, too."

"I guess Moe got it."

"Whatever there was to get. Both the kids went to Western Michigan. I don't think Lorraine ever finished." Nadine shrugged and turned to her work. She could rattle off the life stories of all the Davidsons, even though she wasn't very interested in them.

This echoed the way I'd never been very interested in Moe when he was alive. Joe had mentioned that he had occasionally wondered where Moe got the funds he donated to support all his community projects, but neither of us really cared. Apparently Moe's money had come from his first wife. And the previous evening Emma said Moe had tried hard to get hold of her money as well.

The whole thing had an unsavory aroma. And I felt unsavory for poking around in their affairs.

This didn't stop me from taking time to look Chuck up on the Internet as soon as I got back to my desk. He showed up as selling office supplies at a company based in Grand Rapids.

I tried Lorraine as well. Nothing.

Then I Googled P.M. Development. Nothing. Even their phone listing was missing. That probably meant it was a new company. And the Holland Chamber of Commerce hadn't had much on them. Hmmm, again.

I did Google Philip Montague as well. And to my astonishment, the first item listed turned out to be from the *Warner Pier Weekly Gazette.* I flipped it open.

Philip Montague was quoted in a news release saying that Moe Davidson had made a five-thousand-dollar donation to a community organization.

Triple hmmm.

The organization, naturally, sounded quite worthwhile. It was called Klowns for Kids of Michigan, Inc. The members were raising money for schools, providing library books and field trips. Philip Montague was identified as secretary-treasurer, and Moe, it seemed, had been named a founding director.

"Founding director?" Well, I'd been offered a similar title when I lived in Dallas. All the Junior League members had received a letter from a new group, the Texican Arts Association—or something like that. For five thousand dollars a pop we would be named founding queens or some such fancy title. None of us bit on that particular scam.

I stared at the story. Chuck would have said Klowns for Kids was yet another activity for Moe to throw money at.

That was likely to be the end of the information about Philip Montague, but I thought of one more possibility and tried a popular résumé listing service. When I was looking for new employees, I had found this could be a well of information.

Bingo! Philip Montague was listed.

But none of the information seemed to mean anything. Montague had gone to Michigan State for two years. He was originally from Grand Haven, north of us. He had graduated from a real estate course, and since then had worked in real estate sales, most recently with a firm in Kalamazoo. No mention of P.M. Development appeared.

Chuck had a listing on the résumé service as well. I skipped over the obvious information, such as his high school. Yes, he had graduated from Western Michigan University twelve years earlier. Since then he had worked as a salesman for an office supply company. If he had ever been married, it didn't appear on the résumé.

Neither résumé listed any organizations that might have helped Chuck and Philip meet. Neither belonged to the Kiwanis Club, for example, or was a Boy Scout leader, or even listed membership in Klowns for Kids of Michigan. Which was odd, at least on Philip's part, since he'd been sending out news releases on their behalf. Maybe he simply didn't list service organizations on his résumé, though that would be surprising.

Now I'd looked at all the readily available information on the witnesses to Moe's death and on the person I believed had twice attacked Emma. And what did I know? Of the witnesses, each had a different story— way different. I dismissed Royal Hollis. He was just too unreliable; guilty or innocent, Joe would have to deal with his story face-to-face. As for Emma—well, I thought she believed the unlikely tale she was now telling, and I believed it, too. How about Belle? She admitted she'd been in Warner Pier, that she'd met Moe earlier. But she had first denied it. And how about Lorraine? Could she have been the woman who Elk—or somebody—had seen at the Davidson house the day Moe was killed? Was she in such an alcoholic haze she might not even know herself?

Chuck was another matter. He might be trying to protect Emma, and maybe Lorraine, but he was doing it at the expense of Royal. Not nice. But how could he have anything to do with the attacks by Philip Montague? That seemed to be a separate matter. Two crimes in the same family? Odd.

Unless there was some connection between Chuck and Philip. If they had been working together . . .

But my online research—not exactly comprehensive, true—had discovered nothing that hinted at that situation. Chuck and Philip Montague hadn't gone to either high school or college together. They hadn't belonged to the same organizations, or worked for the same company, or anything, though they were close in age. Both lived in western Michigan, but sixty miles apart. That even made it unlikely that they hung out in the same bars.

If it got down to girls they dated or Chuck's aunt marrying Philip's second cousin once removed—well, there was no way I could figure that out. I'd leave it to the cops. Which was what I ought to be doing anyway.

But I thought of one more source. I went to the state Department of Commerce site and looked up Klowns for Kids of Michigan. If that organization was set up in Michigan, it ought to be in the public listings.

It wasn't.

I stared at the computer screen and wondered if I was doing something wrong. After all, I didn't use this part of the computer world often. Maybe nonprofit corporations had separate listings.

So I went back to my home page and Googled it. There were businesses called Clowns for Kids—Clowns spelled with a C. But no "Klowns" with a K. Not in Michigan. Not unless they had somehow managed to avoid being listed on the Internet.

Had the whole thing been a scam? Had Philip Montague invented this organization the way the Texas scammers had come up with the one that had sent begging letters to the Dallas Junior Leaguers? Had Montague, or someone else, come up with Klowns for Kids of Michigan so he could ask Moe to donate to it? Did Moe have enough money to make it worth Montague's effort?

I wondered how much Moe had given. On impulse I called Joe, thinking that it wasn't likely that he would answer. To my surprise, he did.

"Hi," I said. "I guess you wouldn't have answered if it's inconvenient to talk."

"It's been a hurry-up-and-wait kind of day, and right now we're waiting."

"How's Emma?"

"She seems to like the attorney Mac suggested, and she's apparently eased her conscience somewhat by telling her story."

"Did anybody believe her?"

"They're not confiding in me."

"I've got a question for Emma. I don't suppose she's around."

"She's within walking distance. Do you want to talk to her?"

"Yes, please."

In a minute or so Joe had Emma on his cell phone.

"Emma," I said, "I'm going to ask you a nosy question."

"You already know all my secrets, Lee."

"It's about Moe's donations. You've complained that he gave away money he couldn't afford to donate."

"He certainly did."

"Did he give much to Klowns for Kids of Michigan?"

"Lee, I was stunned when I saw how much he had donated to them. Of course, most of it was before we were married."

"I found a story in the *Gazette* saying he'd given one donation. Were there others?"

"Oh yes! I'm afraid so."

"Do you mind giving me an estimate of how much?"

"An estimate?"

"Yes. Ten thousand? Fifteen?"

"Oh no, Lee! Much more than that."

The figure she named curled my hair. "Oh! I see why Chuck was upset," I said.

Emma handed the phone back to Joe. I was still stunned. "Joe! I think I just stumbled across a motive for Moe's murder!"

"Another?" He lowered his voice. "Besides general obnoxiousness?"

I quickly told Joe about Philip Montague's connection to Klowns for Kids. And the amount of money Moe had given an apparently nonexistent organization.

"If Moe figured it out, he would have raised hell," I said. "In fact, I can't see any reason he wouldn't have immediately gone to the cops."

Joe whistled. "You can ask Emma."

"She said she was shocked when she learned how much he had given. But she didn't say anything about his thinking he'd been scammed." I thought a moment. "Did you say Clancy is over there?"

"He was a few minutes ago."

"If you can find him, tell him about it."

Joe spoke in a very low voice. "He's on the phone trying to get Holland to put out an arrest warrant for Montague."

"Great! I wasn't sure he took me seriously."

"He did, Lee. And you be careful!"

"As far as Montague goes, Joe, he has no reason to know that I figured out he tried to kill Emma."

"Maybe not. But you try to stay around people until they arrest him."

I promised that I'd be cautious, then hung up. Stay around people? I hoped that wouldn't be a problem. The tourism committee had spent months trying to encourage people to gather and have fun at Clown Week. And to eat fun foods . . .

"Yikes!" I jumped to my feet. "I've got to get those chocolates up to the high school!"

It was three thirty. Time to move along. I ran to the workroom. As I had expected, the trays of chocolates were ready. "I'm sorry," I said to Dolly. "I'm just no help at all today. First a little emergency came up, and now I've got to get ready for that Clown Week kickoff. Are you still planning to work the shop this evening?"

"I'll be here!" Dolly boomed.

"Dolly, I really appreciate your filling in like this. I'll come back as soon as I can get away from the reception up at the high school."

"Glad to do it, Lee! Now scoot! You've got to get into that funny costume!"

I loaded the boxes of chocolates into the back of my van and headed for the high school. It wasn't easy to get there. Traffic was thick, almost like summer, when Warner Pier streets are bumper-to-bumper. Of course, I knew the back ways, but I didn't want to get stuck. The main streets had been carefully cleared, except for the street that had added artificial snow for the sled run. But the alleys might be iffy.

I made it, however, going around to the street at the back of the school. It took two trips to carry the chocolates inside. My pal Lindy was setting up the refreshment room.

"Hi, Lee," she said. "Have you seen the sled run?"

"No, I came in the back. Are your kids out there?"

"Tony thinks he's the boss." She laughed. "I mean T.J. I keep forgetting his new name." Lindy looked proud. "He's keeping everyone in line. He's quite officious about it. You ought to take a look."

"That's all I'll take! I'm not getting on a sled!"

"Do kids in Texas ever get a chance to sled?"

"In our part of Texas—northwest of Dallas—we usually have snow every couple of years, but we're more likely to have ice. You can kill yourself getting the paper from the front porch. But kids in my hometown used to slide down the back of the football bleachers."

"The bleachers!"

"Sure. The bleachers were built against an embankment. You'd call it a dune."

Lindy and I are always kidding each other about our hometowns. Prairie Creek and Warner Pier are about the same size, but with major regional differences. Prairie Creek raises cattle; Warner Pier grows fruit.

"The back of the embankment forms a very nice slope," I said, "and kids slide down it on anything they can find. Some families do own sleds, but sledders also use garbage can lids, plastic bags, sheets of cardboard. Whatever works!"

"Go take a look at *real* sledding before you leave."

Lindy walked out the front of the high school with me so we could see the sled run. She nudged me as T.J. positioned a sled at the starting line and ordered a slightly younger kid to sit on it. He checked the clasp on the kid's helmet, then counted importantly—"Three! Two! One! Go!"—and shoved the sled down the trail.

The kid gave a loud whoop as the sled took off down the icy chute. The sled went really fast.

"Oh golly!" I yelped the words out. "I'm sure glad I don't have to go on that thing."

"Oh, it's fun," Lindy said. "You're talking like a Texan!"

"No, Texans are brave. I'm talking like a coward, and I don't care who knows it. I learned my lesson at your sledding party two years ago."

We watched the sleds and the tubes for a few more minutes. There was a little lull, and T.J. took the opportunity to demonstrate snowboarding for us.

As he trudged back up the slope, I drank it all in. The lights, the music, the colors—it was going to be great. We could see the ice rink at the bottom of the hill, strung with colored lights. Tony Senior was swooping around the ice. A few clowns had already shown up, and a couple of them were also skating.

The weather was even cooperating: it was cold enough to keep the snow and ice frozen, but the air was still.

"This is great," I said. "But I'm not getting on one of those sleds! I'll be back in half an hour with a big bow on my head."

I left to get into my clown costume. I couldn't help wishing that I could add a bulletproof vest to the getup. I hoped that Philip Montague would be arrested quickly. Joe's warnings about staying around people I knew had scared me more than I wanted to admit.

Chapter 23

I went home and made myself a peanut butter and jelly sandwich, in case the tourists ate all the refreshments at the Clown Week opening. Eating it gave me a few minutes to further think about Moe's death and the attacks on Emma.

Point number one: Emma said she had angrily shoved Moe, knocking him down, and he had hit his head on the step. He was bleeding, but not unconscious. Royal Hollis, she said, had not hit Moe but had simply run away. Chuck had then urged her to leave, saying he would look after his dad, and she had driven off. It was hours later that she learned that Moe was dead.

Several things in that scenario were worth thinking about. First, Emma was plump but short. She didn't seem strong. It was hard to believe that she could have killed a fairly vigorous grown man such as Moe by shoving him. But stranger things had happened.

Second, Emma said Chuck had assured her she shouldn't confess; she hadn't intended to kill Moe, and there was no need for her to be punished. But after she found out that Hollis was accused of the killing, according to the story Emma had told us, she planned to confess and clear Hollis. Once she learned Joe had been appointed to represent Hollis, she began to try to reach him.

Third, Harry Vandercool had said Royal Hollis ran off and came to his house after Moe attacked him. But Hollis had lost his shoes in the fracas. And even though Harry gave him another pair, Hollis had apparently gone back to get the first pair. This was understandable. To a homeless man, a pair of shoes was a prized possession.

Question: Did Hollis ever get the shoes? And if so, when? Did it matter?

Fourth, by the time Harry went over to Moe and Emma's house, Moe was dead. Chuck told Harry and the investigators that he had gone out for gas and had just come back. He saw Hollis running off. There was no sign of Emma, and Chuck never mentioned her earlier presence to Vandercool.

Fifth, the medical examiner's report had indicated that Moe's injuries were much more serious than a cut on the head. He had had several blows to the head, and the investigating officers had found a rock that they believed was the weapon. This did not jibe with Emma's story.

So? Which person was the sheriff going to arrest? Who had had the opportunity to kill Moe?

Three people: Hollis, Chuck, and Emma. Joe believed Hollis' story: Hollis said he had never struck Moe. I believed Emma's: She said Moe cut his head on the step, and that she had not hit him with a rock or other weapon.

If they were both telling the truth, then Chuck had

to be the killer. He was simply the only other person
there. And according to Emma, he had lied about several parts of his story.

I'm sure I rolled my eyes as I rinsed the crumbs from
my sandwich off the plate. It was hard to picture
Chuck—friendly Chuck—killing his own father. Besides, I was positive that Chuck hadn't been the clown
who had tried to smother Emma. He'd been working
in the Clowning Around shop that day, along with Lorraine. Dolly Jolly and I had seen both of them there.

I went into the bedroom to get dressed. It was going
to be a cold evening, and I'd be outdoors for most of it.
I took off my office clothes and started with a set of
lightweight long johns. Wool slacks and sweater. Heavy
socks. Forget the clown shoes; I'd wear my warm winter boots. Ski jacket. Scarf. Knit cap. Finally, the baggy
red-and-white clown suit. The hat, complete with
floppy red bow, perched on top of the whole shebang,
and red mittens suitable for a clown went over leather
driving gloves. The final detail was bright red lipstick.

I looked in the mirror and saw a gigantic red-and-
white tub. With a big red bow on top. Oh well. Maybe
I'd make somebody laugh, and that was the whole purpose.

I didn't want to carry a purse, so I put my cell phone
and some money in pockets inside the clown suit, but
still accessible from the Velcro opening down the front.

I got in the van and headed for downtown. By then
it was growing dark, and I was happy to see that traffic
was still heavy. In fact, the traffic forced me to drive
slowly. I parked in my reserved spot, in the alley behind TenHuis Chocolade, and went through the shop
to fill a bag with giveaway chocolates. They were
wrapped in foil, and I could hand them out as I climbed
the hill, heading for the high school to get my assign-

ment from our clown chairman. Dolly, who was behind the cash register, laughed at my appearance. She already had customers, I was happy to see. I wouldn't want to look like a complete fool and not make money by doing it.

All the way up the hill to the high school, I was handing out tiny chocolates wrapped in foil and waving at sledders and tubers coming past me down the slope. And they were coming steadily, too. The sledding and tubing slope was already a terrific hit. It was still too early for a line to have formed, but kids were flopping onto sleds and tubes, then heading down the snowy slope. Fast.

"Look out, Lee!" Although I was safely off the path of the sleds, I jumped when I heard my name. T.J. shot past me, waving. He was riding one of the larger sleds, accompanying several small children. They were all squealing with delight, and T.J. was one big grin. I waved back. Luckily, one of the horse-drawn sleighs came by just then, and I hitched a ride the rest of the way up. That hill was definitely easier for going down than for going up, at least for people who had the nerve to ride on a sled.

But through all the fun—the snowmobiles, the sleds and tubes and snowboards, the clowns, the sleighs, and even the chocolate—in the back of my mind I was considering the possibility that Chuck was a killer.

And by the time I was at the top of the hill, I decided I could accept him in that role. Although Chuck was highly personable, he was a salesman: His profession had trained him to seem friendly and easygoing, no matter what he was thinking. I'd been married to a salesman, and his friends had been salesmen, and I had learned that the typical friendliness to customers didn't always come home with the salesman. In fact, the salesmen I'd known tended to come home so tired of people that— Well, that's enough about my past problems.

In other words, I could believe that Chuck had a temper and could lose it.

But I still doubted Chuck had killed his dad, because I was sure Chuck wasn't the person who tried to kill his stepmother. No, that had been Philip Montague, the so-called developer. I didn't know *why* he had done it, but he certainly was the right size and had the right eye-brows to be the clown who tried to smother Emma. And I had witnessed his attempt in the hospital to give her a pill I thought was a fake.

Of course, if Chuck and Philip Montague were work-ing *together*, that would explain everything. Chuck might have killed his dad, and then Philip Montague could have tried to kill Emma. But I had no reason to think that they even *knew* each other. They hadn't gone to the same high school or the same college. They hadn't ever worked for the same business or even in the same field. Their résumés showed no overlap at all.

No, I couldn't bring that possibility up—not even to the most sympathetic law officer. I had no evidence at all.

The sleigh let its load off at the front door of the high school, and I went inside. The tourism committee members were supposed to meet at the trophy case, the big one by the main door of the high school, to get our assignments.

But when I got there, instead of the committee mem-bers I met Clancy Pike. When I greeted him, he replied absently, "Oh! Lee Woodyard."

"Yes. It's me. Silly hat and all."

"I'd never recognize you if you'd painted your face like some of these clowns."

"I drew the line at that. But I thought you were in Dorinda for a big confab."

"The sheriff sent me back." He leaned close and lowered his voice. "There's an arrest warrant out for that guy you think tried to kill Emma Davidson."

"Oh! I sure hope you catch him. But what connection does he have with the Davidsons?"

"It seems he's linked up with some organization that Moe gave a lot of money to."

"Klowns for Kids of Michigan?"

"Keep your voice down. Sheriff Ramsey found out the organization doesn't exist. Moe had been making a lot of phone calls about it. He must have found out it was a fake."

"What about Royal Hollis?"

"Joe and the prosecutor are arguing that out with Ramsey." He smiled. "It looks like Hollis finally got the representation he should have had all along."

I didn't say anything, but I felt a little thrill of victory. It's nice to see the good guys—such as Joe—win one.

"Clancy, what are you doing here? I mean, why here at the high school?"

"Why not? Everybody else in Warner Pier seems to be here." Clancy grinned. "Let's be friends, Lee."

"Sure!" I grinned back and handed him a foil-wrapped chocolate. "Have a big time, Chief!"

He walked off, pulling his hat over his bald head, and I moved over to the trophy case. The chairman of the clowns wasn't in sight, but the crowd of people getting out of the cold was growing. I moved down to the end of the case, trying to stay out of the main bunch. Since I had nothing to do but feel triumphant, I looked in the case.

One of the first things I saw was a trophy: STATE CHAMPIONS. WRESTLING. Sure enough, behind it was a group shot of a wrestling team, ten guys in those silly-looking one-piece suits they wear to compete. Right in the middle of the back row were Joe and Tony Herrera, T.J.'s father. Tony towered over Joe and all the other wrestlers. He's a big guy, and he's still all muscle today.

The picture made me smile. Here we were, nearly twenty years later, and Joe and Tony were still friends. Tony Junior—I mean T.J.—was going out for wrestling himself this year. When he wasn't tormenting his father by pretending to be a professional wrestling fan.

I hoped the wrestling team had better outfits these days. Then I caught a glimpse of myself reflected in the glass case and laughed. A nearly six-foot-tall woman dressed in a clown suit has no right to criticize someone else for looking silly.

I moved along the case. Apparently only state champs rated the trophy case by the gym, because all the teams pictured had earned honors. Baseball, basketball, more wrestling, a football team—trophies for all were on display, backed by photos of the teams. I was surprised by the number of Warner Pier people I recognized.

Until I got to the final photo. And that one didn't surprise me. No—it astonished me, amazed me, dumb-founded me, hit me between the eyes, and nearly knocked me off my feet.

It was a photo of a group of clowns. And, like the other photos, it was matched with a trophy.

Clowning is certainly a skill, but it's hard to see it as a competitive sport.

The trophy was marked with the year, and was engraved BEST CLOWN UNIT—CHICAGO CHRISTMAS PARADE. Smaller letters below read WEST MICHIGAN STUDENT CLOWN CORPS.

I said "Huh" out loud.

The picture did look good. The costumes were beautiful, and the makeup was original and clever. For one thing, each clown's makeup was different, but each included teardrops, in imitation of Moe's. Then I read the cutline. The clowns were from a half dozen southwest Michigan high schools. As I had guessed, the hobo clown in the middle was Moe Davidson, identified as "Sponsor." He had never varied his makeup. At one end was Chuck Davidson. Not too surprising. But the tall clown in the back—his name was Philip Montague, and his hometown was listed as Grand Haven.

I was knocked into a heap again. I couldn't yell; I whispered. "Oh! My gosh!"

This was the link. The link between Chuck Davidson and Philip Montague. They had been in a high school clown group sponsored by Moe.

I had to find Clancy. I whirled around and found myself face to face with a clown—a tall hobo clown with teardrops on his left cheek. He had heavy black eyebrows.

I tried to act casual, as if I hadn't recognized him.

I pushed past him. "Excuse me," I said.

But the clown grabbed my arm. "Not so fast," he said.

And even through all the clothes I had on under my costume, I could feel something small and hard against my side.

I looked down. He held a pistol. And he was shoving it into my rib cage.

I didn't scream. Maybe I should have.

"Don't move," the clown said. "Not a muscle."

I obeyed.

"Now," he said, "we're going outside. We're going down the hill. Not on a sled! We're going to walk. Everything will be okay as long as you do what I say."

He shoved the gun into my side harder. The floppy sleeve of his hobo coat hid it. "If I have you with me, the cops will let me alone. Do you understand?"

I nodded.

He still had hold of my arm, and he shoved me ahead of him, toward the door of the high school. Three clowns were coming in. I recognized them as fellow members of the tourism committee.

They all greeted me. "Lee, you're going the wrong direction," one said.

"I'll be right back."

I had a vague hope that one of them would notice I was being held at gunpoint, but they merely turned away, talking among themselves.

My brain began to function again. This clown was Philip Montague. He had left those thick black eyebrows untouched by makeup, and they were unmistakable.

Then we were outside. I stopped. "Listen, Philip," I said. "This is not smart. There's a warrant out for your arrest. The police are looking for you."

He swore, but he pushed me ahead of him. "Nothing will happen if you're with me," he said. "You're my ticket out of here. Just keep walking."

I was a hostage.

Montague shoved me toward the path down the hill. We had to swing around several people waiting for sled rides.

T.J. was there. He helped a teenaged girl onto a tube, then shoved her onto the course. She gave a satisfying scream as the tube began to spin.

Then T.J. looked up and saw me. "Hey, Lee! Are you ready for a ride?"

I tried to sound natural. "Not now, Tony—T.J. But it looks as if you're doing a great job."

But the darn kid came closer. "Aw, c'mon, Lee! You can take a sled ride."

"Not tonight, T.J.!"

Now he was right in front of me. And Philip Montague spoke. "Get out of the way, kid!"

T.J. stiffened all over. He looked at the big clown, and there were hurt feelings in his eyes.

I put my hand on his arm. "T.J., we have an important errand. I'll come back if I can."

But T.J. wasn't giving way. He stood still. His eyes narrowed. He knew something was wrong, but he didn't know how to react.

"T.J.," I said. "Tony. Let us pass. Please."

"Yes, kid." The giant clown growled the words. Then he shoved me a step ahead.

T.J. dropped his head, as if he was giving in to our demands, and I hoped he was going to cooperate.

Then T.J. head butted the big clown. Right in the belly. Just like the professional wrestlers his dad despised.

I did scream then. Philip Montague dropped my arm and threw up the hand that held the pistol. He waved it over his head.

Somehow I got the gumption to shove him sideways. He landed in a heap on the sidewalk.

But he still had the gun.

I yelled, "Everybody get back!"

Instead of dropping back, the people standing around began to hoot with laughter. I heard all sorts of shouts and calls.

"What are the clowns doing, Mommy?" "They're just playing, darling! Aren't they funny?" "Beat 'em up, babe!" "Maybe a flag that says 'bang!' will come out the front of the gun!" "Ha! Ha! Ha! Ha! Ha!"

Nobody got the real joke. If Philip Montague began to spray bullets around, they could all die.

Philip was still looking at T.J. and me. I grabbed T.J. and swiveled around, so that I was between him and the gun.

Then the giant clown was back on his feet. His lips were moving, but the crowd was so loud that I have no idea what he said. He dodged left, then right, then left again, apparently unsure of which way he should go.

Suddenly, he seemed to realize that the way to the sleds was open. He dashed across the twenty or twenty-five feet to reach them and flopped onto the one that was first in line. He shoved off and went flying down the sledding course.

He still had the gun, but at least he was away from T.J. and the crowd of people at the sled run.

But he was getting away. I heard my voice yelling, "Stop that clown!"

Before I could stop T.J., he darted forward, grabbed a snowboard, jumped onto it, and took off down the hill.

"Oh no! Tony! T.J.!" I could have killed the kid. He was chasing a man I knew had at least twice tried to kill Emma Davidson. And the man had a gun.

"Darn you!" I had to do something. I ran to the pile of sleds, grabbed one, threw it down, flopped onto it flat on my stomach, and took off down the hill.

Chapter 24

I will never know what in the world I was thinking. After all, the only time I'd ever ridden a sled down a hill I'd crashed and been buried in a snowdrift. But I was so frightened for T.J. I couldn't bear to stand by and do nothing. And what else could I do?

But I kept remembering that Philip Montague had a gun.

As I began to slide, I remembered that proper safe sledding position is sitting up on the sled. No way! That would make me into a target. No, I lay as flat as a tall woman in a clown suit can lie, and I kept my head down—floppy red bow and all.

There was nothing I could do about T.J. standing erect on his snowboard. But he was dipping and swooping with such verve, I doubted the world's greatest sharpshooter could have hit him.

We were breaking some of the carefully written safety rules for the Clown Week sledding course. Two of us had no helmets. It's also not proper to be waving pistols around as you head down the snowy hill.

Of course, what I dreaded during this wild ride was that T.J. would catch up with Philip Montague. He'd already head butted the jerk; who knew what he might decide to do the next time. And while I might admire his courage—in reality it terrified me—T.J. was only fourteen. He couldn't go up against a grown man with a gun.

But what could I do about it? If I caught up with T.J.—well, then I might be able to stop him. I'd gladly let Philip Montague get away. I just didn't want T.J. to get hurt.

I also didn't want to get hurt myself.

While all this was racing through my head, I was hurtling down that hill at what seemed like super-speed. Maybe I wasn't going that fast, but it sure seemed like it.

Philip Montague was still ahead of me. Also ahead, closing in on Philip, was T.J.

I began to yell. "Tony! Tony! Stop! Stop! T.J., he has a gun!"

But the slope was lined with spectators. People were walking up and down the path beside the sledding area. The sleighs were also going up and down the hill, carrying visitors.

And the walkers and riders were pointing at us. They were applauding. The spectators thought we were part of Clown Week.

"Tony! Tony! Stop!" It didn't matter how loudly I yelled. T.J. couldn't hear me because of the music, the applause, and the shouting. Nobody could hear me.

I was still yelling when Philip Montague reached the first rise. He crested it with only a minor wobble, eased over, and went on. The darn man had been reared in

Michigan. He'd probably come home from the maternity ward on a sled.

Tony was swooping onto the rise. He knew every inch of the slope, of course, and had already made at least two dozen trips down it. He took the rise and started down again without hesitation.

That left me, and I didn't even know how to guide the dadgum sled.

It had handles of some sort at the front. I grabbed them and moved them to the left. The sled responded and went left—but not far enough to miss the huge pile of snow on the right of the track. The sled flipped over, and I went rolling into a snowdrift. My sled stopped fifteen feet farther down the slope.

I wasn't hurt, but something was digging into my ribs.

My cell phone.

I could call someone. But who? During the three seconds it took me to dig my way out of the snow, I thought about that. And I came up with an answer.

As soon as I wasn't buried in snow, I ripped the Velcro open down the front of my clown suit and reached into the side pocket of my ski jacket. Thank God the phone was still working. I punched the right buttons and found the right number.

"Answer! Answer!" I spoke out loud and used mental telepathy at the same time. "Emergency!"

"Hello."

"It's Lee! There's a guy in a hobo outfit coming down the slope!"

Two blocks down the hill, at the skating rink, I could see Tony Herrera—Tony Senior—turn around to look up the hill.

"So?"

"Tony, he's got a gun! He's the guy that tried to kill

Emma Davidson! And Tony Junior is right behind, chasing him!"

"Huh?"

I wailed. "I know it's hard to believe, but when the guy jumped on a sled, Tony jumped on his snowboard right after him!" I was on my feet by then, and I waved my arms. "Can you see them?"

"I see them." Tony Senior's voice was grim. And immediately—*immediately*—I heard the loudspeaker down at the skating rink. "Clear the ice! Now!" I knew Tony Senior had the portable mike, so that was his doing.

As I watched, Tony Senior sped across the ice, his skates seeming to strike sparks. He didn't pause when he reached the edge, but kept going, running through the snow. He ran right over the flimsy picket fence that was used to keep waiting skaters in line. He was headed for the sledding slope.

I ended the call to Tony and punched 9-1-1. I kept the message simple. "Mayday! Mayday! I'm in Warner Pier. There's a guy with a pistol on the sledding slope!"

Then I plunged through the snow to recapture my sled. I looked at the gadget and wished I had an ax to chop it up with. I was scared to death of it. But I needed the darn thing. I had done all I could do from that spot.

I sighed, aimed the sled in the right direction, and pushed off.

By the time I reached the bottom of the hill, Tony Senior had Philip Montague in a headlock. Montague's pistol was ten feet away, and he was whining like a little girl.

Nobody could understand whatever he was trying to say. This was because Tony was talking louder than his captive. And his words were addressed to T.J.

I didn't catch much of it, but I do remember his saying, "And you're grounded for life!"

When T.J. made a motion toward the pistol in the snow, Tony Senior roared even louder. "Don't touch that!"

Tony didn't let go of Philip until Clancy Pike had him handcuffed. Then Tony got to his feet. In skates, he towered even higher than he does normally. He grabbed Tony Junior and shook him like a rag doll. Then he hugged him—though the word "hug" doesn't quite express the strength of his embrace. And tears ran down Tony Senior's face.

I grabbed his arm. "Tony, cut him some slack! He saved my life!"

So Tony hugged both of us. "I don't even want to hear this story," he said. "But I guess I have to sometime."

By then all three of us were crying.

Over the next few days everything settled into place.

First, T.J. and Tony Senior seemed to be much better friends. And T.J. was grounded for only a weekend.

Chuck was arrested at Clowning Around just as soon as Clancy could get there. He and Philip turned on each other at the first opportunity, of course.

Chuck claimed Philip came up with the plan to defraud his dad by getting him to donate to Klowns for Kids of Michigan. Philip claimed it was all Chuck's idea.

"Chuck said his dad stole money from his mom's estate," Philip said. "Money that should have gone to him and to Lorraine. He said it was only fair for him to steal it back."

They also blamed each other for killing Moe. It seems Philip had been inside the house when Moe, Emma, and Chuck arrived. Chuck had arranged to meet his dad there, claiming he and Philip had a good explanation for the Klowns for Kids of Michigan caper. After Emma shoved Moe, and Chuck urged her to leave, Chuck and Moe got into a fight. Chuck claimed Philip appeared from inside the house and killed his dad; Philip claimed he was only a witness and that Chuck killed him.

Each of them had tried to kill Emma, who apparently has nine lives, because she escaped three times. I hope she doesn't try for six more.

When Emma said she was going to confess to killing his dad, Chuck knew that no one was likely to believe her story; he also knew that if they did believe her, he was probably the next suspect in line. So he laced a Bloody Mary with an overdose of her medication, then urged Lorraine to push the drink on her. He took the groggy Emma down to the Clowning Around shop and left her to die, but Tilda VanAust and I ruined his plan. Lorraine apparently passed out and didn't know he had taken her to the shop.

Philip got involved because of his link to real estate. He set up a fake development company and pretended he wanted to buy the Clowning Around building. This was a ploy to raise the price, to convince Aunt Nettie and me that the building was worth more.

I never got a chance to tell Philip that wouldn't have worked. I'm not a complete idiot.

Philip made two attempts to kill Emma. He first tried to smother her, wearing the only kind of clown makeup he knew how to do—the kind he'd used back in Moe's clown club for teenagers. A picture of the club hung in the shop, though I had never noticed it. Apparently Philip was afraid I had recognized the makeup and would realize who he was. I don't think Philip had any idea it was the hair-dye disguise, not the teardrops painted on his cheek, that gave him away when he tried to poison Emma. The teardrops only confused Emma, making her drugged mind think that Moe had returned from the dead to further torment her.

Philip tried to take me hostage just in case he needed a shield to make his escape from Warner Pier.

Philip and Chuck haven't been sent up yet, but they will be, and for good long sentences.

Surprisingly, Lorraine and Emma have become closer friends. During Clown Week they managed to sell almost the entire stock of Clowning Around, which gave them some badly needed ready cash. Emma offered to send Lorraine to a rehab program for her drinking problem, and Lorraine agreed to go. So far, I hear, she's sticking to it. They sold the Warner Pier house, and Emma's back in Indiana.

A few days after Chuck's arrest, Aunt Nettie called from Australia. She agreed enthusiastically to the purchase of the Clowning Around building. TenHuis Chocolade has now taken possession of it, and we're looking for an architect.

Royal Hollis was released the day after Chuck and Philip were arrested. I didn't witness his meeting with Belle, but Joe said it was "very touching." Belle offered to rent an apartment for her dad in Saginaw, and he agreed to live in it—at least for the rest of the winter. He's also back in treatment for his mental problems.

I just hope he doesn't give up the harmonica.

Chocolate Chat

One of the most intriguing bits of chocolate trivia comes from St. Louis folklore.

An old story there claims that the custom of placing chocolates on the pillows of hotel rooms was instigated by Cary Grant while staying at an elegant St. Louis hotel. It seems he used the chocolates to tempt a woman into visiting his room.

Aw, c'mon! Cary Grant didn't need chocolates to get a lady friend to come to his room. The movie queens of the 1940s were pounding at the door, begging to get in. And Cary would have at least provided his own chocolates.

I confess to a weakness for the leading men of my childhood—Cary Grant among them—and I think lots of women, young and old, feel the same way. I recall once finding my sixteen-year-old daughter sighing over an old movie starring Clark Gable. Clark Gable had been the screen idol of her grandmother's generation! But the guy still had it, forty years later.

The inspiration for Joe Woodyard is Gregory Peck. Joe is less scrawny than Mr. Peck—and is just as good-looking.

Read on for an excerpt from JoAnna Carl's
latest Chocoholic Mystery,

THE CHOCOLATE FALCON FRAUD

Available now in hardcover from Obsidian.

When Jeff Godfrey came in the door of TenHuis
Chocolade, I didn't know if I should shake his
hand, kiss him, or call the cops.

My relationship with Jeff was closer than handshak-
ing—or it had been—but not as close as kissing. And
the last time I saw Jeff, he'd barely escaped being accused of murder.

Of course, I had to look at Jeff closely before I was
sure who he was; I hadn't seen him in three and a half
years. Now, at twenty-two, Jeff looked quite different.
More mature, of course, but also more handsome and
more confident. And he'd gotten rid of the enormous
eyelets in his earlobes.

So when he appeared, I stared for a moment. Then I
called out, "Jeff! What are you doing there? I mean,
here!"

Jeff grinned shyly as he walked across the shop. He
probably felt as ill at ease as I did. By the time I was
standing up, leaning against my desk, he was beside
me. We settled for the handshake-chest-bump-air-kiss
ritual, as if one of us were a talk show host and the
other a featured guest.

I motioned him into the chair on the other side of my
desk and sat back down. "You look great," I said. "Let
me guess—you're here for this weekend's film noir festival, aren't you?"

"That's right. I read about it online. How could I pass up the lectures on *The Maltese Falcon*?"

The Warner Pier Film Festival was always a big success at increasing our tourist traffic. And this year, as a member of the Chamber of Commerce Tourism Committee, I was even invited to the big kickoff party at the yacht club. "And how are your folks?"

"Well, they're still together—again. And you married that Joe guy, right? The boat builder?"

"Yep. We seem to have gotten it right this time. And Joe's now just a boat builder part-time. He's back in the lawyer game three days a week. How about Tess? Do you still see her?" Tess had figured importantly in Jeff's life four years earlier.

"Tess and I see each other on campus. And she works part-time for my dad."

I realized I was beaming, and that Jeff was looking pleased, too. That made me beam even harder. After all, not every ex-stepson is happy to see his ex-stepmother.

I'm Lee McKinney Woodyard, and four years earlier I had moved from Dallas to Warner Pier, Michigan, the most picturesque resort town on Lake Michigan. Here I was business manager for a luxury chocolate company owned by my aunt, Nettie TenHuis Jones.

One reason I'd made the move was to cut all ties with Jeff's dad, my ex-husband. But I still liked his son.

Jeff did look great. At eighteen he'd been a scrawny kid with sandy hair, gray eyes, and an enormous hole in each earlobe. He'd also had a gold ring in his left eyebrow, and he'd worn thick glasses.

Now he was at least two inches taller—I guessed his new height at six feet—and thirty pounds more muscular. He'd definitely lost the scrawny teenage look, and he'd also lost the piercings and the glasses. I could barely see the scars where the earlobes had been repaired. He blinked, and I diagnosed contact lenses. Instead of ragged jeans, he was wearing a brand-name polo, khakis, and boat shoes. The result was a great-looking guy.

I counted mentally. Yes, Jeff would have been a senior at Southern Methodist University this year. "Did you just graduate?"

"Yep, I squeaked through. BA in history. And I even got into graduate school at UT."

University of Texas; all us Texans know those initials. "Wonderful! What's your field?"

"Maybe Texas history. I think I want to teach. I got a slot as a graduate assistant. And I had an offer of an internship at the Texas Museum of Popular Culture. I had to turn that down because I had a conflict."

"That's still great." I leaned toward Jeff and dropped my voice. "What does your dad think of a history career?"

He laughed. "He'd rather I got an MBA, of course, but he said he'd pay my grad school tuition and books."

"He's proud of you, Jeff."

"Maybe. Most of the time he hides it. He'd still like me to sell real estate."

"Do your own thing." I shook a finger at him. "I'm really tickled to see you. Joe and I live in the old cottage now. I hope you'll stay with us."

Jeff straightened his shoulders a little. "Thanks, but I already have a hotel room. I'm actually doing a research project this trip. Warner Pier was all booked up, but I've got a room in Holland. And I hope you and Joe—and Aunt Nettie and her husband, too—will let me take you all out to dinner tonight."

I knew Aunt Nettie would want to cook for Jeff—she wants to feed the whole world—but I could see Jeff was spreading his grown-up wings a little. I assured him we'd all love to be his guests.

"And I can legitimately write it off as part of my research," Jeff said.

"What are you residing? I mean, researching?" Yikes! I'd pulled another one of my tongue twisters.

Jeff didn't react to it. "Did you ever hear of anybody around here named Fal-cone? Or Fal-cone-ie? I'm not sure of the pronunciation."

"Sounds too Italian for Warner Pier. You know nearly everybody around here is Dutch."

I picked up the phone book and thumbed through, hunting for the *F* listings, but Jeff stood up. "I already checked the directories and the Internet. No person or business with that name is listed."

"We can ask Aunt Nettie. She knows more people than I do. She's in Holland for a dental appointment. She'll want to see you as soon as she gets back."

"She was so nice to me. Before. Is the Inn on the Pier still a good place to eat?"

"Sure."

"Seven o'clock?"

"That sounds fine."

"See you there."

We exchanged cell phone numbers, and I added a warning. "Big areas around here still have no cell service. Including our house. The only place Joe and I have reception—most of the time—is on the roof! They blame the lake, but I have my doubts. They put a tower on one of the highest spots in Saugatuck and reception around there improved dramatically." I stood up. "Wait a minute, and I'll walk you to the door."

I reached for my crutch. For the first time Jeff saw that and my orthopedic boot.

"Hey, Lee! What have you done to yourself?"

"Nothing serious. I sprained an ankle on those steep stairs at the house. I'm sure you remember them."

Jeff nodded. He'd slept in an upstairs bedroom on his previous visit to Warner Pier, and once or twice he had nearly fallen down our steep stairs himself.

"They tell me no permanent damage has been done," I said, "but the doctor wants me to keep weight off the ankle for a while."

I stumped along behind Jeff as we passed through our retail shop, and I insisted he select a chocolate. He went for a dark chocolate falcon, a two-inch replica of the famous film bird that we had created especially for the film festival.

When we reached the street door, we did our belly-bump-air-kiss-hug act again.

"Seven o'clock," Jeff said.

"Seven o'clock," I answered.

And at seven o'clock four of us—my husband, Joe, my aunt Nettie, her husband, Police Chief Hogan Jones, and me—met in the bar at the Inn on the Pier, ready to have dinner with Jeff. I had told everyone how good he had looked, how mature he had seemed, and how pleased he had been at the prospect of seeing all of us again.

So it was quite a letdown when he didn't show up.

We waited in the bar until eight o'clock. I knew, because I checked my watch—again—the third time the hostess came to tell us we could have a table.

"I don't understand this," I said. "I can call Jeff's cell phone again."

"Let's take this table in any case," Hogan said. "Dinner will be my treat."

Aunt Nettie looked worried. She had beautiful curly white hair and a sweet face. "I'm afraid something has happened to Jeff."

Joe laughed. "Something has! He's run into someone more interesting. Despite the changes in his appearance, Lee, I'm afraid Jeff is still the irresponsible kid who showed up on your roof nearly four years ago and tried to break in through the upstairs window."

"Hand me my crutch," I said. "Once we're seated, I'll try his cell phone again."

But there was still no answer.

Hogan left his menu closed and began to make noises like a cop. "Do you know where Jeff was staying?"

"A Holland motel."

"That narrows it down to maybe fifty, sixty places. Does he have your cell phone number?"

I nodded.

"Did he say why he came to Warner Pier?"

"He said he was going to catch part of the film festival, and that he was doing a research project. But he didn't explain anything about it. He asked me if I knew anyone named Fal-cone or Fal-cone-ie. He wasn't sure of the pronunciation."

"Falconi?" Aunt Nettie looked surprised. "That would be an odd name around Warner Pier. Valk, maybe."

Valk? What could Valk have to do with Falcone? I started to ask Aunt Nettie to explain, but the waiter interrupted. We all put our attention on the menus, and after we had ordered dinner some unwritten rule of good manners inspired us to stop discussing Jeff.

But why had Jeff invited us all to dinner, then failed to show up? I had no explanation. But then, maybe I didn't know Jeff all that well.

His parents, Dina and Rich, had divorced when Jeff was nine. Three years later I married Rich, who was then in his early forties. I was twenty-three. Dumb. Dumb. Dumb. Marrying Rich was the stupidest thing I ever did, though the age difference was the least of our problems.

Today I understood that I fell for Rich because I wanted stability in my life. He fell for me because I was six feet tall and a natural blond who had been in a Miss Texas competition.

Also, I think, he liked me because I have malapropism. This means I get my tongue twisted, saying such things as "residing" when I mean "researching," as I did when talking to Jeff. Rich thought "dumb" and "blond" were synonyms, and he didn't want any mental competition from his wife. He loved it when I goofed.

In those days Jeff was a bratty adolescent. Rich had his custody one or two weekends a month and on some holidays. Or maybe I had his custody. Rich was a successful real estate developer in Dallas, and he often managed to be playing golf with a client at the times when he should have been paying attention to Jeff. I will say he was careful not to miss any of Jeff's swim meets. The kid could swim and dive like a dolphin.

There's a fine line between getting along with an adolescent and keeping one from bossing you around. Jeff was a nice enough kid, but dealing with a stepmother who was only eleven years older than he was—well, it wasn't an ideal situation for either of us.

After some sparring around, Jeff and I developed an informal truce. We spent a lot of time on neutral activities such as playing board games and watching old movies. Even in those days Jeff was a fan of forties and fifties noir films and books.

For five years I struggled to make my marriage work. But my relationship with Rich got worse and worse. I wanted to think of marriage as a partnership. Rich wanted to think of me as a possession. I'd become the proverbial trophy wife, and I didn't like it. And I couldn't get Rich even to discuss the situation.

Finally I left, and I didn't take anything with me. I abandoned my jewelry (selected by Rich), my snazzy car (picked out by Rich), my elegant house (gussied up by a decorator Rich chose), even my wardrobe (though Rich had allowed me to pick out my own clothes, provided I went to the stores he approved of).

When I left Rich I drove away in a junky car somebody had abandoned at my dad's garage. I was wearing an old pair of jeans and a T-shirt. I moved in with my mom, who was on Rich's side, and I begged until she bought me a tank of gas. Then I took a job as a waitress because I could start work that day and keep my tips.

My plan was to convince Rich that I loved *him*, not his money, and thus save my marriage. This did not work. It took a couple of months with a counselor for me to understand that Rich regarded his money as part of his personality. In rejecting it, I had rejected him.

When I discovered Rich had put detectives on my

trail, I accepted the end of my marriage. I wasn't seeing anyone else, but Rich couldn't believe I'd leave one wealthy man without having a new one lined up.

About the time my marriage ended, my wonderful aunt Nettie—world's finest chocolatier—offered me a job as business manager of TenHuis Chocolade. I moved to Warner Pier. I met Joe Woodyard—who had also had some unhappy romantic times. Now we'd been married three years. And I loved my life.

But apparently my decision to get a divorce brought a personality crisis for Rich. He went into counseling and must have done a lot of self-examination. Then he began to see Dina again. A year and a half after our divorce, the two of them remarried.

I wished them all sorts of happiness. But that part of my life was over. I didn't want to see them ever again. However, I could hardly refuse to meet with Jeff. He and I had watched a lot of Humphrey Bogart and Alan Ladd.

But why had Jeff invited us all to dinner, then failed to show?

I went to bed that night puzzled by Jeff's nonappearance, but trying not to worry about him. Unfortunately the scrabbling of my thoughts was echoed by some darn animal making noises in the attic (a chronic problem of semirural living) and I had trouble falling asleep. I insisted to myself that Joe was right; Jeff had simply found someone more interesting to have dinner with. I shouldn't be wringing my hands over him.

I was still sleeping when the phone rang at seven the next morning. Joe was already awake, and he answered it.

"Oh, hi." He sounded wary. "Sure. She's here."

Where else would I be at that time of day? I took the phone and mumbled my greeting. "It's Lee."

"Lee, it's Alicia."

"Alicia?" I sat up in bed. I had recognized the Texas accent immediately. "Alicia Richardson!"

"Oh yeah. The same old gal. How you doin'?"

"Fine! It's good to hear from you."

And it was good. Alicia was a part of my life in Dallas I remembered with pleasure. At one time she'd helped me out a lot.

Alicia was office manager and head of accounting for Rich's company. I guess every business has one key person, and at Godfrey Development, Alicia was it. She had worked for Rich for at least fifteen years. She knew where all the bodies were buried, where all the money was socked away, who couldn't stand whom, and how to Get Things Done.

On a day-to-day basis, Alicia ran the company. Rich made the deals, and Alicia made them happen. Rich didn't admit this out loud, but the salary he paid Alicia proved he appreciated her abilities. Their relationship was strictly professional. Alicia was married to a terrific guy named Tom who was a surveyor, and they had two great kids. She was perfectly capable of telling Rich she couldn't stay late because it was her daughter's birthday, and Rich would say, "Yes, ma'am."

Back when I was married to Rich, Alicia had saved my fanny lots of times. If Rich and I were going to a party, for example, she'd give me tips on what was really going on in the world of property development, and which subjects to avoid with whom. She kept my foot out of my mouth most of the time.

If I had a role model in my job as business manager for TenHuis Chocolade, it was Alicia. I was glad to hear from her, though I knew she hadn't called simply to chat.

Sure enough, she went right to the point. "I don't suppose you've heard from Jeff," she said. "That little booger seems to have misplaced hisself."

"Misplaced himself? Alicia, I thought he finally grew up enough to be allowed out of the house alone."

"As a general rule he does pretty well. But his parents are in South America until the end of the week, and something has come up. He mentioned you before he got away."

"Actually Jeff did drop by yesterday."

Alicia gave a dramatic sigh of relief. "Thank the Lord! Is he there with you?"

"No, he said he had a motel room in Holland."

"Was he okay?"

"Sure. He looked great and seemed to be in good spirits." My mind was racing, and fear was settling in the pit of my stomach. It was stupid, but I'd always had a terrible fear that something would happen to Jeff and that it would happen on my watch.

But what should I say to Alicia? Jeff had made a date with us, then had failed to show up. Should I tell her that? I stalled.

"I guess he told you he was common—I mean, coming! He must have told you he was coming to Warner Pier."

"No, he didn't tell me! He's living at home this summer. He gave up his apartment, because he's going to move to Austin in August. Rich and Dina are skiing, of all things, in Peru, of all places. Jeff was supposed to mind his mama's store."

Dina owned a high-end antiques business, and Jeff had worked part-time for her since he was fourteen or so.

Alicia was still talking. "He found someone to fill in at the store, then went off—I guess to Michigan—and apparently didn't tell anybody where he was going. Not even that sweet little Tess. I finally found a message from him on my line at the office. It said something about seeing you. And he's not answering his cell phone. Do you know what motel he's in?"

"I'm afraid not. All he gave me was his cell number."

"Dadgum it!"

"Alicia, is there some emergency?"

"I honestly don't know, Lee. The girl who's at Dina's shop called me to say Jeff was getting these strange phone calls. I went over there and listened to a couple of messages, and, Lee, they sound a lot like threats! Like 'If you miss this opportunity, you'll be sorry forever, because the black bird may come after you.'"

"Who on earth would threaten Jeff?"

"I can't imagine. I don't know what's going on. But I need to talk to him about it. If anything happens to Jeff . . ." She left the sentence incomplete.

I decided that I wouldn't tell Alicia about Jeff being a no-show for dinner. She was worried already, and that wouldn't help.

"Listen," I said, "as soon as I'm a little more up-and-at-'em, I'll get on the phone and call a few Holland motels. Maybe I can track him down."

"Oh, would you? I'd really appreciate it."

Alicia gave me her cell number, and I promised to call back by noon, even if I didn't find Jeff.

I hung up, then slumped down in bed and looked at Joe. Darn, he was fun to look at. Dark hair, brilliant blue eyes. Definitely the best-looking guy in west Michigan. With the best shoulders. Also smart.

"Good morning," I said.

Joe rolled his eyes. "Why do your friends and relatives call so early?"

"They forget we're in the eastern time zone."

"But that would make them call later, Lee. Not earlier."

"Then I don't know. But you were already up. Why did the phone bother you?"

"I guess I just don't like to see you get mixed up with those people."

"What's wrong with Alicia and Jeff? At least *Rich* didn't call."

"He doesn't bother me. You're not friendly with Rich. It's other people who want favors."

"I haven't heard from any of them since Jeff got in all that trouble on his last visit. Three years ago. Three and a half."

"But yesterday, when he showed up, you said Jeff knew we were married."

"Yes, and he knew Aunt Nettie and Hogan were married. So what? Oh, it's odd, because he didn't get it from me."

"He's been keeping track of you, Lee. It's creepy. Plus, last night you and Aunt Nettie were talking about meeting with that architect today. You don't have time to look all over Holland for Jeff."

TenHuis Chocolade ("luxury chocolates in the Dutch tradition") had recently acquired the building next door. We were in the early stages of expanding into the additional space. Even the early stages were taking a lot of time.

I sighed. "Joe, I can't refuse to help Alicia find Jeff. She's obviously worried about him. And Alicia is one of those people I owe."

I sat up and rested my chin on my knees. "This is one of those recurring nightmares."

"Why? I'm sure nothing's happened to Jeff."

"It's a holdover from when I was first married to Rich. I admit we hadn't dated nearly long enough. He hadn't bothered to mention that he had a twelve-year-old son."

"What a jerk!"

"True, but . . . Anyway, a month after I met Jeff, Rich asked me to pick him up for weekend visitation and bring him out to the club and drop him off to have dinner with Rich. I had to go someplace else. So I took Jeff to the club and dropped him off at the front door. I had barely gotten where I was going when Rich called and asked where Jeff was. He'd never gotten inside the club."

"That was scary!"

I blinked away a tear. "Actually he'd just gone out to the driving range, but it frightened the something or other out of me. All I could think was that he'd been kidnapped. And it would all be my fault!"

Joe sat on the edge of the bed and took my hand. "Jeff's a grown-up now!"

"Is he?"

"Legally he is. You didn't ask him to come to Michigan. He's responsible for himself."

"Thanks, but this is a topic I'm not always rational about."

Joe gave me a kiss and another dose of reassurance. Then I got up, hoisted myself onto my crutch, and limped through my morning routine. As soon as Joe left for work, I started calling motels in Holland, thirty miles away, looking for Jeff. It only took four calls. He was registered at the Holiday Inn Express.

But when the front desk rang his room, Jeff didn't answer. I left a voice mail, telling him Alicia was trying to find him. And I added a sentence. "We were sorry that we missed you last night, Jeff. Don't leave the area without calling, guy!"

I began to dress for the office, telling myself I'd hear from Jeff within a few minutes. He had probably been in the shower.

But I didn't hear from him. By the time I left for the office, thumping my crutch irately at every step, there had been no word from Jeff.

After Joe left, the only sound I heard was the animal in the attic.

Anyone who's ever lived in the country knows about the animal in the attic. And if Joe and I didn't live in the country in a legal sense, we did in a physical one. Our house was inside the city limits of Warner Pier. We had city water and sewer, plus all the police and fire protection available in a town of twenty-five hundred souls. But our neighborhood was semirural and heavily wooded. It looked and felt like country. We were surrounded by country things like bushes and trees and animals.

Deer, turkeys, raccoons, rabbits—even the occasional badger and fox—hung out in our neighborhood. And they considered our house part of their territory. A squirrel had come down our chimney. We'd had chipmunks move into our basement. Every fall the mice invaded, trying to avoid cold weather. Don't ask me how they found cracks and holes to get it; we tried to plug 'em up.

We were experts on amateur extermination, and we also knew whom to call if professional action was required. In fact, we'd had the exterminator the previous week, and he thought he had de-animaled the house completely. But I was already hearing noises from the attic.

This situation, of course, was not found only in Michigan. My dad had the same problem in north Texas. It's just part of country living, so we tried not to pay too much attention to stray scratchings and thumpings.

But I wrote a note to Joe with a big, fat Magic Marker. "Please check attic for annie-mule!" Then I taped it to the window over the kitchen sink before I left for the office.

I made sure my phone was on; I didn't want to miss Jeff's call. But by noon I still hadn't heard from him. When I talked to Alicia, she hadn't heard from him either.

"Listen," I said, "I'll go to the Holiday Inn and see what I can find out."

"If that kid is lounging around the pool and letting us worry, I'll have his hide."

"I'll hold him while you kick him."

I told Aunt Nettie I was making an emergency trip to Holland and would be back to meet with the architect. I worried the whole thirty miles to Holland. But I was on the outskirts of town before I gave in, stopped the car in a parking lot, and called Hogan for a little informal advice from law enforcement. Luckily it was a slow day for crime in Warner Pier, and I caught him in his office.

I quickly sketched the situation for him. "We can't make a missing person report on Jeff yet, can we?"

"Not unless you find something scary."

"Scary?"

"Yeah. Like his car with a pool of blood in the front seat."

I shuddered. "I don't even want to think such a thing!"

"Then don't. But if he's simply not there, the cops can't do much. He's over twenty-one, isn't he?"

"Oh yes. He's supposedly a grown-up."

"And the motel isn't likely to give you much information."

"That's what I thought."

"The only way you could get a look in his room, for example, is if there was a possibility he's sick."

"Sick?"

"Some chronic condition. The possibility of a diabetic coma maybe. He's a little bit young for you to tell them he might have had a stroke. And you don't want to say he'd threatened suicide. The motel might toss him out. Motels don't like dead guests." Hogan laughed. "But don't make it too elaborate, Lee. You don't look old enough to be Jeff's mother."

"Even though I was. Sort of."

When I got to the Holiday Inn I cruised the parking lot, looking for Texas license plates. Nary a one. So I parked and went to the desk, where the clerk tried calling Jeff's room. No answer.

I took a deep breath and pulled the stunt Hogan had hinted might work.

My stepson, I told the clerk, was diabetic. "We really didn't want him to tackle this trip, because his blood sugar has been up and down, but you know kids! We couldn't talk him out of it."

The clerk nodded sympathetically.

"Is there any way a staff member could check the room? Make sure he's all right?"

"I'll ask the manager."

The manager wasn't happy, but he got a special key card from a drawer. I didn't ask if I could go along. I just went.

The room was on the third floor. I tried to follow the

manager inside, but he gestured at me. "Please stay here."

So I stood in the doorway, though I did manage to edge inside far enough to see into the bathroom and most of the bedroom. By then I had talked myself into real concern about Jeff's disappearance, and I was holding my breath as the manager made a circuit of the room, checking behind the shower curtain, between the beds, in the closet. I felt a genuine sense of relief when he spoke. "No sign of him."

"Thank goodness." From my place two steps inside the room I could see Jeff's luggage—a medium-sized wheeled duffel bag—on the foot of the bed. I could peek inside the bathroom and see his shaving kit on the counter. But neither bag looked as if it had been opened.

Jeff had apparently checked in the previous day, dropped off his luggage, then left. There was no sign that he had ever come back to the room.